DAMIA'S CHILDREN

ANNE McCAFFREY
DAMIA'S CHILDREN

BCA

LONDON NEW YORK SYDNEY TORONTO

This edition published 1993 by
BCA
by arrangement with Bantam Press
a division of Transworld Publishers Ltd

CN 8604

Printed and bound in Great Britain by
Mackays of Chatham PLC, Chatham, Kent

Reverently dedicated to

Richard Woods, O.P.

aka *Pendragon, Fullfret Faxdragon,*
Captooth Fangbite the Whistler
Hurryfast Rushdrake
Sir Walter McDragon
Slipknife Ouchblend the Reckless
Shortblast Spleenfume the Apoplectic
Dragonrabbit Eggsnitcher the Wily
Thickhead Diddlewit the Forgetful
Snatchfinger Jewelheist the Avaricious
Snapdragon Fastsnatch

Harpmaker, Storyteller, GOOD Friend

1

Laria reined Saki in at the curve, to let Tlp and Hgf catch up. She deliberately kept her eyes forward, curbing Saki's intention to gallop up the last hill to home, because she knew the 'Dinis would have dropped to four legs to make the steep climb. Tlp and Hgf were awfully sensitive about being caught on all fours. Like humans, the Mrdinis assumed bipedal stance as soon as their back muscles were well enough developed to support the long trunk. Her father said that he thought the 'Dinis had been much relieved to learn that human children also had to learn how to walk upright.

When Saki's twitching ears and a waft of a musky leathery scent on the breeze announced their arrival, she acknowledged them with a whistle/click. She couldn't quite make the sound as well as her brothers Thian and Rojer, but she did better than Zara who hadn't the hang of it at all yet. Kaltia wasn't even trying though she signed well enough to be understood by the 'Dinis as Morag did. Her youngest siblings, Ewain and Petra, were too young to have more than the most rudimentary contact with their pairs.

Despite saddlebags full of the day's catch, Saki marched vigorously uphill, careful not to tread on the flipper feet on either side of her. Tip and Huf – which were Laria's mental tag for her 'Dinis – had taken holds on Laria's stirrups to assist them up this steepest part of the climb. Well accustomed to hauling 'Dinis, Saki accepted the additional burden.

Dropping the reins now that Saki was behaving, Laria had hands free to sign to her companions in excitement over their success hunting. They'd never hear her well enough over the clopping of Saki's hoofbeats if she spoke aloud. Tlp and Hgf clicked and clacked happy sounds which echoed in their skulls. They could produce any number of identifiable noises that way, ranging from fear to bravado, agreement, dislike, curiosity, concern, enjoyment and what passed for 'Dini laughter.

Neither species could quite manage the varied sounds needed to reproduce the subtler nuances of the other's speech but human body language could add emphasis to words and so could 'Dini body movements. Their five fingers were as dextrous in reproducing arbitrary patterns as their oral cavities were in producing understandable, pitched noises that humans could copy. Both languages, as spoken by the other species, were refined to somewhat limited vocabularies that fortunately could be extended into quite a few technical areas: such as space travel, basic engine design, biological and meteorological sciences, metallurgy and mining.

Laria's mother and father, Damia and Afra Raven-Lyon, had spent the past fifteen years developing and refining this communications bridge – apart from the Dreamings – with Mrdini colleagues. Laria had been the earliest human test subject. Constantly surrounded from birth by adult Mrdinis, and then young Tip and Huf, she had absorbed posture and sounds just as any child learns another language from early exposure. By the time she was six months old, she had had Tlp and Hgf as cribmates and had dreamed the pleasantest dreams in their company at naptime and at night. All the Raven-Lyon offspring had been similarly paired when they were six months old with 'Dini young.

On Iota Aurigae, such partnering had become normal. Even before much interspecies communication had become viable, miners – who were so overworked they were glad of any assistance – had taken adult pairs of 'Dinis into the pits and shafts when the Mrdinis had 'dreamed' their willingness to do so. The tough and suspicious Aurigaean miners had discovered that the 'Dinis were instinctive colliers, hard workers, and unusually strong.

'Hey-YO,' cried someone behind her. Turning, Laria saw her brother Thian, his white lock flopping across his face, on his chunky black pony, Charger, round the bend, Mrg and Dpl trudging along beside him.

Not for the first time did Laria regret that the conformation of the 'Dini made it impossible for them, with their stout short legs and stumpy tail, to straddle the hardy little Denebian hybrid ponies that humans employed. When they were younger, she'd occasionally put Tip and Huf up on Saki, Tip in front where she could hold on to it, and Huf riding pillion behind, its fingers latched tightly to her belt. But it wasn't the most comfortable way to travel and now her mates were too heavy to ride Saki with her.

'Good hunting, Thian?' Laria called back.

'Plenty for pot and spit,' her brother yelled, grinning hugely. 'Rojer's right behind us, with their bag. He must have some secret source of scurriers the amount he's bringing in.'

Hunting was a weekend occupation for the three oldest Raven-Lyon children who were good archers while the 'Dinis were clever with traps. With such a big household to feed, small avian species and burrowing animals, scurriers and the variety of rabbit that had adapted well to Aurigae were welcome additions to protein requirements, not always as well satisfied by the huge gardens.

The Tower could, of course, have brought in any

3

supplies needed but it had become a matter of family pride and honour for *this* household to supply its own needs – human and Mrdini – either from the high plateaux and valleys behind Aurigae City or from their fields.

Saki was too eager for her warm stable and supper to be held back to wait for Thian so Laria let her walk out, her tired young 'Dini mates hauled alongside.

As they finally reached the terrace level, lights were already beginning to augment the dimming day and illuminate the broad courtyard. Saki's hooves clattered across it, summoning the resident pets: Coonies, Darbuls and what Laria had termed Slithers, the Mrdini equivalent of a pet.

Neither reptile nor bird, neither furred nor feathered, but loving, affectionate, dependent on assistance to survive anywhere, Slithers had – to everyone's great astonishment – become accepted by Coonies, ignored by Darbuls, and endeared themselves to the humans as useful household creatures. Their existence and nurture by Mrdinis had been a curiously important factor in the acceptance of the aliens: 'Any critter that cares for a pet – even one as repulsive as that slithery reptiloid er . . . ah . . . entity – ' the Fleet Commander had remarked, 'can't be all bad.'

As Slither diet consisted of Aurigaean insects and small bugs unappetizing to other life forms, the creatures kept the large sprawling Raven-Lyon residence and neighbouring fields clear of pests that often caused humans on Aurigae considerable discomfort or nuisance when they fed on the crops.

Laria was already giving Saki a rub-down when first Thian and then Rojer arrived in the stable, to tend their own beasts. While one 'Dini brought the catch up to the kitchen wing, the other helped with hay and feed for the horses. That set the already stabled animals to stamping and snorting.

Have all the ponies been fed? Laria asked, broadcasting her thought more than directing it to either parent.

4

Please, darling? Had some late Tower traffic, replied Damia. *What splendid hunting you've all had!*

Laria 'ported the feeds into the mangers, adding the special vitamins and salts that two of the newest ponies required until their digestions altered to Aurigaean grasses. As usual, the four 'Dinis clacked in loud appreciation of her kinetic skill.

WE FEED PONIS, WE MAKE PONIS 'APPY, Tip and Huf chanted, although they themselves had done nothing, but as Tip and Huf were hers, any of her achievements were also theirs. Laria gave a small, almost inaudible sigh of resignation: for all their years in a Talented household, the 'Dinis were always more charmed by small teleportations like this than any major workings from the Tower. Cargo and ships just disappeared from or appeared in cradles whereas now the 'Dinis could *see* the movement from one place to another.

WE FEED PONIS PLUS, Thian's pair, Mur and Dip, added.

WE FEED FIRST, Tip began, turning its poll eye back over itself to pin Mur with a steely glance.

She signed it quickly not to be so silly and *tlocked* with her tongue a disapproving note. Tlp shrugged that off, swaying its upper body and head in reaffirmation.

As her parents had cautioned her as soon as she began to experiment with her telekinetic abilities, Laria was careful in their usage. The young Raven-Lyons did 'path more than most Talented parents would recommend for family communications but then the circumstances were unusual. Conversations between humans – when the 'Dinis could not follow verbal speech – would be rude so they often 'pathed rather than discourteously 'spoke' what their guests could not understand.

The entire Raven-Lyon family, including eight-month-old Petra, was considered by the Governmental Authority to be acting as official liaison representatives to Mrdini. Telepathy allowed the family the privacy and ease to discuss intimate matters which might have to exclude the 'Dinis.

5

As soon as Laria, Thian and Rojer had seen to the comfort of their ponies, they and the other 'Dinis went up the ramp from the stable complex to the Hall where most of the combined household's activities took place. With their 'Dinis' help, Morag was already plucking, skinning and eviscerating the catch. Zara, who would not butcher animals, was washing and preparing vegetables and greens. Afra and Flk were trussing bird and scurrier beast for the spit while Damia and Trp were doing multiple tasks with the rest of the meal. The 'Dinis were also carrying on a voluble conversation with their returning young. Despite the differences in shape and origin, there were many similarities between Mrdini and human in the care, education and nurture of their progeny.

Laria caught only half of what Flk and Trp were saying to the younglings but the sounds merrily ranged up and down the pitches available to 'Dini vocal cords so she knew that nothing was amiss. 'Dinis might not use body-language supplements when speaking to their own but tone could be interpreted in this home of sensitive Talents.

Anything new? Laria asked.

Nothing at all, darling, Damia said. *Can you do some more carrots? You know how Flk and Trp adore them but they haven't got the hang of using scrapers.*

Vitamin A! Laria replied with a mental grin, and 'ported two more bunches from the storeroom, holding them up for her mother to approve the quantity. A nod sufficed and Laria began preparing them.

Tlp and Hgf immediately came to her assistance, their single poll eyes glittering, for they were as fond of carrots as the adults. Once she had scraped, they sliced, Tip and Huf twitching their upper torsos happily, their 'heads' bent so that their single poll eyes were focused on what their hands were doing. Ordinarily, 'Dinis brought whatever they were working on up to eye level but when attempting a human task, they tended to adopt human postures.

Some people said they couldn't tell one 'Dini from another but that's because they didn't work closely with a pair. Laria recognized, and knew the names of, every pair living on Aurigae. 'Dini pairing was another mystery that hadn't been adequately explained, though biologists were trying. They had had to accept the fact that Mrdini always came in pairs. Laria did not know if Tip and Huf were the young of her parents' Flk and Trp: she didn't know if Flk and Trp were birth pairs, or had paired off by mutual choice when mature. There were still gaps in communication levels.

The Mrdinis dreamed explanations but these did not explain their biology. Mrdinis reproduced during their annual hibernations. Whether mating occurred before or during was still debatable; the Mrdinis did not seem to understand 'gestation' as a concept of time or even a process. They did not understand 'abort' or 'impotence' as a reason why not all 'pairs' reproduced. Nor why there were always twin births. Diplomatic courtesy denied humans the right to 'observe' in the hibernatorium. No-one was certain that these were live births, or if the Mrdinis might be oviparous. But the young were born 'adult', in that they understood the basics that all 'Dinis instinctively knew. They had to wait until their muscles strengthened to walk upright but they needed only to be 'reminded', Laria thought, of sounds – words – to reproduce them properly. As Damia once said, 'Dini young went from 'oh' to 'oration' in nothing flat. And they left the hibernatorium 'house-trained' and with mouths full of sharp teeth.

Mrdini builders had constructed the special hibernation facility well up in the hills behind the sprawling Raven-Lyon home. To this, all the Aurigaean Mrdini retired for their two-month-long period of inactivity. Not all pairs reproduced in that time. Not all remained for only two months. When all had left the facility, it was scrupulously cleaned and ready for the next hibernation period.

Laria was both relieved and lonely during the absence

of Tip and Huf: relieved because she didn't have that extra worry about doing or saying something misleading; lonely because she enjoyed their company and the fun they could get up to. 'Dinis had whimsical humour and a special rippling wheeze that was their amused noise: not quite a laugh, not a sputter, but definitely laughter. Fortunately 'Dinis and humans had comparable notions of comedy.

Though she had learned to get her tongue around the vowelless Tlp and Hgf, Laria used Tip and Huf: Thian called Mrg and Dpl, Mur and Dip. Her parents called Flk, Fok, and Trp, Tri. Evidently 'Dini made do without vowel sounds, though they certainly had innumerable consonant sounds, glottal stops and fricatives to produce all those clicks, clacks, dongs, bongs, tlocks and infinite varieties of whistle. Laria had become so deft at interpreting, that her parents often asked her to verify their understanding of conversations with Flk and Trp.

Then dinner was ready and served with rapidity to the hungry horde. 'Dinis had clever blades that served as spoon, fork and knife. Laria was adept with the instrument and kept one on her belt as Tip and Huf did. Fingers were permissible at home, Morag and Ewain employing theirs to good use and even remembering to use finger-bowls and napkins. Zara was more fastidious even at nine and her 'Dinis tended to imitate her. The fact that the 'Dinis were also accustomed to finger-bowls and napkins had at first astonished humans. Afra had carved the first bowls from Denebian hardwoods, decorated with the first Dream which the 'Dinis had sent him and Damia. While he still entertained everyone in the household with his paper-folded origami designs, he had added woodworking to his leisure time.

He had done 'Dinis in origami. Fok and Tri carried theirs in their belt pouches and would often exhibit them to 'Dini guests. While all the family liked to watch him create his animals and forms, only Rojer and Zara showed enough interest to learn to do the intricate paper-folding. Fok and

Tri had attended the first two lessons and then retired. Their digits were too powerful for the delicate movements needed and they tore more paper than they folded.

Mrdini mental processes apparently differed from human – though the results might be similar – but areas of mutuality were in constant development, and double households like the Raven-Lyons' contributed hugely to interspecies' understanding. It wasn't their Talent that was exercised so much as their innate empathy and objectivity.

'Dad,' Thian began when he had assuaged the first edge of hunger, 'we've about hunted out the nearby ranges. Aren't I old enough to use a sledge?'

Afra thoughtfully regarded his eldest son, all bony ribs, elbows and knees in his latest growth spurt and likely to match his father's height soon. *It would be useful, considering the fact that we may not 'port our friends about the place.*

Laria held her breath, for though she didn't begrudge Thian the opportunity . . .

Both Laria and Thian are responsible youngsters, Afra went on, nodding at them in the manner both knew was cautionary as well as challenging. *I shall apply to the City for licences. You two will have to qualify on your own merits but I'll arrange with Xexo a time to give you trial runs . . . Study the operation manuals.*

Sure, Dad, both Laria and Thian chorused, delighted. Considering both had the family eidetic memory, they'd be through that requisite in an hour or more. And Xexo, the resourceful T-8 Tower engineer who kept all the machinery running smoothly, had known them since their births and was a special friend.

Then, as Thian turned to Mur and Dip, Laria signed to Tip and Huf that soon they wouldn't have to climb the hill: transport was going to be arranged. They would be able to reach new hunting grounds without effort. The 'Dinis clicked and wriggled enthusiastically – Tip almost falling off its bench in its exuberance.

Laria, you must also become familiar with the management of

Mrdini ground effects machines, Damia added, cocking her head in her daughter's direction. *I'll arrange that with the Coordinators.*

Then I will be going to Mrdini?

Damia nodded, a resigned twitch to her lips. *That has always been the plan. Thian will follow when he reaches sixteen. You will be the first* young *human to go.* She sent a flood of pride and encouragement to her eldest child. Then she, in turn, felt the warmth of love and reassurance from Afra, salving the ache of that separation.

Sixteen is old enough for one of us, Afra said in the very tight focus that meant his thought was for her alone. She was also aware of his mental caress.

I was no older when I was sent to Altair, she answered as discreetly.

The difference being that Laria does not resent the duty.

I think we've done what we could to be sure she wouldn't, Damia added with a resigned sigh. *You've made such a good father.*

Afra grinned openly, his smile including every child at the table. *They've had their mother's help.*

I shall miss her, though.

Why? She'll be only a thought away.

It's the thought that she will *be* away. Damia diverted herself by 'porting the dirty dishes from the table and extracting the final course from the larder.

With the exception of Terran bee honey, the Mrdinis did not find sweets palatable. Honey was, however, a luxury item *when* it was available. So, while the humans ate fruit, the 'Dinis cracked nuts and picked the meats out of the shells or nibbled at the unsweetened mealy crackers made of imported 'Dini flour that Damia baked for them. From time to time, 'Dini delicacies were shipped to the exchange personnel but today was not an occasion.

DAMIA! Keylarion called and the Aurigaean Tower's T-6 managed to cram excitement and alarm into her shout for the Prime.

Damia and Afra immediately excused themselves and 'ported down the slope to the Tower control centre where the generators were beginning their upward climb to full power.

'Earth Prime ordered me to get you both here,' Keylarion said.

Father? Damia sent across the vastness of space, her thought boosted by gestalt with the generators and Afra's immediately accessible T-3 thrust.

Mrdini scouts have crossed the path of three Hive ships! Jeff Raven said.

Three? the Damia–Afra link cried in an almost fearful tone.

Three! The theory is that these must have originated from the Home System, for their directions began to diverge just as the Mrdini scout ship crossed their ion trail. Fortunately the scout was well out from any Alliance colonies or worlds. The Hivers are heading even further out.

The Damia–Afra link let out a cheer, all apprehension dissolved at this tremendous news. For fifteen years Mrdini and Nine Star League ships, now called the Alliance, had been probing systems to locate the homeworld of the Hive culture, aliens whose prime directive of ruthless propagation of their species had once attempted to invade the Mrdini colony in its Sef solar system. The attack had been repulsed but only with the extreme sacrifice of 'Dini ships and personnel. The colony had been devastated and had to be rebuilt and repopulated. Thereafter 'Dini had kept ships in constant patrol about their colonized worlds and sent out squadrons to patrol nearby space to make sure no 'Dini ship ever got so close to a 'Dini world again. Over two centuries they had maintained such a vigil, constantly expanding the parameters of 'safe space', their whole culture dominated by the dire threat of Hive penetration.

The Mrdinis had also searched vainly for allies of sufficient spatial sophistication to aid them. The resources of their home and colony planets had been stretched to the utmost in the constant vigilance.

As desperately, the Mrdini sought new weapons to destroy the predatory Hive ships. The effective tactic was to use a suicide ship which would plunge midships in the spherical Hive ship and detonate itself in order to achieve total destruction of the Hiver. Not every suicide mission was successful, for the Hive gunners were skilful and often six suicide ships had to attack to be sure one got through. Such punitive losses had naturally used up tremendous materiel as well as 'Dinis whose genes should be perpetuated.

But still, elements of the 'Dini fleet searched and would track down any Hive ion trail located in the vastness of space.

Then, both a marauding Hive ship and the 'Dini ship following its ion trail discovered the Denebian system.

Jeff Raven, an unexpectedly Talented telepath and teleporter, had single-mindedly held off three scouts from an intruding Hive. With the assistance of the Primes of Earth, Altair, Procyon, Capella, Betelgeuse and the Rowan on Callisto Moon, the mind-merge focusing in Jeff Raven had destroyed two of the scouts and sent the third back to its Mother ship. Two years later, the Mother Hive had been on a collision course with Deneb which had been thwarted when the Rowan, leading the female minds, had paralysed the dominant Hive 'Many'. Then Jeff Raven, being the focus for the male Talents, had diverted the Hiver into the blazing whiteness of the Deneb primary.

Alarmed, the Nine Star League had prepared distant early warning devices around all its inhabited systems to forestall another incursion by this dangerous species. The Mrdini had been able to circumvent the device by staying just beyond its sensor range and inserting instructive dreams in the sleeping minds of Damia, Afra and four other Denebian Talents. The Mrdini were not only triumphant to find a species that could destroy a Hive

12

ship with no loss of life and without collecting a flotilla of space vessels and suicide crews in doing so, but also Allies in their long struggle against the depredations of the Hivers. Deneb had been unknowingly selected as an excellent Hive colony society. The press for acceptable worlds on which to propagate themselves meant the annihilation of any life form they encountered. Sadly, not all emerging species had the weapons to counter such tactics and the method which the Talents had used – telepathy and teleportation – had seemed magical to the Mrdinis. While the 'Dinis had no 'Talent' as the Nine Star League understood it, they were able to superimpose their dreams on susceptible human minds.

Through these dreams they had communicated an outline of their history and their hopes, and the Nine Star League, with the help of all Talents, began to establish a viable communication level, starting with the most pliable and least resistant humans – children of both Talented and unTalented families.

Damia and Afra had been one of the first families to accept Mrdini youngling pairs in order to establish a useful form of communication between the species. As it happened, Talent was an unimportant factor since the Mrdini mind could not be read even by as powerful a Talent as Jeff Raven, or his wife, Angharad Gwyn-Raven, the Rowan. But when Damia realized she was pregnant, shortly after the first 'Dini contact was made, she was one of the first to suggest that the young of each species, brought up together from infancy, might absorb the 'Dini language as easily as Basic. So Laria had had cribmates from the time she was six months old, as had each of her siblings.

Almost as prolific as her Denebian grandmother, the Healer Isthia, Damia had had no problems with pregnancies though, unlike her mother, the Rowan, she had been careful to space her children two or two and a half years apart. Then, too, her duties at the Iota Aurigaean Tower

13

had not been as demanding as her mother's responsibilities at Callisto Moon Station. And Afra, being partnered in the Tower with his mate, had been able to devote as much time as required to his increasing family.

If Jeff Raven twitted his son-in-law about overdoing paternity, Afra would merely shrug and remind his friend that he himself had urged the Capellan to marry and have children.

Maternity had mellowed Damia as much as paternity had relaxed Afra. If his family never understood why their Talented son had had to leave Capella and the promise of a good position in Callisto Prime Tower, he could at least find alternative Towers for those nieces and nephews of his that might also wish for a life unrestricted by Capella's methody ways.

He did insist, however – and often smiled as he did so – that his children behave within the courtesy protocols in which he had been raised. But he did not fall into the error of his own parents – in believing that they knew best for their children.

Consequently the Raven-Lyon home was easy-going, friendly, and totally unselfconscious in the practice of Talent and the inclusion of an alien species into their familial structure.

That life-style might undergo drastic change with the Mrdini discovery of the putative route to the Hive Home System. Damia had no precognitive Talent but she didn't need any to recognize that a new era had just begun: an era that would, hopefully, eradicate the threat of the Hive species for both human and Mrdini.

So, what happens now? Damia and Afra asked Earth Prime.

Well, and there was a wry note to Jeff's tone, *your mother and I are to send all available Fleet ships of Galaxy and Constellation class to a rendezvous with the Mrdini scout. They're sending as many of their own heavyweights as possible.*

Afra snorted. *And what good is that going to do without*

Talent support, Jeff? We all know the extrapolations of confrontation. Who's going to supply sufficient power to overwhelm them?

We may follow, Jeff replied in a droll fashion.

You AND Mother? Damia's concern and alarm flowed out of her despite Afra's tight reassuring embrace.

When you consider how much larger a Talented population we can draw on now than we could twenty-odd years ago, daughter dear, stop being negative. Much has to be decided. But we cannot deny the use of Talent when it can be of tactical advantage.

First the Hive Home System has to be found.

And every other one they have overpowered, Jeff added, seemingly unconcerned at the monumental task facing the Allies.

How in the universe can we do that? Damia demanded, appalled at the prospect.

That is what must be discovered. The strength of resolve in her father's voice provided Damia with fortitude. *The event which we have entertained for so long has occurred. We cannot be lacking in courage now.*

No, Dad, of course not. Aurigae Tower supports you one hundred per cent.

The warning has been limited to those who need to know, of which Aurigae Tower is one. The official position will be announced in due course but prepare yourselves and the Tower for unusual activity.

The Hive System is near Aurigae?

No, but the mine production will be increased as fast and as soon as possible. Expect to transmit huge and continuous ore drones.

And what explanation is to be given? Damia asked for she knew they'd be interrogated by the mine syndicates.

Tell them a new design of interstellar transport has been approved and production of the units is a top priority. Jeff chuckled. *That won't be a falsehood, either, for our people have just commissioned a prototype long-range Constellation-class vessel, the* Genesee. *There are four more in construction and they'll be finished as fast as possible. Your miners don't have to know where their ore goes, only that they'll be paid for it. How good are your eldest two in Tower disciplines?*

Laria and Thian? Damia asked, once again experiencing that stab of irrational maternal concern.

They're steady enough for anything we can handle, Afra replied. *Why?*

You may have to lob big-daddies about the League again.

What a blessing my eldest are both T-1s then, isn't it?

Jeff Raven chuckled over his daughter's sardonic remark. Then his mental tone abruptly altered to one of great pride and dignity. *The Allies will be made fully aware of how blessed we are with Talent.* There was a pause and then one of Jeff Raven's inimitable chuckles reached their ears. *Gwyn-Ravens and Lyons to the rescue yet again!* Then his mental tone disappeared from their minds.

Damia was buoyed up by Jeff's imperturbable optimism but she looked to Afra for further reassurance. Tenderly he pulled her into a deeper embrace, gently pressing her head into his shoulder. With one hand he pushed back the vagrant silver lock of her hair that always seemed to fall into her face when she was distressed. Patting it into place, he kissed her, making contact on every level that bound them to each other. She felt herself respond, as much out of habit as need.

I didn't raise children to fight Hives. Does Laria have to go to Mrdini?

We have promised the exchange. We have intrinsically benefited by the exchange. We will make it as planned. Don't fret. Laria's a well-balanced, sensible and responsible chi . . . young woman, nearly – as we both know. She is in no more danger on Clarf than she would be here.

Especially if she has to help us shift big-daddy drone pods, and Damia tried to sound facetious. Afra knew she was not and tightened his arms about her in appreciation of the attempt.

The daughter of the girl who overwhelmed Sodan will not fail in whatever she is required to do.

Damia shivered in recollection of her battle with the Sodan mind which had been dangerous to her, fatal to her beloved younger brother, Larak, and come very close to destroying the other Talents in that focus. The Hive menace was even more dangerous to the Allies.

'Damia,' Afra said aloud, releasing her enough to tip her head up so she made eye contact, 'count, if you can, just how many more Talents are available now than there were thirty-eight years ago. Between your brothers and sister, and David of Betelgeuse, Mauli and Mick, Torshan and Saggoner. Why, the uncles, aunts and second cousins on Deneb alone constitute a brigade!'

Damia allowed herself to be comforted because she couldn't refute Afra's logic. And definitely there was safety in the numbers of Talented minds that could be counted in Federated Telepathy and Teleportation alone: not to mention the higher Talents in every other occupation that made use of psionic abilities. Only how to bring such a mental weapon against a far distant enemy homeworld? As clever and powerful as a massed mind focus of Talent had proved itself, there were different parameters now that did not favour such use of Talent.

'Consider also that our Allies have certainly not been idle in the past twenty-five years, always with the goal of defeating the Hive ships.'

'But they died to defeat a Hiver!'

'Yes, they did die, but that was before we Dreamed!'

Damia *felt* Afra's conviction. Was it just a masculine certitude? Her father's mind had been coloured with it as well! Damia wondered if she should ask her mother what *she* felt. No, she decided, she should solve this confusion within herself. And soon! Her doubts must not impinge on her children's confidence and courage. They might all need those soon enough.

'Yes,' she said aloud, looking calmly into her mate's yellow eyes, sparkling with purpose, 'that was before we Dreamed Mrdini.'

17

2

The very next day Aurigae Tower accepted a message, containing an immense order for tonnes of metal ore from the Allied Commands. Afra forwarded it to the Miners Main Office and sat back, waiting for the explosion.

Within minutes of receiving the message, Segrazlin, Master Miner and head of the various mining organizations on Aurigae, requested an urgent meeting with the Prime to discuss transportation requirements. His manner was a combination of gratification for the quantities ordered and astonishment and concern at the delivery dates expected, trepidation over how to approach the Prime on the matter of the tonnage to be shifted, all mingled with intense curiosity as to the finished form of such massive quantities of metal.

Damia grinned at his promptness and told him he could come along right then, as the morning's traffic had been despatched.

Segrazlin arrived with his personal assistant and the owners of the major mines to be involved.

'All very well to want this kind of delivery, Prime,'

Segrazlin said, nervously folding and unfolding the message sheet, 'but, one, we don't have enough miners, even working flat out, to supply the ores within the delivery frame and, two, there aren't enough small and medium carriers to deliver half of what's required. Now, we don't want to lose such a contract, but first off, we'll need more miners.' He was hedging around asking her to transport the big-daddy drone containers. 'And my principals,' at which point the five owners nodded their heads, 'want to be sure that the metal's being properly used.'

'Ah,' Afra said, broadcasting reassurance, 'I asked Earth Prime that myself. Some new Constellation-class vessel has been designed, long-journey capability, and enough for a squadron has been authorized. Replacing some of the older space vessels. And not before time, I understand. FT&T may cut down on the normal wear and tear of space vehicles, but the problem of metal fatigue is still vexing.'

Damia sent a mental smirk to her husband for that smooth explanation.

'There is also the happy fact that the Tower is now in a position to transport bigger drones,' Damia went on, 'a good training exercise for our oldest children. Having standardized the size and shapes of most containers, any Prime, given the mass within, can shift it anywhere within the Alliance. It's new and unfamiliar objects that cause problems, because they have to be *seen* and preferably touched by a Prime before 'portation can be guaranteed. However, we can shift most anything you need to send because your drones are standard. As you know, both Laria and Thian are T-1s . . . '

'But are they old enough?' Segrazlin asked, his eyes protruding in surprise. Having expected resistance, he'd lost his prepared stance.

'They are old enough and will be under our guidance, but their assistance will make it possible to lift such weight. Linkage is good training for their future duties.' Damia inclined her head graciously.

'That still leaves us with the worst problem, Prime,' one of the mine owners said, clearing his throat, and glancing at his colleagues for reassurance. They nodded their heads and murmured agreement. 'Enough workers.'

'I thought your work force was up to strength, Yugin,' Damia said, frowning in well-imitated surprise.

Yugin snorted. 'For normal production, yes, but the last quota of immigrants haven't been trained for deep seam work and that's what we'd need. Also more qualified, and experienced, engineers. We'll have to open more shafts . . . ' He trailed off.

'We can't supply those prodigious quantities,' Mexalgo said, 'from existing facilities.'

'Would you accept more 'Dinis?' Afra asked.

Mexalgo looked dubious but the others brightened considerably.

'Mex, you treat 'em right, they do you proud,' Yugin said. 'My 'Dinis work like they grew up digging ore.'

'Workers isn't the main problem, Yugin,' Mexalgo said. 'Engineers with the pit experience, if we're starting new seams, is what we really lack.'

'Would you accept 'Dini engineers?'

Mexalgo made a grimace. 'I would if I could understand them.'

'What's to understand?' Segrazlin asked. 'You show 'em where the lode is, give 'em the materials they need, and they dig. They're as well trained, by their standards, as any of our men, and besides,' a grin broke across Segrazlin's craggy features, 'they're built better for underground work!'

'Aye, that's a fact,' Mexalgo said, though reluctantly. 'But how can we be sure, with those little holidays of theirs, that we'll have a work force all the time? We can't make these shipments with part-time help.'

'The Mrdinis don't all hibernate at the same time,' Damia said. 'The hibernation period apparently depends on the continent of origin. The 'Dinis presently on Aurigae all happen to come from the northern Great continent. Or so Flk told me. Should I enquire, on your behalf, if additional 'Dini engineers and workers are available and would be willing to come to Aurigae to work?'

The miners conferred briefly by nods, hand and head gestures.

'Yes, Prime, we would appreciate your enquiring on our behalf.'

'You will of course pay according to experience and training?' Afra asked.

'Of course,' Segrazlin said, slightly indignantly. 'And provide the sort of quarters and hibernation facilities that they prefer. We haven't had any complaints from 'em yet.'

That was true enough because Damia and Afra made certain that the specifications given them by the 'Dinis were carried out.

'I'd like to see the engineering qualifications, though,' Mexalgo said, always cautious. 'In translation.'

'Of course,' Afra replied with a smile. 'Oddly enough, translating scientific data is easier than, say, literature or art forms.'

Mexalgo sniffed.

'Earth Prime agrees to forward your request to Clarf Tower,' Damia said, having spoken to her father during Afra's part of the conversation. 'He'll forward the answer within the current day.'

What Jeff Raven had told his daughter was that, not only were the 'Dinis willing, they were eager. Their own mines were nearly depleted, even those on their colony worlds, and miners, pit men as well as engineers, were as desperate to find work as to supply their homeworld with the commodities it needed.

When Segrazlin and the mine owners had left, Damia was not so sedate that she didn't give a little dance of jubilation for the success of the interview. There had been some criticism – expressed through Flk and Trp to Damia

21

and Afra – that 'Dinis were disappointed that their out-world workers were not given the positions of authority that their experience and training should qualify them for. What the mining community didn't realize was that there were fully trained and professionally able engineers among the 'Dini workers already on Aurigae. Now, with such massive orders, came the chance the 'Dinis had been hoping for to show their true colours. The 'Dinis had been very patient and now would have the opportunity they had long deserved. Damia and Afra had reason to rejoice.

As soon as the miners had boarded their vehicles to return to Aurigae City, Afra went in search of Flk and Trp to inform them of the good news. They clacked, clicked and whistled their joy and then departed towards the city, to spread the news.

'I think we must insist that some of the new pits be 'Dini managed and run,' Afra said.

'We had to go slow or jeopardize the integration,' Damia said.

'I know, I know. We can be extremely grateful for 'Dini patience.'

Damia grinned up at her lover. 'We should really learn more from them. Flk said that it took them nearly ten generations to implant the philosophy of patience in the 'Dini temperament.'

It was again fortunate that 'Dinis were difficult to iden-tify, for when the first shipment of new workers arrived, the 'Dini engineers amazed the mine owners by their grasp of the mining methods currently in use on Aurigae and their incredible dexterity with human-designed equip-ment. They had also brought tools of their own, including large borers to be assembled. The first consultation to organize 'Dini-managed pits erased any reluctance or hesi-tation the mine owners and their engineers might have had about 'Dini professionalism.

'I was impressed,' Mexalgo told Damia, 'very im-pressed. They clicked and clacked when we showed them where we'd located the new lodes, and the next thing they had adit, shafts and quotas all drawn out for us, and the quantities of materials they'd need for shoring, what track, carts, cranes, stuff they evidently knew they didn't have to bring. They've asked permission to send for more of their own mining equipment and I can't fault 'em on that. Showed us schematics of some of the heavy stuff they use and I have to say it looks very efficient. Then, too, they'll be handier with their own mechanicals but they sure understood fast.' He kept shaking his head. 'Now,' he added quickly, 'I always knew the critters were smart. I just didn't realize how smart.'

Damia and Afra managed to respond appropriately.

Wouldn't he have a fit if he knew the 'new' 'Dinis engineers had been working in his mines for the past sixteen years! Damia said, her mental tone rocking with laughter at the deceptions.

Later. We'll confess to Mexalgo later, Afra promised.

The 'Dinis were also impressed by the quality of accommodation supplied by the mine owners, including a 'Dini-staffed medical facility. That had been an extra which Segrazlin had insisted on providing.

'You house and feed a man and his family decently,' the miners' rep said, 'and you make pits as safe as possible, but you damn better have emergency facilities available, too. Man works better because he knows he's valued. Same has to apply to 'Dinis. They got feelings, too.'

During the settling-in period, Laria, Thian and even Rojer did translating duty. Zara, though only nine, wanted to have some part in the family activity and thought of donating the young eggs from her Slither's latest lay to the new arrivals.

'To make 'em feel at home,' she'd said very solemnly as she signed Tip and Hug, explaining her gift. All the Raven-Lyon 'Dinis took turns expressing how grateful they were for her generosity. They had Slither nestlings too, and so an expedition was planned.

'I think this ought to come from the young of humans to the young of Mrdini, Laria,' Damia said, 'so you can drive – carefully –' and Damia reinforced that caution mentally, 'and make it an outing.'

She's fully competent to drive that sort of sledge, Damia, Afra told his wife when she began to regret her suggestion. *You've driven with her enough to know she's well able. And we've got to let her have some experience on her own. Not that she's exactly on her own right now.*

I know, I know, Affie, Damia said, unable to suppress all her maternal agitation, despite his logical reassurances. *It's just that . . .*

I trust her and I'll be with her every kilometre of the way.

If you really trusted her, you wouldn't be with her all the way, Damia added, darkly accusatory.

Afra laughed and ruffled her hair as they watched Laria load her passengers into the big sledge. The girl kept looking over her shoulder at her parents.

See? She expects you to renege, Damia. Smile, wave, encourage her!

She doesn't really need encouragement, Damia replied, still dour, but she smiled and waved vigorously. She held her breath as the sledge rose, without a hitch, on its air cushion. Laria turned it competently and Damia began to relax a little. Especially when Afra chuckled teasingly in her ear.

We can't stand here watching, Afra added and gently propelled her back towards the Tower. *And don't peek!* At that admonition, Damia had to laugh because he had caught her tendril of thought reaching out to maintain a very light contact with Laria's mind. *We've got those first drones to despatch and I want your entire attention on that transfer, my little love!*

Afra was right about keeping her mind on the work at hand, Damia knew. Not the big-daddies yet but some very heavy mothers. The mining industry was determined to deliver on time and this first shipment was in earnest of that intention.

The generators were already at peak when Aurigaean Prime and her T-2 mate took their Tower positions. Damia contacted David of Betelgeuse who gave her a cheerful greeting.

I understand we're back to big-daddies soon in this rearmament, David said.

Is it advisable, Damia replied cautiously, *to bandy about such terms?*

Who'd be able to hear us, Damia?

Here you are then, David! With the skill and ease of long practice, Damia caught the generators at peak and teleported the ore drones from the mine yards directly to David who would shift them to the refinery awaiting the metal.

Motherhood certainly hasn't slowed you down, has it?

Why should it?

Catch you later!

Catch, you'd better! was Damia's response and then Keylarion sent her up an urgent incoming load.

In the rhythm of work, Damia forgot about her daughter's first major driving experience.

Laria found the drive exhilarating, only minimally conscious of her passengers or even her brother who shared the front seat.

It was one thing to teleport herself, which she had done often enough to make it routine, and quite another to be *driving* others in a mechanical apparatus: even if she knew all Tower vehicles were maintained at top efficiency. The sledge was dead easy to manage, with a yoke for steering and pedals for speed and braking. Even if the power, for some unforeseen reason, went off and the air cushion failed, her reflexes were fast enough to switch to kinetic mode and avoid a hard or abrupt landing. Her father had drilled her on such emergency measures – even before he had allowed her any solo time in one of the smaller sledges.

25

The most important aspect was that neither of her parents were 'peeking'. She, on the other hand, could tell they were both involved in Tower work. They really were allowing her to exercise independent action, which she felt to be appropriate since she was so nearly sixteen, and then would be considered 'of age'.

The 'Dini village had been constructed on the far side of the city, where the land sloped up to the western plateau. It had been a consolidated effort: Flk and Trp had overseen the project, with some assistance from their human colleagues and more from the 'Dini professionals in various skills. Once the materials had been assembled, the entire population of Aurigae City had devoted three days to the building of the village, complete with hibernatory, medical and recreational facilities from the 'Dini-originated designs. The plans had drawn admiring support from the human construction crew which had passed on their enthusiasm to the whole community. The result was a village of a high standard, with every comfort that 'Dinis would find on their homeworlds.

Laria had a little flurry of nerves as she approached the village vehicle park because 'Dinis were flitting about in the air, using the personal flying equipment they had brought with them, but in a totally random fashion that didn't appear to follow any traffic pattern. Laria was afraid that she might inadvertently cause an accident. Tip clicked encouragingly at her while Huf slid open a window and started crackling at the nearby fliers who then did make way for the sledge. Laria landed with no further obstacles.

'Those belts are great, Lar,' Thian exclaimed, craning his neck to watch the rapid manoeuvres of the airborne. 'D'you think we could get some?'

'When we can teleport anywhere we want to?' asked Laria in amazement.

'Teleporting's not the same thing, Lar,' Thian replied wistfully and ignored his sister's wry snort. 'I *like* mechanical things,' he added defensively.

26

Which his sister knew was very true. Thian was always taking things apart and putting them laboriously back together. Sometimes not so laboriously, if he knew the equipment well enough to use kinesis in reassembly. Their father encouraged the activity, though their mother had always appeared sceptical.

Tip, Huf, Mur and Dip joined them on the hard dirt of the park, each carrying precious baskets of Slithers. Zara had hers cradled against her narrow chest, her eyes wide both with her responsibility and her inclusion in this journey.

Tip clucked and pointed one flipper in the direction they were to take – towards the 'community' hall. The 'Dinis had opted for a main feeding service and that building also became their meeting and assembly facility. Chairs, and tables for that matter, were not a necessity for 'Dini dining customs. Stacks of bowls were neatly stored to one side and cushions dotted the open floor space. The cushions were occupied as Laria and her brother and sister entered with their 'Dini friends, and their appearance occasioned much noise from the expectant 'Dinis. Laria could see that the majority here were young 'Dinis, apprentices who wouldn't work as long hours as the adults but the very ones who would cherish the Slithers. The creatures provided endless amusement to 'Dinis though Laria didn't very much appreciate Slithers crawling on her bare skin: it gave her such an odd feeling.

The clacking, clicking and whistling of the eager young 'Dinis made the distribution of the pets urgent, so that was done, Zara and Thian deeply thanked, with Tip, Huf, Mur and Dip doing the translating. The youngsters were sent off with their new acquisitions and the adult females offered the humans suitable refreshments. Laria, Thian and Zara were asked to seat themselves on the cushions and became the object of much poll bowing and eyeing.

'What's so funny about us?' Zara wanted to know.

'I don't think these 'Dinis have seen many humans,'

27

Laria said quietly. 'Yes,' and she caught Tip's hand signals, 'these are just mature attendant females who haven't gone out of the village yet.' She signalled another question to Tip. And grinned at the answer. 'They thought humans were something the elder 'Dinis had made. They are astonished to see that we are real. Tip says they come from a southern continent that isn't very forward. But they needed employment so badly that they couldn't afford to pass up the good pay. They are very pleased to find that the accommodations are every bit as good as they were promised.' Then she laughed again, blushing.

'What's the matter, Lar?' Thian asked, surprised, for his sister rarely coloured.

'Tip likes the buff-coloured one with the leg stripes.'

Thian pretended to subject the 'Dini to intense scrutiny and then grinned. 'She is rather charmingly marked.'

At which point, both young people laughed because the 'Dini mistook his attention and came hurrying over with her tray of bite-sized edibles.

You're being mean, Zara said in a scathing tone, narrowing her eyes at her brother and sister.

We aren't, really, Zara, Laria said, somewhat chastened. Then she turned to Tip and asked if there was a chance to see the 'Dini living quarters, or would that be considered an intrusion.

Tip got to its feet, chattering a comment to the marked 'Dini, and the others were instantly off their tails and gesturing the humans towards the door.

'I gather we're to inspect,' Thian said, grinning from ear to ear and signalling Tip that he was very pleased to be accorded such an honour.

Having had 'Dini roommates in their own quarters all their lives, it was somewhat of a surprise to see what 'Dinis considered suitable accommodations. Heated pools were featured on the lowest level of the five dormitories they were shown. Hatches led from the spacious pool area back into service areas, or so Thian suggested to his sisters. In the foyer of the main entrance, the walls were full of racks fashioned to hold the flying belts which 'Dinis used for transportation. On the two upper levels, for the 'Dinis preferred to spread out rather than up, long dark corridors bisected and, on either side, were doors into smaller apartments. These included a main room, never very large, the 'Dini equivalent of a water closet – which was, in truth, a closet – and several sleeping rooms, with what Laria called bunk beds, usually four in each tier, two and three tiers across every wallspace. A small locker was fastened to the end of each bed and in that special personal possessions were kept. There seemed to be no blankets or pillows and Laria wondered that their 'Dinis had always used such comforts.

Adaptable, aren't they? Thian told his sister as they did the rounds, expressing appropriate approval by signals. Their four 'Dinis returned with signals of pleasure at their responses. Zara was too awed by her surroundings to have any other reaction than a good long look around her.

I wonder why they don't have any windows at all, Laria said to Thian, having noticed the omission. *That'd be smarter than those lighting bars.*

For us, maybe, but let's not ask until we leave here, Thian said.

I wasn't going to, Laria said, a little miffed that her brother thought her so lacking in tact.

Didn't think you were. Hey, they do have exhaust fans in the ceilings. Or that's what they look like. Small ones over each bed unless those round things are lights, too. So have our 'Dinis been living in the lap of luxury, or slumming it?

Thian!

He grinned, unabashed.

Their spontaneous tour ended near the entrance to one of the hibernatories. Thian asked Mur if there were five facilities to accommodate the numbers of 'Dinis or to accommodate different continents. Continents, he was informed, so that there would always be a full crew of workers

29

available in the mines. 'Dinis would honour their contracts.

'Never doubted that for a minute,' Thian said, smiling and nodding approval at Mur.

Although the three young people would never have intruded on such a sacred place, the 'Dinis were suddenly herding them adroitly back to the parking area. The mine whistle blew for a change of shift which speeded up their farewells.

That evening while dinner was being prepared, Laria had a lot of questions for her parents.

Mother, would you say that the 'Dini quarters are luxurious? Or just basic?

Flk and Trp informed us in no uncertain terms, Damia replied, *that the quarters are of a very high standard and everyone is very pleased with them.*

Afra grinned, looking over at Laria from where he was feeding Petra her supper. *Their real delight are the heated pools. Those would apparently have made up for many other shortcomings.*

Of which we made sure there were none. Though some of the amenities they did request were a bit odd, Damia said, frowning slightly.

Like what? Thian wanted to know. *The exhaust fans or those tube lights?*

Damia paused for a moment, considering her answer. *You know, I'm not quite sure.*

They don't seem to use bedding or pillows or anything, Thian went on. *They do here.*

Cruel and unusual torments, they are, Afra said, judiciously spooning mashed vegetables into his daughter's mouth.

Ah, Dad! Thian said.

They adapt to our ways, Damia said, shooting a quelling glance at her lover.

And I'll have to adapt to their ways? Laria sounded dubious.

When in Rome . . . her father said.

Afra! Damia turned to reassure her daughter. Laria's time to exchange was nearing and such questions must be answered truthfully. *We asked and asked all the 'Dinis what comforts they needed.* She gave a sigh of exasperation. *They said they needed no special ones. They are quite happy with everything we do for them.*

But will I be happy? Laria replied, wondering how she could ever cope with windowless rooms, exhaust fans and long tube lights. She hadn't really thought about the conditions she'd be faced with on Clarf even if she had never been uncomfortable for a moment with Tip and Huf. At least on her own turf. Or even when they vacationed on Deneb with Great-Grandmother Isthia.

The Tower personnel at Clarf have assured me that they have spacious and elegant quarters, Damia said so emphatically that Laria began to feel less insecure.

But Lar won't be living at the Tower, will she, Ma? Thian asked, looking as innocent as his youngest sister.

'Thian!' his father said in a firm voice and Thian immediately subsided. *Of course you will be required to enter a hibernatory for two months out of every year just like every other 'Dini.*

His tone was so prosaic that Laria stared at him and then burst out laughing and consequently felt very much better about her future. Another thing: her parents would never have committed her to something that wasn't absolutely safe for her, their eldest daughter. Laria was a little puffed about her premier position in the Raven-Lyon family: not badly, but enough for her to be aware of her seniority.

During the next week, that was put to practical application as both she and Thian joined their parents in the Tower to shift the first big-daddy drones.

'It's the mass that's hard to shift, not the physical weight,' Afra told the two as they settled themselves in the extra couches that had been fitted into the main Tower control room.

Thian was twitching with excitement but Laria was able to control her own, though she'd a dreadful fluttering in her middle. Not that she hadn't already assisted her parents

31

during emergencies. They all had during the cave-in at the Maltese Cross Mine. Telekinesis had saved a hundred and eight miners from sure death by asphyxiation. Afra had even managed to salvage the bodies of the dead: a great comfort to their grieving families. Laria hadn't been quite sure about *that* aspect of the rescue but she'd been very glad when she'd linked with her mother to extricate the live ones: she, Thian, Rojer and even Zara had added their strength to their mother's in a spontaneous link. They'd practised such joinings – for just such an emergency as it had been used for – but this had been life and death.

Today's exercise was merely a union of the four high Talented minds to lift dead weight of refined iron ore and fling it across the galaxy to Betelgeuse and the manufactories there. They had four to transport.

'This is by way of being a practice session, children,' Afra said. 'Easily within your present abilities and strengths.'

'You'll be doing it often enough and with considerably more drones so that this could become a boring exercise,' Damia added as she settled herself in her couch. 'It is *never*,' and she waggled a finger at each of them, 'to become either boring or an exercise. You are to pay strict attention to the protocol and the technique now and whenever else you are required to teleport: especially such masses as these.'

Laria and Thian nodded solemnly. They knew how proud their mother was of her Tower status as Aurigaean Prime. She'd held it since she was barely eighteen and had never lost a cargo or mishandled one, inanimate or animate. They had been trained since the first time they'd 'lifted' with mind power alone.

'Now, settle yourself comfortably,' Damia said, putting her head back on the rest, shaking her hands to relax them.

The generators were coming up to full power. Laria knew the sound intimately. She waggled her hands and let them drape beside her, giving her head a final scrunch. She listened intently to the generators, felt the touch of

Mother-Father in her mind, let the link happen and felt part of that accord, then felt the addition of Thian's. Only it was no longer four separate minds, it was a Mind, much, much stronger than one raised to the fourth power. This Mind was directed to the first of five puny-looking drones, lying like swollen slugs in the paved court of the Trefoil Mining Corporation. The Mind gripped the drone and lifted it up, up, and then, as a youngster would skate a flat pebble across the still waters of a lake or river, the drone was skipped out, beyond the planet, beyond its moon and further, further, further, gathering speed until speed was a blur, until the Mind felt a resistance.

Betelgeuse has it! said the Mind that was directed by David of Betelgeuse with his grown children behind him.

The first of five, her Mind announced formally.

Receiving.

Lifting.

Pause.

Receiving.

Lifting.

Pause.

Receiving. The pattern continued until all five drones had been delivered to their destination.

That is all today.

That is enough today! the Betelgeuse replied with feeling.

Tut-tut, David. We must set the example for our young.

We are our young today, Damia! Salutations, Afra, Laria, Thian.

Salutations, David, Perry, Xahra, Morgelle.

The subsequent silence was as rigid as the exchange had been fluid: almost painful. Laria felt a subtraction, knew that Thian had been dropped from the Mind. Then sensed her own exclusion and opened her eyes, rolling her head to release taut neck muscles. Saw Thian doing the same exercises.

'Thank you,' Damia said warmly. 'That made a hard task much easier.'

'I've got the hang of it now, Mother,' Laria said shyly. 'No headache.'

'That only comes when you resist the link,' Damia said, reaching across the intervening space to ruffle her daughter's hair. 'All right, Thian.'

The boy shook his head, rolled his eyes dramatically. 'I must have been resisting. My head's drumming.'

Immediately, Damia swung off her couch and went to sit on his, her long fingers massaging the column of his neck and up into the head, down again into the shoulder muscles. Thian made faces at Laria who sympathized because she knew how strong her mother's fingers were even as she envied Thian the special treatment.

'Comes with practice,' Afra said, sliding beside his daughter and giving her a gentle massage.

Thian grimaced again. 'We'll get plenty of that now, won't we?'

'Enough to *learn* the technique required,' Damia said. 'There, that should do the trick. Off you go, now. You've studies to do as well today!'

Thian groaned and Laria was certain that he only pretended to have the headache, hoping to be excused from lessons. Mother was a lot smarter than Thian! She kept her notion to herself, however, for she wasn't in the mood to pick a fight right now. Being part of the Mind might be just part of the work of the telekinetic Talent but the merging, being part of her parents, her brother, being tuned to the generators exalted her – yes, exalt *was* exactly the word – in ways no other facet of her Talent did. She'd once tried to explain the complexity of that rapport to her father and stumbled badly. But they weren't telepaths for nothing and he had cradled her in his arms, assuring her, telepathically, that he knew exactly what she meant. That that was how it should be, a transcendence of self. She had been much reassured.

Despite the fact that she had grown up among high Talents, had shown evidence of very strong aptitudes by the time she was three, there were certain aspects of the gifts that were occasionally overwhelming.

'And that, my little love,' her father had said, cradling her gently and tenderly, letting his love for her wrap like a warm soft shawl about her, 'is exactly how it should be. It doesn't do to become arrogant and that's a danger we must studiously shun.'

Now she made her way down from the Tower into the main room of the complex, waved to Keylarion the Tower's T-6, and Herault the stationmaster who looked inordinately relieved that the transfer of such mass had gone so smoothly. Xexo didn't look up from the gauges of his beloved generators and Filamena, the expeditor, was busy watching a scroll of incoming cargo assignments.

Tip and Huf looked up from the complicated stick game they were playing with Mur and Dip when she appeared on the steps. They whistled and began to gather up the splinters in front of them. Mur and Dip protested, and Laria had to laugh. No matter how often the two sets played, Tip and Huf were always the winners and Mur and Dip never seemed to figure out how. She signed to Mur that she couldn't beat Tip and Huf either but that didn't much appease them. Thian's arrival did and the sextet set out back to the terraced house and the tutorials awaiting them, for all six young creatures had lessons to attend and that was how they occupied themselves until it was time to prepare lunch.

3

When her parents told Laria that she would shortly be going to the Mrdini homeworld, she was at first ecstatic. At the same time, Tip and Huf had been informed by the Aurigaean Mrdini chief and their joy to be going home was expressed in the form of incredible joyous acrobatics of such complexity that everyone in the Raven-Lyon household stopped whatever they were doing to see their display. The other 'Dinis joined in with suitable support gyrations, not as complex as Tip and Huf were managing for, after all, it was Tip and Huf who were going home.

It was perhaps seeing such antics on her home terrace that made Laria realize that she would be leaving it. Leaving Saki, the Coonies, the Darbuls, even the Slithers: leaving her brothers and sisters, and most of all leaving her parents and all that was familiar and homely. Laria suppressed the rising doubt and nebulous anxieties about her ability to handle all she would now experience. The exchange pact had been explained to her the day, at five years of age, she'd asked her parents why some people didn't have 'Dini friends. But, oh, how she would miss everyone!

We would be terribly hurt if you didn't, her father said gently, obviously speaking only to her. She managed a smile for him as she turned to where he stood on the top of the terrace steps with her mother. *You will be only a thought away, dear heart,* he added. *We have that advantage.*

Yes, we do, Daddy, she replied stoutly and resolutely turned her thoughts to positive ones. The first was to fix in her mind's eye the scene around her; their house with the mountains looming behind them in an unbroken stretch, the city below her with the faint rattle and clang of mine machinery (a constant background noise), the 'Dinis dancing, the admiring audience of her brothers and sisters, Coonies and Darbuls, and even a few Slithers who carefully kept to the banks where they would be less apt to be trampled by flippered feet.

The evening sky was a particularly beautiful shade of azure, darkening slowly to the vivid depths of night. There was even a breeze, flowing down from the mountains, that was cold and redolent of the pungent vegetation that was welcoming Aurigaean spring. And, as ever, the faint acrid whiff that left a metallic aftertaste at the back of the throat.

Laria would remember this scene, this moment for ever. She knew it, and sighed deeply.

Laria's sisters, Zara, Kaltia and even five-year-old Morag, helped her pack while the 'Dinis watched. They didn't have more to take home than a small pouch apiece: oddments that were valuable only to them: pieces of pretty rocks and sea shells, beaded panels of unknown usage and uncut gemstones which were their particular favourites. When their fondness for jewels had been noticed, Afra had located a lapidary among the Aurigaean miners but, while the 'Dinis displayed a keen interest in the process, they were not at all intrigued with the formality of cutting their gems. The 'Dinis on Earth had evidently cornered the market in pearls, nacre and other iridescent marine shells, items not available on Aurigae.

Leaving Saki was the hardest part although Laria knew that Zara, who would inherit the amiable horse, adored her. She would be leaving Saki in the best possible hands. Zara's pony would now pass to Morag who was just old enough to manage. But once Laria had accepted that necessity, she began to get excited about the adventure. For it would be one. She felt it from both her mother and father, including a touch or two of envy that she would be having an experience that they couldn't. Thian was particularly strong in his envy aura but he'd only a year or so to wait before he could come too, so Laria didn't mind him. Rojer was the most unhappy because he hadn't been part of the 'Dini exchange and he really, really wanted to be. Laria tried projecting soothing thoughts to him but he caught her at it and disappeared on one of his solitary hunts. Dismayed, she kept a light touch on him, but Rojer, although only twelve now, was clever and eluded her.

Sometimes Laria felt like the 'Dinis, leaping about with excitement; at others, she wondered just what she was getting into. Whether or not the 'Dinis had had simi-lar trepidations she didn't know, but she received such supportive dreams from Tip and Huf that gradually an-ticipation became wholly positive. She almost couldn't bear the wait until the hour she was to depart.

As several other 'Dini pairs were making the trip home, a large carrier was to be used. Almost too keyed-up to contain herself, Laria hugged each of her siblings, her mother and father, and practically dived into the capsule.

As he closed the hatch, her father winked in such a conspiratorial fashion that she was startled. *Glad you stayed around to go by carrier, love,* he said. *You looked about ready to make the jump unaided.*

She wriggled with impatience and grinned radiantly back at him. She *had* felt that way. *I've got more sense than that, Dad!*

If you hadn't, we wouldn't have considered sending you, Laria, he replied in his droll fashion. *When in doubt, use that good common sense of yours, Coonie, and you'll be fine.*

Calling her 'Coonie' was his especial endearment and a flood of prideful love enveloped her. She widened an already cheek-breaking smile and he completed the closure, slapping the roof of the carrier as the cargo handlers always did.

Laria wiggled again, scrunching herself more comfortably on to the padding. Then she turned her head to be sure that the 'Dinis were all secure in their specially made hammocks.

Ready? her mother asked.

Ready, Laria answered, dying for the protocol of sending to be finished so she could *go!*

For all of her excitement and anticipation, she couldn't help hanging on to the mind-touch of her parents as they inaugurated the lift. So she knew the second in which the personnel carrier was taken from the cradle, as it hovered and, with a split second to prepare herself, was thrust across the void in the teleportation that would end at the Mrdinis' world.

Clarf, which was the nearest that humans could come to the sounds which Mrdinis made for their homeworld, was in the usual third position of an oxygen-hydrocarbon world about its primary. The system, however, was in the midst of a very populous area of the galaxy. It was no wonder the Mrdinis had achieved star flight, with so many near, bright and sparkling neighbours to encourage them to explore other worlds. Clarf's position in such a teeming cluster also gave the Mrdinis some protection from the encroaching Hive: there were many other worlds to attract that species' interest.

When the transfer of teleports occurred, Laria was involved in the exchange.

Hi there, small stuff, a cheerful baritone voice said. *Allow me to introduce ourselves: Yoshuk is me, and Nesrun is my happy otherself.* There was an alto chuckle.

Yoshuk has his joke, the alto voice said. *Be welcome, young*

39

Laria. And there! You're landed. Quite a welcoming committee so be ready.

Since the capsule's controls were for human manipulation, Laria unsealed the hatch and cracked it. The blazing light that poured in made her squint while the 'Dinis sneezed, honked, crackled at a high level of joy and excitement. Shielding her eyes, Laria pushed the hatch back, and then stood aside. Tip and Huf were most insistent in sign and sound that they emerge first. Noise poured in on them as well as light, almost as violently as the assault of light on her eyes. But she couldn't see well enough to locate the source. Then the other Mrdini filed past her, clicking softly with polite appreciation of her courtesy. The moment they stepped out, they added their own sharp barks and shouts to the external din. She blinked furiously to adjust her eyes. She wondered how the 'Dinis had been able to see at all on Aurigae if this brilliance was constant on their world.

Ooops, said Yoshuk, *try these.* A pair of wraparound lenses floated in through the open hatch to her. *Someone should have warned you.*

Laria put the glasses on and the light abated to a much more comfortable level. The noise outside, however, crescendoed and, just as she peered outside, four pairs of 'Dini paws reached in towards her. The clicks and squeaks of welcome were abetted by signs of 'come out', 'come here', 'join us' and 'where it' – meaning herself.

Laughing at the conflicting salutations, Laria stepped out and had her first view of Clarf. Or rather the Tower complex, reassuringly familiar despite the alien sky, the incredible sun making the flat apron a heat-trap. She was right beside the Tower which had been one of the first such installations on the Mrdini-controlled worlds. The shapes of the Tower and its auxiliary buildings, even the cradles, were familiar but the materials from which they had been made were most unusual. Rock, orange slashes with black and red, had been used for the walls: some deep-blue material slated the roofs. The cradles were iron black, not alloy blue, and the plascrete was a greeny black – and the yellow-white of sun soaking up light and throwing back glare.

Laria had only the merest glance at what panorama lay beyond – low and layered buildings of complex geometric design, great triangular mounds which she assumed were entrances to immense hibernatories and, overhead, buzzing like so many angry insects, the unmistakable figures of airborne 'Dinis, using their personal lift belts. Occasionally, a vivid orange line shot across the sky and a flying figure veered abruptly out of its way. There seemed to be uncluttered air space over the Tower Complex.

We'll be with you as soon as incoming traffic eases, Yoshuk said. *They may paw you to death but it's an enthusiastic way to go.*

She could see what he meant for she was now surrounded by a horde of 'Dinis of all sizes and colours, all wanting to touch her, as if to reassure themselves that the human child they had been promised had actually landed.

A very loud crack and the 'Dinis crowding about her stood still, with only one or two small noises of what Laria interpreted as dismay. Another crack and the 'Dinis made a respectful corridor as the largest 'Dini she had ever seen made its way to her. It had great loops of pearls about its neck and an incredible tiara-like construction ornamenting its poll eye which was tilted in her direction.

Just as she was wondering what sort of movement she should make to indicate respect to this superior 'Dini, she felt paws lift her two hands and bring them forward. Tip and Huf had become her escorts? sponsors?

The big 'Dini lowered its upper section so that the liquid, purply poll eye was level with her face. The eye began to twirl slowly. The 'Dini brought both of its paws forward to touch her out-held hands, folded them to its chest and said firmly 'Plsgt!': the 'Dini way of exchanging names with humans.

Laria copied that gesture and said 'Lr!', well pleased

that she had managed both the liquid 'l' and the rolled 'r' sounds.

Recoiling in what was a very good approximation of human surprise, Plus (which she decided to call it in her own mind) gave that burbling noise that signified 'Dini pleasure.

Well done, Laria, Yoshuk said. *They'll love you here with those ells and arrs.* Another alto chuckle from Nesrun.

Beyond her a second large personnel carrier glided gently to rest in a cradle. Behind her an almighty thunder shook not only the air but the ground and, whirling around, Laria saw her first self-propelled spaceship take off. It was far away, probably ten kilometres or more, despite the tremendous sound. The flames from its massive rockets grew longer and longer as its upward movement proceeded. Laria couldn't help but stare and wonder why such an antiquated and wasteful method was still in use when Clarf had its own Tower. But it wasn't, she reminded herself, a Prime Tower. Yoshuk and Nesrun were T-2s, not T-1s and would be unable to thrust such a behemoth on its way. Beyond it, a second, then a third, and fourth spaceship rumbled skyward.

A little shake of one of her 'Dini-held hands and Laria recalled herself to her surroundings. Tip and Huf had gathered attendants: much the same coloration as they were, so Laria figured they might be related. No-one knew how many constituted a 'Dini family group.

Plus now tucked her hand under its arm, against its warm silky side and turned, so she followed. Unobtrusively Tip gave her a quick sign that this was an honour – which she had already gathered. She lengthened her stride just as Plus shortened its and she didn't know if she should laugh at their cross-purposes. Then she saw Huf make amusement signs and so she felt able to grin up at the big 'Dini.

Oh, my dear, you are landing on your feet, Yoshuk said. *Led out by Plsgt itself.*

42

What's going to happen now, Yoshuk?

You're to be escorted to your new quarters by Plsgt who's always been the strongest proponent on this planet of the experiment. Then you'll be part of the welcome home banquet for your pair.

Tip and Huf?

Yes, and we'll meet you there. We won't leave you unsupported, Laria.

Not unless we want our ears singed off by the Rowan or the Raven, added Nesrun, colouring her tone with a mock malicious grin.

Plus handed Laria into the open-air passenger compartment: Tip, Huf and several of their colour group joining them. The vehicle moved smoothly forward on airjets, the driver carefully manoeuvring through oncoming traffic that was mostly crated, bagged and boxed materials, piled high on floats. How inefficient it was to have no kinetics available, Laria thought. Her presence distracted one or two drivers to near-accident situations. Surely, since their two species had been in contact for more than sixteen years, the sight of humans was not *that* unusual for 'Dinis. Tip and Huf wiggled with amusement at the near misses and flicked signs at her, crackling at their kin who apparently were more concerned about the situation.

Then the vehicle turned out of the spaceport facility on to a very broad 'roadway' teeming with traffic of all kinds: pedestrian, vehicular and a single-wheeled affair that riders handled with exceeding skill and daring, darting in and around slower, more cumbersome road users. Laria was so fascinated by their antics that Tip had to whistle a warning to her. Plsgt was signing and she'd missed its opening remarks. She shot a frantic glance at Tip who repeated it behind Plus' back. Fortunately, Plus was only identifying the buildings they were passing.

The spaceport was, quite rightly, surrounded by support and service agencies. Then their vehicle pulled into the centre of the road to allow the passage of a block of

43

what Laria had to identify as 'soldiers' though she had never seen any. Unlike other 'Dinis, these wore heavy bandoliers, with tubes and other ominous-looking devices slung across their backs. They looked tougher and many had odd cicatrix along their bodies and limbs, suggesting healed wounds. At least, that's what the marks appeared to be to her. Sometimes one didn't need familiarity with a thing to recognize it.

Then Plus was pointing out apertures on either side of the broad roadway, and smaller avenues leading off the main thoroughfare. These were the domestic quarters of the spacefield technicians. These residential facilities formed the usual 'Dini quadrangle about the workplace. Separating the various dwellings were the great slanting mounds of hibernatories. No-one had far to go. Where did food and other commodities come from, Laria wondered, but Plus evidently didn't feel it necessary to comment on such particulars.

Behind them came the roar of more ships taking off, and the air was once more filled with the smell of hot metal and fuel exhaust. Really, Laria thought, it was too bad there weren't enough Talents available to loft the 'Dini vessels, and reduce noise and air pollution. Maybe she should concentrate on fitting herself for that. With no immodesty, Laria knew that she'd be a Tower Prime when she'd finished her training.

The journey to her new home took over an hour, as Plus' vehicle drove them steadily deeper into the capital of Clarf – a sprawling metropolis – past flat open spaces whose purpose was not mentioned. At one point, she also caught the unmistakable odour of rotting vegetables and the cloying sweetness of fruit. She couldn't isolate from which building of the many small structures they passed such smells issued and it amused her that Plus seemed either oblivious or unwilling to comment on that side of 'Dini ecology. It was tactful of Plus not to show her the downside of life on Clarf. It did point out plinths and columns, or pillars, with a great deal of pride and an explanation which she couldn't quite grasp and neither could Tip nor Huf.

Between the air pollution and the intense sunlight, Laria began to develop a fierce headache and did her best to dampen it. She would have liked to close her eyes to rest them. Plus wouldn't notice she had with the dark lenses covering her from brow to cheek but she had to watch its signings or be rude. She was overwhelmingly grateful when the vehicle came to a stop before a large and new-looking building – new because the intense sunlight had not bleached it – with an odd annexe perched on the roof.

It took her only a moment to realize that the annexe was odd because it had windows, a feature which no other 'Dini building had, as well as a door, some sort of a glassed-in porch and potted plants. Or, at least, that's what she thought they must be. That's when she realized she had seen nothing, absolutely nothing, green, growing or vegetable-looking on the long ride from the Tower. There was probably an explanation for that. Being of a practical turn of mind and having hunted for the table for years, Laria did sort of wonder about food resources and distribution. Maybe hunger was part of her headache.

Now Plus opened the panel in the vehicle and stepped to the ground, turning to assist her in the most chivalrous fashion. Then she saw a double file of 'Dinis come out of the building, poll eyes bent respectfully in the presence of Plus and herself. Tip and Huf became a close-drill escort behind her, their flippered feet aligned with hers as if, and Laria managed to suppress a grin, they were to make sure she didn't put a foot wrong!

The file reached them, proper greetings accorded Plus and then the lead pair turned to her with carefully enunciated sounds which she understood perfectly, so that she could respond in kind to their welcome and good wishes. She, and Plus, were invited inside to enjoy guest hospitality, and she and Plus accepted. She waited a second to see what Tip and Huf would do and felt their pressure on her feet. She could move forward, staying slightly to the rear of Plus, as they progressed to the building.

She clicked and clacked to either side of her, nodding politely to each poll eye, saying either 'Your welcome honours' or 'Pleased to meet you' with an occasional 'Thank you'.

It was on her passage up this gauntlet that she suddenly realized something which she felt was significant. Though there was considerable variety in the 'Dini pelts, they were all the same basic hue. Plus, however, was covered in fur of a shade that almost 'fought' with theirs, having an orange hue whereas theirs had a bluishness to it. She glanced furtively at Tip and Huf and realized that they were 'blues'. So 'colour grouping' was more critical than anyone had known.

Good girl! Got it the first day! Yoshuk's tenor was triumphant. *Many are still trying to find the connection.*

It is significant?

As you'll discover now you're here. Don't let it worry you. You're above the colour bar, being human. And Nesrun's alto voice was cynical. *You might be more cautious with broad generalizations when in mixed colours, though I really don't think you'll be unduly troubled by this little quirk.*

Colour bar? Laria found the concept disconcerting.

Then Tip's foot trod heavily on her heel and she stopped making tangential conversation. They had passed the portal and were now in the usual broad foyer where appurtenances, single-wheeled bikes and fly belts were in a state of inspection readiness.

The Mrdinis had been on a war-basis for centuries now so she shouldn't have been surprised by the military flavour, even if she wasn't all that familiar with it: undoubtedly one of the adjustments she would have to make.

The place was spotless – not that one could see too many details in the semi-light in which all 'Dini accommodation was kept. Laria was glad that she had been such a frequent visitor to the Aurigaean village. And this, of course, was the reason she had been encouraged.

She followed in Plus' wake as the official tour continued, to the bathing rooms on both sides of the main entry, to the apartments, and finally to the standing lift that gave her access to her own. Plus would not fit on the two-person affair – no more than a piece of flooring and the central shaft that lifted the floor up to her quarters or down to the level. It was an ingenious amenity. Tip gestured for her to take her place, took the other side and made a big show of pressing the control button. There were two, each with luminescent paint – one marked D, and one marked U. Laria signed her approval and appreciation.

Sunlight poured through the wide windows of her own special apartment and she looked about her, clapping her hands, which was fortuitously just the way 'Dinis expressed delight. And it was an amazing surprise. She had fully expected to be living in 'Dini-style quarters, had made up her mind to that necessity if the exchange was to be properly honoured. But to have her own space and place was unforeseen.

There was a human-style bed, with beautiful thick covers (for 'Dinis never used any), pillows, a chest, a small press for garments, a desk, a terminal (displaying a map of the city with her current position shown by the pulsing red cursor icon) and audio equipment, shelving, two human chairs and two 'Dini-style stools, with tail-holes. There were two doors: one led out to the roof area and the other most probably to sanitary facilities.

'OH, TIP, BEAUTIFUL LIVING SPACE! MUCH BEAUTIFUL FOR SINGLE HUMAN. MUCH EFFORT DESIGN AND THINGS. BEAUTIFUL. THOUGHTFUL. CONSIDERATE. FRIENDLY!' In her excitement she had trouble getting her tongue about the 'Dini phrases.

You're doing all right, kid! Yoshuk said, his voice warm with approval.

Can you understand 'Dini?

47

I can understand your surprise and pleasure, Laria, and the syntax has to be 'Dini. I'll do my best to learn it from you. They want you happy here and, as you see, they went to a great deal of trouble. Obviously worth it.

Oh, it is, Yoshuk. It is. But . . . I'm going to need drapes on these windows. The light is blinding.

Didn't know what colours you liked, Nesrun put in. *Got some things for you to pick from soon's you get over here.*

Tip was signing at her, too, stating that, as an adult, she naturally had to have her own quarters. The time for her to share her bed with others was over.

She caught Yoshuk's chuckle at that comment and Nesrun's hiss of censure.

From a 'Dini viewpoint, certainly.

Huf went on to say that they knew she did not require a hibernatory space but she was to make known any other needs that would comfort her.

'THIS ONE TAKES GREAT PLEASURE IN THE QUARTERS. EXPRESSES GREAT PLEASURE AND THANKS. SO KIND. SO CONSIDERATE. SO HONOURABLE.'

Someone had brought the lift down again and now it rose to her level with her carisaks. With Tip's help she cleared them.

'Hang on pretty now,' Huf said with a forward jerk of the head, meaning this was very important. From its own pouch, Huf began to take necklaces of shells and stones, bracelets with uncut gem charms, and what her mother had told Laria was an old mantilla comb, carved of ivory, which Tip carefully secured above its poll eye.

Understanding came and Laria rummaged in her cases for the pearls her father had given her for her birthday: a double-stranded necklace, earrings, bracelet and two rings, one pearl and one of a fire opal. She had been astounded by such a lavish present – and one of jewellery – but now she understood that the jewels were as much a part of her role here on Clarf as her fluency in the language.

One of the areas in which human and Mrdini compared

favourably was in their sociability. 'Dinis loved to have eating sessions with their kin and peripheral groupings. That was the reason for the large empty squares she had seen on the way here. And it was to the nearest of these that Tip and Huf now led her. Huf had put on its special treasures, the mother-of-pearl crown, various chains of uncut gems and other pretties, with coil upon coil of shell bracelets. Huf nodded approval as it saw how bedecked Laria was and then her old friends led her to the square.

A 'Dini percussion band was in place and rivalled even the continuing thunder of departing space vehicles. Food had appeared, spread out on great tables which had been set up during the inspection, and hundreds of the small cubes and rounds that were 'Dini seats.

As honoured guest, she sat – on a conspicuously human chair – by Plus who had added extra decorations to its display and several smaller versions of itself, also much bejewelled. It was very polite to examine in close detail the jewellery of another 'Dini and so Laria performed that social obligation, exclaiming in admiration and managing to find something new to say about each ornament presented for her inspection.

By the time these courtesies for Plus' entourage had been acquitted, her jaws ached and her tongue was dry in a parched throat.

'Drink?' she asked Tip who had been hovering close by: possibly for just this requirement. She turned her head away from the main group and rubbed her jaw muscles, yawning to ease the tension in her mouth and lips: actions which could be misconstrued by 'Dinis if seen.

The sun was beating down again and she resolved to find herself a hat as soon as possible. She'd never needed one but somehow she had to protect her head.

Sunstroke is what you hazard, Yoshuk told her, *but we've allowed for that.*

49

Distance meant nothing to a Prime telepath but Laria was instantly aware that Yoshuk 'sounded' closer. She peered around her and saw the two humans entering the square. They were instantly lost in the mêlée of 'Dinis dancing to the rhythmic percussive beats. In fact, the rhythm was very difficult to deny and she'd had to keep her feet from tapping as she made the diplomatic jewel inspection. 'Dinis were very susceptible to cadence and the adept 'Dini dancer could perform incredible feats in tempo with drums or other tapped surfaces and objects. She'd danced at home but she also knew that there were certain protocols about dancing which she had to respect while on Clarf. Tip and Huf had been unable to explain the ramifications but she'd been promised full instruction once she arrived on Clarf.

Suddenly the two humans emerged out of the gyrating crowd of 'Dini, and the man both wore and carried headgear. The woman, who was taller than the slender little man, wore some sort of ornate turban about her head. The yellow and white fabric made the perfect frame for her dark skin and dark eyes.

'I am Nesrun of Betelgeuse,' the woman said and her smile of very white even teeth was even more impressive against the dark chocolate of her skin. She held out her hand, palm up, and Laria made the formal contact, brief and somewhat electric as it was. Nesrun had a startling touch: vibrant, deep yellow, with a curious acid taste. But she nodded as if she approved of however she perceived Laria in the tactile contact.

'I am Yoshuk of Altair,' the man said, grinning broadly with some secret amusement as he held out his hand.

As he was quite the most beautiful man Laria had ever seen, she was curiously hesitant to complete the courtesies. His smile deepened as if he had caught her diffidence, though she had instantly shielded. He was softer than Nesrun had been, deep blue, and lemony: a combination which startled her almost as much as his beauty.

50

The skin touch was swiftly replaced by the hat he put in her outstretched hand, a hat similar to the one he wore.

'These are specially developed against harsh tropic suns, Laria. Our welcome gift to you.'

Laria was properly grateful, especially as the hat was an excellent fit, shading her eyes as well as the back of her neck with its slanting brim. There was air space above her pate: neither heat nor the pressure of the sun was so intensely felt.

'With all we know about Clarf, no-one thought to mention the sun,' Nesrun remarked.

'Though, God knows, I have mentioned it innumerable times and so has every human visitor,' Yoshuk added with a droll grin of resignation.

Laria was aware that she was staring at Yoshuk, but he continued to smile pleasantly as if accustomed to such scrutiny: even inviting it, the way he turned his head so she had the full benefit of his classic profile. Then Nesrun, apparently by chance, trod on his foot and he danced away from it, much as a nervous colt might. That analogy interrupted Laria's daze and she fell into a more normal manner.

'Were you two responsible for my marvellous quarters?' Laria asked.

Yoshuk shook his head and Nesrun answered. 'No, the design is all their idea. They know what humans require. I did suggest that you might be happier picking the final touches yourself.' She rolled her eyes upwards. 'They learn quick, though.'

'You should have seen what they'd rigged up for us!' Yoshuk grinned.

Trouble was, Laria thought, the grin doesn't spoil his looks, except I'd hate to annoy him. She grinned back.

'What did you mean, Yoshuk,' she said, searching for a safe topic to end the pause, 'by saying you'd be happy to learn syntax from me? Don't you speak 'Dini?'

Nesrun's laugh was pure malice which Yoshuk totally ignored. 'Neither of us speak 'Dini, Laria,' Nesrun said. 'Can't clack, click or whistle with any fluency. We get along by signing – our own brand – but it suffices. Or we ask for a dreamer. That,' and she glared at Yoshuk, 'is the port of last resort.' She gave a controlled shudder.

Laria regarded her with some surprise. 'Don't you *like* 'Dinis?'

'I've got accustomed to them,' she said sardonically, 'but they are certainly *not* my chosen bedmates.' Again another little shudder.

Yoshuk leaned forward, almost conspiratorially, shielding his hand from those around them. 'She's not *exactly* xenophobic . . . '

'You're lucky to have been raised with them, Laria,' Nesrun put in. 'Saves a lot of adjustment.'

'Don't you want to *learn* 'Dini?' Laria asked Nesrun. It seemed terribly impolite to live in the midst of a new culture and not *know* about it; be unable to communicate with the inhabitants, especially when so much was at stake!

'I'd like to learn signing,' Nesrun said reluctantly, compressing her lips briefly, 'but you're going to have to teach that, too, you know!'

'I do,' Laria said and sighed.

Yoshuk gave her the kindest smile imaginable. 'Don't worry, Laria. You'll cope!'

He said that with such sincerity and sympathy that Laria got a second wind of resolution!

'I'm to work out Tower times with you . . . '

Yoshuk's smile became mischievous. 'You'll be on *call*, certainly. But the real work won't come right away. It's almost more important for you to teach right now. In fact, it's imperative.'

Laria took a deep breath. 'I can see that it is.'

Then Plus leaned sideways to attract her attention and she politely concentrated on what it was saying. With the dark lenses and the hat, her headache was reduced to a mere pulse. Or maybe that was her blood throbbing in time to the percussives?

She lasted out the celebrations and was ready the next morning for the students of both races.

4

When his sister came home for his sixteen-birthday celebration, Thian was even prouder of her than her parents – if
that could be possible. She was tanned a warm ruddy shade
– up to midbrow – where her hat sat. She was extremely
fit, and showed them all up by leading them a merry chase
out hunting on Saki. Nor had she lost her skill with arrow
and dart for, at the end of the day, she had more in her
hunting bag than anyone else. She was the same, and yet
she was *more*, Thian decided. Better, and not the least bit
smug like some of his Denebian cousins who were being
trained by his parents in Aurigae Tower.

He was scheduled to take over Laria's teaching duties on
Clarf so he wouldn't have to put up with cousins Roddie
and Megan, who were only T-3s and shouldn't take on the
airs and poses they did. The one time he had tried to take
the wind out of their sails, his parents had jumped on him
with all four feet and threatened to send him to Coventry
if he ever pulled another stunt like that.

'But they . . . ' he began in self-defence.

It is what you *do that concerns us and you may* not *retaliate*

54

in that fashion no matter what the provocation!

There could be no question in Thian's mind that his mother meant exactly what she said. Worse, he could feel his father's mind confirming the rebuke.

They didn't say anything when he began bringing in more game than either of his cousins could find. He studied the tactical games in which Roddie was said to excel and beat him consistently in all of them. He kept his scholastic record higher than his obnoxious cousin's – and Roddie was supposed to be the engineering brains in the family, taking after his famous namesake uncle. With quiet satisfaction, he saw that Roddie kept trying but he could never quite reach Thian's level and that was fine by Thian. There are many ways to outmanoeuvre an enemy and Thian was perfecting one.

He wasn't sure that he actually envied Laria, for she now was scheduled to do a final three months' training at Callisto Tower. Grandmother Rowan was known to be picky to work with, a perfectionist, endlessly demanding that all her Tower staff operate on the highest possible level, especially now, as there was so much traffic. But that was why Laria was recalled from her teaching assignment and given this intensive course. If she met the Rowan's high standard – which no-one doubted – she'd return to Clarf as Tower Prime to help bring in the great assault ships, built of Aurigaean ores in the satellite construction-yards of Earth, Betelgeuse, Procyon and the Mrdini worlds of Clarf, Sef, Ptu, Kif, and Tplu.

On quite a few occasions, while Thian had been standing a listening watch at the Tower, he had received important and secret messages. In point of fact, the first three times, he had been told to get either his mother or his father to accept the communication. Either his mother or father must have vouched for him because, after that, he'd been given the direct message. He never discussed them with either parent, and never knew if they were aware of these developments. But he treasured the trust shown in him, and tried to fit the substance of the messages into his overview of the Hive pursuit.

He was cautious with those think-files and always erased any notes thoroughly before he left his room screen. Thian was aware that most of the Federation did *not* know that contact with the Hive Migration ships had been made or that 'Dini and human pursuit ships were attempting to find the Hive Home System.

Before he'd been born, before Laria had been born, the Mrdinis had made contact with his parents on Deneb where they were spending a well-deserved rest and re-laxation leave. There was something else about that point in time Thian hadn't been told: he just sensed that there was more explanation due him. Probably when he was older and a Tower Prime himself. The Raven-Lyon children knew when, and when not, to probe for information.

At any rate, Damia and Afra had Dreamed Mrdini and made contact with the alien race, discovering that the enemy which had ravaged their worlds was the same menace that had attacked Deneb, Granddad's planet. The assault had been repulsed by the massed, merged Minds of every T-rating on every planet in the Federation. The Many Mind of the sixteen queens on the Hive ship had been overpowered and then the ship plunged, helpless, into Deneb's sun. But there were more than one Hive ship and the Mrdini wanted human help in preventing more worlds from falling under Hive domination, for the Hive species stripped any suitable world of all other life forms, propagated at an incredible rate, and then sent its excess population out into space to find yet more worlds where it could repeat the process.

While there were estimated to be millions of carbon-based planets in the galaxy, such uncontrolled expansion – to the detriment of other species – had to be limited.

At tremendous cost in personnel and materiel, the Mrdinis had struggled to keep their own worlds free. They had been overjoyed to find that humans were also involved in, and capable of, species' protection. They were fascinated by the special psionic Talents used by the Federation to reduce loss of life without diluting the effectiveness of the deterrent with which they had defeated the initial attempts of the Hive ships to intrude on their spheres of influence.

With such vastly different species and for such a common purpose, unambiguous communications had to be established. This was being done through the young of both life forms who paired early in order to instil mutual respect and form a basis for the mutual understanding required for the undertaking.

While this programme was maturing, the military arms of each species were searching space in a joint operation. Though dissimilar in style and operation, the means to trace the Hive ships' ion trails back to their point of origin had been available to both navies, and had finally been productive.

FT&T Primes had forwarded a squadron to a rendezvous with the Mrdini ships which had intercepted the Hive vessels' trails. Each of the 'Dini ships had several strong dreamers who could communicate on a basic level with Talents on board the human ships. While hoping that following the ion trails back the way they had come might result in discovering the location of the Hive homeworld, the more pessimistic of both species recognized that the trails might dwindle to nothing – considering the period of time involved – and the effort would be wasted. But others argued, and won, that this was the best opportunity to at least *try*. They'd be no worse off, and at least would have identified where the Hive were *not*.

A second contingent, six fast ships from each fleet, had set out in pursuit of the marauding Hivers. It was as critical to know their destinations as to discover their origins. And possibly come to the assistance of whatever planet was the target of Hive attentions.

No-one yet, of either species, had suggested the way

to destroy the Hive culture. Or, at the least, contain it. Another ethical point on which Mrdini and human were agreed: neither found it morally acceptable to undertake the total annihilation of another sentient species, even one as inimical to both their life forms as the Hivers.

'That's because they haven't been physically threatened,' Jeff Raven had said grimly in the privacy of his mother's home on Deneb. 'One can indulge in such moral stands at several removes.'

'There must be some humane way to remove the threat of Hive invasions,' his oldest son, Jeran, had replied.

'We're working on it, though I'll argue the point that "humane" applies to the Hivers. Seemingly, they have only one method of colonizing and that's fatal to any other life form inhabiting the planet they choose.'

'It'd be very difficult to change the goals of a species you can't even talk to,' Isthia said.

'I don't even want to talk to them,' the Rowan had said, giving a shudder as she vividly remembered the moment she, as focus of the merged female Talents, had briefly touched the Many Mind of the Hive queens. 'There was nothing *there* to talk *to!*' she added, after a moment's thought.

'We could just pick off each ship that's found using the same methods, couldn't we?' Cera Raven-Hilk asked.

'We could,' Jeff replied. 'But that would be a life's work in itself . . .'

'Besides tying up Primes and whole bunches of Talent, quite likely at the most inconvenient times,' the Rowan added, with a little sniff. 'I certainly wouldn't like to have to keep doing it, time after time. The 'Dinis' estimate of how many Hive ships there could be is unnerving.'

'How many is that?' Jeran asked diffidently.

Classified, said both parents at once.

Oh, well, you can't blame me for trying, Jeran said.

'At least we do now have a great many more Talents to call on than we did when you had to execute the first one,' Cera said, placidly. Her parents gave her such a long look that she blinked, wondering why she had incurred their disapproval. 'The Two-Level mass mind-merges didn't *take* very long, after all.'

'It took more than you think,' the Rowan said, remembering that Cera had been affected *in utero* during that brief, but exceedingly intense, assault. Maybe that was why she came out with such peculiar sentiments.

The human ships following the ion trail were now far beyond any friendly system. The traces remained strong, indicating excesses of speed which made the ion trail so easy to follow. The human flagship, the *Vadim*, and her consorts, the *Solidarity*, the *Reliant* and the *Beijing* were experiencing supply shortages which must be remedied if they were expected to continue. Captain Ashiant of the *Vadim* made it very plain that he and the other human captains insisted on continuing towards the Hive homeworld no matter how long it took. To transport such long distances, the Towers involved – Deneb and Callisto – were also going to need reinforcements. There was even the hint that a Prime Talent would be required on the pursuit flagship, to facilitate future transportations and communications over the immense distances now involved.

'All the old military commanders say it's wrong to have too long a supply line,' Thian said when the subject of Tower augmentations came up.

'This is the twenty-fourth century, Thian,' Roddie said, dismissing that concern. 'We have skills and abilities those ancients never thought of. And,' he added pompously, 'we haven't had a land-war in generations.'

'Thian's point is well taken,' Afra said at his most mild and Roddie flushed, hearing the subtle rebuke. 'Neither species has explored the areas through which they've been passing. There've been no yellow stars, which are systems the Hivers seek, or where our folk could land and replenish supplies from natural materials. Naval hydroponics can only supply so much to augment frozen, dried and canned comestibles. Water's been recycled far too often for it to be potable. That's actually the main problem, though fuel supplies are also dwindling and must be replenished.'

'Ice planet? Ice asteroids?' Roddie suggested.

'Requires detours from the course into a system with an expense of fuel that might not be justified by results,' Afra said. Roddie's face fell. 'But it is an alternative that's being considered.'

'But that's not a viable one, is it?' Thian said thoughtfully. 'If yellow stars generate the kind of planets that the Hive wants and that we'd need to find drinkable water. There'd be the possibility of a confrontation.'

Afra nodded solemnly and Thian sighed at the complexity of it all.

'We'll think of something,' Roddie said proudly.

'The 'Dinis might beat us to it,' and Laria's grin was mischievous. 'They're very clever.'

Roddie decided he had other things to do than argue with cousins.

'Is it being a Denebian that makes him like that, or being just a T-3?' Laria asked her brother in a low voice.

'Deneb does inculcate certain characteristics in its children,' Afra said, rising, 'just as Aurigae instils others, not necessarily exemplary ones, in hers!'

'Whooops!' Laria said, grinning at the subtle rebuke. 'A few years in a Tower and he'll probably turn into a quite bearable young man.'

At that both her father and brother laughed and moved off to mingle with other guests.

Several days later, Damia and Afra sent Thian a telepathic call to join them in the Tower room. Family matters were generally dealt with in the house, so Thian was instantly aware that this was an unusual summons. With some trepidation and a quick inventory of recent misdemeanours, Thian 'ported himself the short distance into the upper

Chamber where his parents conducted all FT&T business.

He didn't dare probe his own parents but he could, and did, establish their mental tone: Damia was sad and worried, and his father seemed coloured by regret and reluctance but was also containing pride, being more apprehensive than worried.

'Thian,' his mother began, pausing to fingercomb over her shoulder the silver tress that even her son knew misbehaved when she was upset, 'we've had a request . . . ' She glanced for assistance to Afra.

'Jeff Raven makes few,' Afra said, 'and it *is* only a request which we three can examine, forget or accept, as we decide.'

Thian mastered the impatience with this roundabout talk and waited. He couldn't even catch a hint of what this request was about.

'What does my grandfather want?' Thian said, rather pleased with his adroit phrasing. It might generate the sort of response he wanted. It did.

'Earth Prime,' and his mother corrected him firmly, 'requires a T-1 to accompany the reinforcements to the rendezvous.'

'Wow! I was right about supply lines, wasn't I, Dad!'

What are you talking about, Thian? Damia asked, sharp with worries she tried to hide.

He made a point the other day and it's come to roost on his own shoulders, his father said, grinning. *Going to honour it?*

'You mean, Granddad's really considering me?' Thian couldn't believe his great good luck. Wait'll he told Roddie. His silly coz would be mouldy with envy.

That remark doesn't become you, Afra said in a very tight voice and Thian shook himself, sharpening his attention to the matter in hand. *That's better.*

'You know how few T-1s there are . . . ' Damia began, fiddling with the curl on the end of her silver tress which had found its way back over her shoulder. That automatic

61

gesture reminded Thian that he often fiddled with the silver streak that was a genetic legacy from his mother. Even the baby Petra had a tuft of silver hairs at the temple, the cause of some amusement in the Denebian side of the family.

'There's nearly a hundred of us now,' Thian began in protest.

'Not of working age,' Damia said. 'You're barely sixteen and while you've been trained to very high standards, you've only worked here in Aurigae . . . '

'And Deneb in the summers,' Thian added, afraid she might not remember that.

'Not the most active of Towers,' she replied. Then she gave him a little smile. 'But you did well, and you've always done well here. It's just that . . . '

'Mom, you know I've read everything there is on naval histories, even military ones from the early centuries,' Thian said earnestly. 'You know I'm the best there is at strategy games . . . '

'Strategy is not involved here,' she said rather sharply. *What is involved are very long lonely distances for my eldest son who has only just reached manhood.*

Then she let Thian *feel* what she was feeling and he almost burst into tears, despite his sixteen years. She was terribly afraid – afraid she might never see him again – that he'd die before his time, as her brother Larak had done. Larak often figured in Damia's sadder thoughts: a pain that never really eased, in its own special corner of her mind.

She let him have that brief glimpse, then shut it, giving herself a little shake of self-reprimand. His father had one hand on her shoulder, as he often did when his mother was upset about something.

'Mother,' and Thian laid his hand on her arm, 'we're only a thought away no matter how far apart our bodies are.'

She gave a little cry and embraced him, now letting him

feel her pride in his response, her constant love and caring of him, and how immensely pleased she was to be able to supply a child of her body for this service.

'Spoken like a true Lyon,' she said, laughing and crying at the same time, as she tightened her arms one more time before releasing him.

'Why blame it on Lyons, Gwyn-Raven?' Afra said in a low, but teasing tone.

'It *is* a tremendously responsible position, Thian,' Damia said, restored to poise and dignity.

'Don't think I don't know it,' Thian said. 'And Grand-dad suggested me?'

Afra nodded. 'Oh, we've run through all the training squirts,' and his cocked eyebrow took the sting out of his words. 'You can thank Gren for it. He made the final assessments. *He* considered you the best candidate – if we'd let you go.'

'You mean you mightn't've?' Thian was aghast at what he might have been deprived of.

Damia gave his father a sour look and pursed her lips for a moment. 'No, you should know us better than that, Thian Lyon! But we do believe that you've a good head on your shoulders, a fine sense of responsibility and sufficient training to be an effective member of FT&T.'

A sudden thought caught Thian. 'But what about Mur and Dip?' He was appalled that he had forgotten his 'Dini companions even during that moment of personal success.

'I told you,' Afra said, teasing his wife.

Damia sighed and then smiled to relieve Thian's growing concern. 'They will accompany you. You've actually a double purpose: providing the search with a Prime and a working 'Dini team plus some language instruction. That should help ease relations between human and Dini.'

'Why? Are they bad?'

Afra cleared his throat. 'Not bad, exactly, but with inadequate communication, unnecessary problems have arisen that accurate interpretation could have avoided.'

'Oh!'

'You are young for such responsibility but your mother and I feel you have a mature enough attitude and certainly you communicate well with 'Dinis. You are well grown and you don't *look* wet behind the ears – which is aided and abetted by the infamous Gwyn streak,' and Afra gave Thian's silver lock a gentle tap. Afra cleared his throat then added, 'I believe that, and your interest in naval history and protocol, tipped the balance in your favour.'

Thian lifted his chest, grinning as he remembered all the teasing he'd had for blurring his eyes over ancient texts and stupid manuals. You never did know when something you studied for the fun of it became very useful indeed.

'Now, I suggest that you give yourself,' his father said, 'say, half an hour, to appreciate this unexpected honour before you get your head back down to size. Because you're not allowed to mention this to anyone. Not even your 'Dinis, until the formalities are observed and your official orders are cut.'

'Not even Laria?'

'Especially not your sister, Thian, since she's slated to depart to Callisto in two days' time,' his mother said. She gave his hair a brief stroke at his disappointment. 'She'll hear through the appropriate sources, dear.'

'Consider this your first exercise in naval intelligence. You'll soon hear many messages you may never even hint you've received.'

'And I used to wonder why I had to help you with those big-daddies all the time.' Thian's active mind had also been cataloguing the sort of materiel he'd be having to 'port to his squadron.

'To every thing its use and season,' Afra said, obviously quoting.

Just then a tray with glasses and a basket of tidbits came floating into the Tower room.

'A celebration is obviously called for: quiet, necessarily limited to immediate family members but none the less a celebration, son,' Damia said, and herself placed one glass in Thian's hand.

Three glasses chimed melodiously as they met: their contents then ceremonially drunk.

Thian found it was harder to keep his mouth shut over this than he'd anticipated. It was even harder to suppress the inner excitement that threatened to bubble up whenever he considered his altered status. Fortunately, Laria was involved with renewing contacts with her siblings and their 'Dinis. She also 'ported frequently to the 'Dini village to spend time with relatives of those she knew on Clarf.

The first time Thian had accompanied her, he had been awed at the sophistication of her 'Dini vocabulary. True, they had been paired with young 'Dinis, who were also learning their language from their adults, but vocabulary and complexity had reached a mature level even before Laria had gone to Clarf. But now . . . Thian went with her whenever he could, listening to the new combinations of sound and sign. He wouldn't be talking baby-talk to the naval 'Dinis.

Look, Thian, Laria said, turning on him before she went off for the fourth morning to the village, *I'm real pleased you like my company but haven't you something better to do with your time?*

Gee, Lar, I have missed you, he began, caught without a glib excuse ready. *And it's a real treat to hear you speak 'Dini. You've learned a great deal. I thought I was fluent . . .* And he paused, hoping the flattery would cover his genuine need. *But you've been using complex constructions I've never heard before.*

Laria gave him a long measuring look. *Thian? You're my brother and I know you well enough to know you're covering. What?*

Could we just leave it that I need to improve technical 'Dini-speak?

You'll pick it up very quickly once you're on Clarf, Thian, she began. *You're pretty fluent as it is.*

In day-to-day stuff, but not the technical jargon and I will need that, won't I?

She frowned slightly, cocking her head at him, and he could feel her mind push against his. He waggled a finger at her.

'That's not good manners,' he said.

'You've never minded before. And you *are* hiding something.'

'Not hiding,' he said with a grin, 'but you know that we never talk Tower business.'

'Oh, all right, Thian, you can come today – for the last time.'

It would be, Thian knew, but he couldn't indicate that either. It was getting harder and harder to suppress his inner excitement. Still, if he couldn't handle this minor incident, he oughtn't to accept the assignment at all.

You are the best candidate for this job, son, his father said softly. *Never doubt that!*

Laria knows a lot more technical lingo than I do. Wouldn't she be better?

Having doubts is normal. Overcoming them is part of maturing. I would be more worried about your success if you didn't question yourself. Your training and experience are more than adequate for this assignment. Laria would not do as well as you will!

Thian let himself be reassured, especially as he wanted this duty more than anything. Very softly even in his own head, Thian added: Roddie would be livid with envy.

Dinner that last evening was not ostentatiously lavish but the meal happened to feature the favourite dishes of Thian, Mur and Dip. No-one made mention of this bias because their special foods were popular anyway.

66

Thian got a bit misty-eyed, though, when his mother served him double-chocolate cake.

I also baked a second one for you to take with you tomorrow, she added very privately and he nearly burst into tears.

They dissipated with a suddenness that suggested 'help', leaving him happy and relaxed but no longer emotionally overloaded.

You have always been an appreciative soul, his father said.

Everyone appreciates double-chocolate cake, he replied, in control of himself again.

The transfer would take place late that evening, when the household was asleep. First they'd land at Callisto.

'Just to keep you humble, Thian,' his mother said as they made their way through the dark still night to the Tower, 'you and your 'Dinis are also-rans with urgently needed medical and food supplies.'

'Thanks, Mom, I needed that,' Thian said facetiously.

I know, and she grinned at him. 'Your grandparents will join with David of Betelgeuse to push the shipment to rendezvous with the starship *Vadim*.'

'At least we'll be pushed by the best,' he said.

They had reached the capsule now and he placed his carisak inside, careful of the double-chocolate cake. His father went on up to the Tower to take his position. His mother hovered as he helped stow the pouches Mur and Dip handed him. They hopped in, clicking softly as they settled into their special hammocks. Then it was Thian's turn to enter.

Thian caught just the glint of moisture in his mother's eyes before, unexpectedly, she threw her arms about him. When, he wondered as his arms closed about her, had she gotten so slender and so much smaller than he?

When you got so much fatter and bigger, she said and shoved him towards the carrier. *You big lunk!* And, on a different level which Thian was astonished to hear, she added, *This is much harder than I thought it would be!*

Almost embarrassed by her remorse, Thian stumbled as

he stepped in and then fell awkwardly across the couch, Mur and Dip clacking concern. He clucked a reassurance and clipped on his harness. The canopy closed.

It's not as if he's gone for ever, his mother's thoughts continued.

Easy, my love, and that was his father answering on the private level.

Firmly Thian diverted his thoughts from this inadvertent contact and squinched his shoulders into the couch.

NOT TO WORRY, Mur said.

TOGETHER US, Dip added.

GOODNESS SPREADS, Thian replied, accepting their encouragement and returning it in the 'Dini idiom.

He caught the 'push' of two strong minds at the onset of 'portation. He held his breath and felt the 'halt' and the almost indefinable alteration as his grandmother 'caught' the capsule from the Aurigaean thrust and brought it safely in. He didn't feel even the slightest vibration as the carrier was placed on the Callistan cradle.

I'm always careful with animate cargo, came the unmistakable touch of his grandmother's 'pathing.

You are indeed, ma'am, Thian answered politely.

This 'port will be longer, remember, but I'll stay with you, if you wish? the Rowan offered.

Thian let a laugh ripple through his reply. *Mother'd snatch me bald-headed, Callisto Prime, if I did that.*

He did give a start when he felt a thud–thunk vibrate through the capsule.

That's the drone capsule locking on, his grandmother said, *not me missing my thrust. Don't break any eggs now,* she added.

On her 'now', he knew that she had pushed because he could just hear the whine of generators. He was also aware of David, the Betelgeuse Prime, when his touch came on line.

Ah! Punctual as ever, David, the Rowan said. *Shall we?*

Why not? was David's diffident reply.

The final thrust of his journey was palpable in Thian's

mind: he expected that both the Rowan and David had done that on purpose. Some Talents, especially Primes, still experienced twinges of apprehension when being 'ported by others. Most of them handled their own 'portations and possibly Thian could have, had he had practice with the coordinates to which he was going: constantly altering coordinates at that. He really was relieved that he hadn't been expected to transport himself.

Then he was there! Inside the battle cruiser.

'Sir,' a loud voice shouted, slightly muffled by the capsule, 'transport and drone are now aboard.'

'Well, well, open up the carrier, man!'

The hatch was cracked and the first thing Thian noted was that the air was tainted. The first thing he did was sneeze, which mortified him.

'Canned air has that effect, sir,' said the uniformed rating who looked in on him. 'You'll get used to it, Mr Lyon.' The grin that followed that warning belied the sentiment.

Mur was convulsed with the equivalent of a 'Dini sneeze while Dip seemed to be gagging.

BE EASY, Thian clacked encouragingly and, pulling the harness release, reached over to extricate Mur from its belt and pull it to a more upright position. Mur managed a wheeze of gratitude and, in turn, assisted Dip.

'Mr Lyon, sir, care to join us?' and a second figure bent down to peer in the open hatch. The face that peered in was young, with that indefinable stamp of perpetual youth that some men seem to retain: regular but undistinguished features, pale blue eyes, fresh complexion and only the hint of down on the upper lip.

'I'm helping my 'Dinis,' Thian said, somewhat relieved as he decided he looked older than his welcomer. Dark hair and heavy eyebrows produced unexpected results. 'Ah, we're coming.'

'You were able to bring 'Dinis, then. By Jove, that is good news,' said this second individual who moved back as Thian swung himself out. 'Welcome aboard, Mr

Lyon,' and Thian was surprised at the crisp salute accorded him. He grinned in return, and then offered his hand. 'Lieutenant Ridvan Auster-Kiely, sir.'

Thian decided that one could be over-sirred but it was only good naval protocol.

Mur was hiccuping in spasms now and Thian felt the first twinge of concern. When Thian touched Mur's sloping forearm, the fur felt very dry. Dehydration! Not good for the 'Dinis who daily consumed quantities of liquid. Thian excused himself to the lieutenant and 'ported both 'Dinis out of the capsule, bracing Mur against his leg until it had cleared its air passage.

'Mur should be all right in a moment,' Thian said with more authority than he felt. 'This is Dip,' he added and handed Dip a clean cloth to mop its poll eye which was streaming, another form of 'Dini reaction to poor air quality and excessive dryness. He had to blink rather furiously himself to clear his own eyes.

'Yeah,' drawled the lieutenant, 'it gets to you if you aren't used to it. Would a puff of the pure do any good?'

'The pure?' Thian wasn't certain he had heard correctly because there was a lot of noise and exclamations from the seamen crowding around the supply drone so he 'reached' for an explanation. 'Oh, oxygen.' Then Thian wondered if his lapse had been noticed but the lieutenant didn't react, just kept grinning sympathetically at the gasping and hiccuping 'Dinis.

'These guys are small,' he said, trying not to be impolite with his interest in them.

'Humans have different growth patterns. 'Dinis do it slower.'

'Oh? Can I assist you with your baggage, sir? Get you to your quarters where it's quieter,' Auster-Kiely said, as Mur's hiccups developed into a distressed pattern that was plainly worrying Dip.

Thian knew he had to get both 'Dinis out of the noise, confusion and bad air as fast as possible.

'Excuse me, Lieutenant,' he said and clutched him by the shoulder just long enough for a quick scan. As Thian had anticipated, the man had a picture in his mind of where he would be guiding this party. 'I'll meet you there.'

He gathered Mur and Dip in his arms and 'ported them all to the cabin Auster-Kiely had envisioned. It was small, but it had what he needed: a bunk on which he deposited Mur in an upright position, propping it with the pillow and sleepsak, before he swung round to the tiny basin, turned the water spigot on to soak the towel he whipped off the rack, and also filled a glass. As he turned back to the bunk, he noticed that the water was an odd off-clear shade and, even a foot away from his nose, he could smell the chemicals used in recycling. But it was moisture. He held it against the appropriate orifice on Mur's upper torso and watched the liquid being ingested while Mur valiantly struggled to suppress another series of hiccups. When partial success was obvious, Thian re-filled the glass and offered it.

Mur clicked in weak protest.

ALL THERE IS, Thian said firmly and proffered the liquid. This time the hiccups completely subsided. Dip had wrung out the towel and was now laying it against Mur's upper torso. Mur sagged into the supports, but its pelt colour was not returning to a normal hue, and the two lids were still covering the poll eye. BETTER AIR NEEDED? Thian asked.

WISE, was Dip's reply but it added a questioning suffix.

DOUBLE WISE, Thian said, feeling a soreness develop in the back of his throat which he knew had to be from the air though what was in the cabin was not as contaminated as the air in the shuttle bay. How the navy could operate in this atmosphere was beyond him. He swung round now to the compact room terminal, wriggling his fingers as he held them above the keyboard indecisively.

Sick-bay! That's what he needed.

There was a hesitant tap on the door.

'Yes,' and he reached out to throw the latch. The young

71

lieutenant stood there, a rating behind him, holding Thian's belongings and the two 'Dini pouches.

THANKS, Dip said in a guttural approximation and both seamen stared down at it in utter astonishment.

'I didn't know they could speak Basic,' Auster-Kiely said in an awed whisper.

'These 'Dinis can, though their responses are limited to the words they can get their vocal equipment to sound,' Thian said. 'But look, Mur here is not pulling round as it should.'

'He . . . it . . . even looks sick,' Auster-Kiely replied, his eyes goggling.

'You don't have a 'Dini medic on board here, do you?'

'On the *Vadim*?' The question startled the lieutenant.

'There *is* a 'Dini ship in this squadron, though, isn't there?'

'Two!'

'How do I contact one? Mur needs more help than I can provide,' and indeed the gasps coming from the 'Dini were causing Dip great consternation to judge by the alteration of its own pelt colour. It proffered another glass of water to Mur.

'No wonder it's sick if you're giving him *washing* water,' cried Auster-Kiely, pointing agitatedly at the basin and then at the small cylinder above it: plainly marked 'drinking water'.

Thian groaned, scrubbing at his face and wondering how he could have been so stupid. Auster-Kiely pushed past him now and began tapping keys.

'Sir, medical emergency in Mr Lyon's quarters. A Mrdini illness. Urgently request contact with 'Dini vessel and their medic.'

'Thanks, Kiely,' Thian said, leaning weakly against the wall. And he thought himself so responsible yet the first thing he does on his assignment is to poison a 'Dini with unpotable water!

'What's this about a 'Dini emergency?'

72

Auster-Kiely came to a rigid attention stance, his eyes once more protruding. 'Yes, sir, there is, sir.'

With an apologetic look, Thian shoved the lieutenant to one side so he was visible to the hoarse-voiced questioner.

'Prime Lyon here,' Thian said. 'My 'Dini companion is experiencing difficulties with breathing. I made the mistake of giving it basin water . . .'

'Damned fool . . . weren't you briefed? Why didn't that young squirt do what he was told to . . .'

Thian could have wished any other circumstances had brought him to the captain's notice so soon but the background noise of Mur's gasps required immediate action.

'Get some oxygen in here, Kiely,' he said to the lieutenant. 'Your pardon, sir, this is an extreme emergency. I need to talk to a 'Dini medic like *right now*!'

'I was told, Lyon, that you were fully capable of caring for your . . .'

'I am, Captain Ashiant, which is what I'm doing, if you will kindly put me through to your communications officer. Explanations must wait.' To Thian's increasing anxiety, Captain Ashiant hesitated. Thian sensed a dislike/distaste/reluctance to communicate with either of the 'Dini ships. 'Now, Captain, before Mur dies!'

That stern threat prompted action.

'Lieutenant Brikowski, sir,' a new voice said and the screen cleared to a new face, a gaunt, hatchet-face topped off by a cap of short dark hair. 'I'm opening a channel but I only have basic 'Dini, Mr Lyon . . .'

'Just open the channel.'

Auster-Kiely had come racing back with a breathing unit – albeit a human one – and didn't know what to do with it. Snatching the unit from the man, Thian turned the cock on the bottle and passed the mask to Dip.

COVER BREATHING ORIFICE, he explained and turned back to the screen just as the view cleared to the 'Dini bridge.

MEDICAL EMERGENCY, CAPTAIN PLR, MRG WITH BREATHING DIFFICULTIES, WATER AND AIR IMPURITIES, COLOUR POOR,

OXYGEN ADMINISTERED, MOISTURE TO BODY PART. OTHER REMEDY?

Thian had no time to be pleased that he got all the words out in the proper order and with good accent. He saw Dip's nod of approval and then Dip ploughed over the screen. On seeing who was answering the call, it bowed first, exhibiting full poll eye to the senior 'Dini in a mark of great respect before Dip added a few medical details to Thian's statement.

GREAT URGENCY REQUIRES DIRE MEASURES, Dip told Thian after a brief exchange. MRG MUST BE IMMERSED IN WATER, ANY KIND, UNTIL MEDICAL CAN ARRIVE. THIAN CAN TRANSPORT? Dip's tone slowed to one of query and entreaty.

ANY TIME ANY PLACE, DPL. REQUEST MEDICAL TO ENTER A PERSONAL CAPSULE, INFORM ME WHEN READY AND I WILL TRANSPORT IMMEDIATELY.

Dip conveyed that message and bowed respectfully again as the screen cleared to the *Vadim*'s bridge.

'Well, did you straighten it all out, Mr Lyon?' Captain Ashiant replied, a scowl still in place on his prominent brow. He was a big-chested man with a heavy neck, big features, and he was probably even more imposing in the flesh. Concern for Mur made Thian more reckless than diplomatic but too much was at stake.

'We need to immerse Mur in water, anywhere will do. It's not a full grown 'Dini, and it needs continued oxygen. A medical person is coming . . . '

'It'll take a day or two . . . ' the captain began.

'It'll take a minute, Captain, once I have a pic of the 'Dini hold, permission to use the *Vadim*'s generators for a 'port to the same hold we arrived in . . . '

'It's that bad?'

Thian had been ready to use any lever required to cut through protocol to get the help Mur required so he was momentarily at a loss.

'Yes, sir, I'm sorry it is.'

'Sick-bay'll have a water bath for you. Come to the

74

bridge as soon as you've settled your friend. Kiely?' and the bark was back in the captain's tone. 'You lend all assistance necessary . . . and I'll see you later, mister.'

Kiely gulped as the screen blanked.

'It wasn't your fault, Kiely,' Thian said. 'I'll explain.' The relief in Kiely's eyes was heartfelt. Thian bent to pick up Mur and carry it over his shoulder before he clasped Dip in the other arm. 'Now *think* of the sick-bay for me, and join me there!'

Startled, Kiely once again flashed Thian the vision he needed and he 'ported them directly into the examining room in the most dramatic fashion.

'You don't waste time, do you?' said the chief medical officer who immediately stepped forward. 'This way,' and hurried the trio towards a cubicle. A small bath was filling with water, the same off-colour stuff. Non-potable, Thian thought bitterly, but water.

MRG, CLOSE ALL ORIFICES, Thian told his friend as he gently lowered the pale, shaking 'Dini into the tub while Dip did its best to keep the oxygen mask in place. 'If there's another mask, Dip will show you where to place it for best effect,' he said to the doctor.

'Certainly,' and a snap of his fingers produced a second breathing apparatus from a very attentive corpswoman. 'I've never dealt with a 'Dini patient before, Mr . . . '

'Lyon . . . ' Thian supplied. 'You don't by any chance speak any 'Dini?'

''Fraid not,' and the physician was genuinely regretful.

Thian saw that the immersion was having some effect for Mur's colour slightly improved.

'Well, Dip speaks Basic. I'll leave it here. I'm getting a 'Dini medic over.'

'But that'll take . . . '

'Not very long, if you'll show me where the bridge is. . .'

The doctor inadvertently visualized the bridge in his public mind and Thian paused long enough to thank him

75

before he transferred. There was no time for the usual protocol or procedures. 'Dinis were rarely ill – especially on humanoid planets – so Mur's unexpected malfunction was of major concern. It couldn't be just the bad air and the inadvertent ingestion of even worse water. Mur must be physically imperfect. It would be like losing a hand, Thian thought, to lose Mur. And far worse for Dip. Maybe the seizure was only passing: the shock of transport, the dehydration of a long passage through space!

He arrived on the bridge to the startlement of all on duty, the security guards reaching for their weapons.

'I'm Thian Lyon,' he said, both vocally and telepathically, reinforcing the thought with an inhibition on them to draw. 'Captain, I do apologize,' he said, rapidly striding to Ashiant's command chair, 'for busting every rule of naval protocol my first hour on the *Vadim* . . . '

'Direct action is sometimes the only course,' Ashiant said, an odd smile tugging at his mouth. He pointed towards an unoccupied chair to the left of the main stations. 'When we were apprised of your joining the *Vadim*, we installed a chair for you in the engineering section. You should have everything you need there. Commander Tikele is standing by.'

Nodding his thanks, Thian strode to the position, smiling with quick gratitude to the wiry little man standing beside the chair. The engineering officer had a slightly supercilious expression to mouth and eyes. Afra had warned his son that he might expect some resistance from mechanically minded naval personnel who trusted their engines more than alternative forms of transportation. Thian managed a respectful bow to the commander as he sat down.

'Generators are already on line?' he asked, though he could also see by the gauges on the board in front of him that they were.

'Ready when you are,' Tikele said in the blandest possible tone.

'May I have a view of the 'Dini ship's shuttle bay?'

'Patch it through,' Captain Ashiant said and the right-hand screen immediately gave Thian the picture he needed.

He reached out with just his mind, sensing the presence of many 'Dinis, and the smooth cylinder that would transport the medics. If he hadn't been rushing around like a Slither after stonelice, he'd have been able to reach across that minimal spatial distance without assistance. But despite the adrenalin coursing through his blood, he leaned into the generators, just as he would have back on Aurigae. At that, his catch didn't place more than a second's strain on the generators.

'There,' Thian said, rising. 'Thank you very much for your cooperation, gentlemen. Captain, with your permission?' he added, belatedly remembering lessons in naval courtesy.

'You haven't needed it yet, have you, Lyon?' But the captain's tone was wry with amusement.

Even as Thian nodded in rueful acknowledgement, he 'ported himself to the shuttle deck where three 'Dinis were debarking from their capsule. They carried considerable equipment. The bay crew were rushing forward, not sure what action to take.

'They are expected. I will lead them,' Thian said quickly before there could be a security incident. He took the necessary steps to the three 'Dinis. They were the biggest he had seen, even larger than the eldest in the Aurigaean village. One 'Dini was nearly his height which was tall enough for a human.

WHO IS SENIOR, O LARGE AND VENERABLE ONES? he asked as deferentially as he could. He knew that some 'Dinis took their size as seriously as some humans took their status.

ESCORT THIS ONE IMMEDIATELY TO THE SICK, the big one said, moving gracefully forward to meet Thian.

'Will one of you escort the rest of them to sick bay?' Thian said, glancing about the humans to see who was in command.

'G'wan,' said one, waving him urgently onward.

HUMBLE APOLOGY FOR INTIMACY, Thian said and, taking a deep breath, put his arms firmly about the middle body of the 'Dini. And 'ported them both to the sick bay corridor outside the cubicle.

They both staggered for balance as they landed in the midst of a group. Thian blamed himself for not checking on a clear corridor but no-one was hurt and the 'Dini, seeing Mur in the tub, ploughed forward to its patient. Dip, bowing nearly double, stepped aside, remembering to keep the breather unit in place as it did so.

While the medical officer and his staff watched with fascination, the 'Dini made an examination: a blur of moving digits and prods and pokings of the mutely coloured Mur who was weakly hiccuping in an irregular pattern.

'Anything I can do?' the medical officer asked without taking his eyes from the big 'Dini. 'Biggest one I've ever seen,' he added in a low tone to Thian.

'Me, too,' Thian agreed, grabbing at whatever lightening he could find in this crisis.

Another blur of motion and the 'Dini medic extracted instruments from the pack it had brought and then quickly shoved small objects in two orifices which Mur obediently opened.

The big 'Dini sat back on its tail, crossing its forward appendages across its upper torso. Dip clicked softly and received an affirmative and, Thian was glad to hear, a reassuring clack.

He inhaled and leaned against the door jamb, abruptly feeling the let-down of recent exertions.

THIS ONE RESPONDS WELL, the 'Dini said, pulling itself to its two feet.

WHAT OCCURRED TO MAKE MRG UNWELL? Thian asked, echoing Dip's more quickly spoken query.

NOT OFTEN BUT SOMETIMES SHOCK OF ADJUSTMENT TO NEW ENVIRONS. TOO DRY AN AIR IMPURE. CANNOT BE PREDICTED. THIS PARTICULAR COLOUR PRONE TO SUCH REACTIONS. DPL

ADJUSTED AS REQUIRED OR WOULD HAVE REACTED ALSO. MEDICATION WILL PREVENT RECURRENCE. SPEEDY HUMAN REACTIONS PREVENTED TRAGEDY. GRATITUDE FROM ALL. IT IS GOOD HUMAN THN IS AHEAD WITH FLEET.

'Will the 'Dini be all right?' the medic asked.

Weak with relief, Thian nodded. 'Seems Mur had environmental adjustment shock.'

'Oh?'

Thian wondered how he was going to avoid criticizing the ship's air and water. 'Dehydration,' he said hurriedly. 'From coming so far in a capsule. It'll be fine once the medication takes effect. You can see how much better its colour is already.'

'Ah, yes, it is. Ah, would you thank the medic for us . . . extend professional courtesies . . . '

HOW IS LARGE ONE CALLED? Thian said, assuming the most courteous posture. THE HUMAN MEDICAL PERSON WISHES TO GIVE THANKS.

THANKS HAVE BEEN PROVIDED BY RAPID CARE AND OBVIOUS CONCERN. THIS ONE CALLED SBLIPK. Sbl bowed politely towards the ship's doctor who quickly bobbed back.

Thian took a deep breath and concentrated hard on pronouncing the 'Dini's name as correctly as he could. A name that long only reinforced the importance of this 'Dini personage.

'He thanks you, Dr . . . '

'Exeter,' the medic supplied.

'For rapid care and obvious concern,' Thian said with a weak grin. 'His name is Sblipk.' Thian managed it creditably and saw Dip flick a digit in approval.

'Exeter,' the medic said, holding out his hand to the 'Dini.

When Sbl took it without hesitation, Thian's relief was compounded. This 'Dini had been among humans long enough to be comfortable with that convention. The fleet might not know how lucky it was to have such a personage as the 'Dini medical officer.

79

EXTR, the 'Dini replied after pumping the doctor's hand three times.

Exeter laughed and, when his expression suggested that he wasn't sure if laughter would be understood, Thian reassured him.

EXTR, MRDINI TYPE NAME, Sbl said in reasonably understandable Basic.

Those listening in – and sick-bay seemed well populated at the moment – murmured in surprise. Thian, who had been holding himself tightly closed, opened up briefly, to sample reactions. There was pleased surprise and relief. There was also some disbelief and incredulity about taking care of 'Dini beasts – and the term had derogatory undertones to Thian's sensitivities – in a human facility. Thian glanced about, trying to see which of the many people in the corridors were anti-'Dini but without either using a broader empathy range or having a particular target, he could not isolate the antagonists in the group.

His parents had obliquely warned him that not all humans wanted to be partnered with Mrdini: that Thian might find unexpected bias against him because of his close association with 'Dinis. He just hadn't expected to come face to face with it quite so abruptly. Then Sbl touched his arm lightly.

WITH MRDINI COMING AND GOING IT IS WELL FOR EXTR TO KNOW NECESSARY REMEDY, Sbl said to Thian. Taking a writing implement from its belt, it swiftly sketched some letters on a pad which it then handed to Exeter.

'These are the remedies to be used if another 'Dini has similar symptoms, Dr Exeter.'

The man was staring at the pad. 'Why, these are chemical formulae.' His jaw dropped.

'There's been a lot of exchange on the scientific levels, Doctor, where it's easier to find means of expressing constants. Sbl here has probably had some intensive sessions on medical practices,' Thian said with just a little pride in his friends.

'Well, I'm pleased to have this. Tell him?'

Thian did so and there was another exchange of warm bows and nods.

Just then the remainder of the 'Dini medical team arrived with their equipment.

MRG WILL NEED SPECIAL ATTENTION FOR THIRTEEN HUMAN HOURS, Sbl told him. ITS SYSTEM MUST BE FLUSHED OF THE POLLUTANTS AND THOROUGHLY CLEANSED AND ANTIDOTES ADMINISTERED REGULARLY TO PREVENT RECURRENCE. DPL MAY REMAIN FOR COMFORT. NO MORE EQUIPMENT WILL BE NEEDED. EXTR MAY WATCH BUT NO OTHER HUMANS ARE NEEDED. THIS ONE MUST RETURN TO KLTL *(which Thian recognized as the name of the 'Dini vessel),* IF THAT CAN BE ARRANGED.

IMMEDIATELY, *Thian replied.*

WITHOUT SO MUCH HASTE, *Sbl added, twitching its head in the manner Thian recognized as signalling good humour.*

WITH GRACE AND DECORUM THIS TIME, *Thian said, twitching his head in what he hoped wasn't a breach of etiquette with so prestigious a personage as Sbl.*

'What's that all about?' *Exeter asked, his eyes darting from one to another.*

Thian explained what treatment Mur would be getting and that Sbl preferred that only the doctor of the human staff attend the patient. Then, because he felt it might do some listeners good, added Sbl's request for a less dramatic return to the shuttle bay.

Exeter chuckled, nodding his head. 'Can't say as I blame him. You don't always pop in and out of places, do you, Prime?'

'Only in great emergencies, I assure you,' *Thian said.* 'And I hope the captain is as good a sport about it as you've been.'

Exeter raised his eyebrows, his dark eyes twinkling. 'Oh, our captain'll doubtless have a few choice words to say but he'd be a lot less pleased if this had turned out fatal.' *His expression was fleetingly more dour than it had been during the worst of the emergency.* 'Don't worry, lad.

You acted with the speed required to save a life. Can't fault that. Now, I am permitted to observe the treatment?'

'That's the general idea. I'll get back in touch with you at . . . ' and Thian checked the clock, '0300 when it will be completed. Or before if you need me for something.' Then he turned to the nursing 'Dinis. THIS SMALL ONE NAMED THN. TELL EXTR NAME AND WILL CONTACT FOR QUESTIONS/PROBLEMS/NEEDS.

GRATEFUL. COMPLY, said the larger of the two nursing 'Dinis without looking up from the apparatus it was setting up in Mur's bath tank.

GO. ALL PROCEEDS WELL NOW, Dip added, fingering relief/approval/affection signs with its left appendage. GO MORE SLOWLY. AFFIRMATIVE?

Thian laughed, resting his fingers briefly on the slope from Dip's head to body before he bowed again to Sbl, and gestured towards the corridor.

The two medics bowed once more to each other.

'Ah, Dr Exeter, can I have directions back to the shuttle bay?' Thian asked as he realized he didn't know the pedestrian route.

'Sally, you take 'em, will you?'

A girl with short red hair stepped up and saluted. 'This way, sirs.' And with a smart about-face, she led them down the passageway, a trip that gave Thian far more time to worry about how to mend public relations than he needed.

5

Thian courteously saw Sbl into the capsule when the corpswoman delivered them to the shuttle bay.

GOOD DREAMS LARGE SBLIPK, Thian said in polite farewell.

DREAMS WILL BE GENTLE was the astonishingly courteous rejoinder.

Even during the brief exchange, Thian sensed, with no great extension of empathy, that the crew were waiting to see what this *civilian* – the tone in which that title was couched was scathingly critical – would do next. He wondered how his father would have handled such a situation. Except that Afra would never *get* himself into such a situation. There was a lot, Thian reluctantly admitted, to be said for the Capellan method of doing things. At that, he didn't wish to admit – by contacting his parents for guidance – that he'd come a cropper within minutes of arriving on the *Vadim*. Fortunately he could also recall some of his father's tales about episodes of Damia's more spontaneous behaviour. Anyway, he could only take things as they came. The important aspect was that Mur would recover.

Closing the lid on Sbl's transport, Thian turned to the

83

expectant crew with a rueful expression on his face.

'Has anyone else ever broken as many navy regulations as I have in the past hour?' He kept his voice humorously self-deprecating, then went on with, 'But I do want to thank you for your help and cooperation because my friend would be dead without it.' He felt a slight lessening of the tension. 'There isn't an engineer crewman among you, is there?'

'Why?' and a man in engineering green leaned forward on the upper-level railing. His manner was more curious than critical and Thian knew he'd adopted the right tack.

He grimaced. 'Because, if I could access the generator power from this level, I'd frankly rather not have to beard the captain on his own bridge right now if I don't have to. But the 'Dini's an important personage and should be sent right back to its own ship.'

'Up here! You can access from the auxiliary station here,' the lieutenant said, ' . . . sir.'

Relieved to hear that 'sir', Thian took the companionway steps, two at a time, noting an odd expression on the ensign's face as he reached the top.

'This panel?' he asked and the lieutenant nodded, half closing his eyes as he did so. There was some quality about the man's faint grin that gave Thian pause: he was likely one of those who resented Talent on the general principle that they didn't have any. This was the auxiliary access to engineering, but beside it was the clearly marked comunit. He might have breached protocol on his arrival, but he didn't intend to continue now the immediate emergency had passed. He depressed the open channel toggle. 'Commander Tikele,' he said in as firm but respectful tone as he could muster. And felt a shaft of irritation.

'Prime Thian, back again?'

'Sir, permission to access the generators to return Medic Sblipk to its ship.'

'Sssbil . . . what?'

Thian repeated the consonants as glibly as if he hadn't

84

any trouble manipulating his tongue through them. 'The medic has diagnosed and provided treatment for the ill member of my group. It wishes to return.'

'That was quick. The generators are yours, Prime, work away.'

Thian caught the pulse of the engines, pressed against them and lightly 'lifted' Sbl's capsule back to its own ship, laying it so gently down that he hoped Sbl would not realize that it had been teleported. He'd had to use more power for the return, which annoyed him, but who else would know?

'Thank you, Commander,' he said.

'Ah, Prime Lyon?' Tikele began. 'Ah, the captain wishes to see you in his ready room. And, ah, Mr Sedallia, please assign a guide to the Prime.'

'Aye, sir.' And the look the lieutenant then turned on Thian was so neutral it bordered on suppressed hostility.

'I really don't just 'port about places, Lieutenant.'

'Couldn't prove it by me . . . sir,' and Thian caught just a hint of resentment before Sedallia grinned. 'Greene, escort Prime Lyon to the captain's ready room.'

Halfway there, Thian found the uninhibited thoughts of the seaman unbearably depressing. Not only did Greene treasure the thought that this *civilian* (an epithet by tone) was going to get reamed by the captain, which he justly deserved in Greene's opinion, but it was just as well that a weasel-lover wasn't going to be long aboard the *Vadim*. Bad enough to have the critters in the squadron and have to share possible glory with 'em, but to have 'em on board, all the time, with their smell and that queer mid-head eye cocked at you all the time, why it was enough to turn a man's stomach! Greene sure wished that he could be the proverbial insect on the wall of the captain's ready room. Ten to one, the guy'd get sent back in disgrace and the ship'd just have to make do with what it had on board, after all. Some inconveniences were just not worth the fuel it took to correct 'em. This cloudhead was really in for it.

Greene wished now that he'd laid a stake on how long this Prime would last on board the *Vadim*.

Greene wheeled smartly at the door to the captain's ready room and rapped twice.

Disregarding Talent protocol, too (in for a half-credit, in for it all), Thian reached out to the captain now sitting behind his desk, both hands flat on its surface, awaiting the interview. He might as well know how to frame his responses. Thian caught a brief echo of another mind before he was thwarted by the captain's natural shield, now firmly in place in anticipation of an interview with a Prime Talent. Withdrawing instantly, for fear the man might be aware of the attempt, Thian gave a convulsive shudder. Fortunately, Greene was busy opening the door and didn't see it.

There was that about the captain's posture that told Thian that Ashiant was totally relaxed. Was he, too, looking forward to the dressing down he was going to give this . . . this *civilian*?

'That's all, thank you, Greene,' the captain said and nodded for the seaman to retire. 'Return to duty.'

The man silently swore as he closed the door behind him.

'Commander Exeter tells me your . . . ah, companion will survive this . . . ah . . . allergic reaction,' the captain began with what Thian decided was a cunningly bland tone.

He'll come down on me like a big-daddy once he's softened me up, Thian thought and tried to relax, matching the captain's urbane air. He could be no worse than Grandmother in her Tower mode. Could he?

'They did the courtesy of sending a very senior medical officer, Captain Ashiant,' Thian said, moving forward to take the seat the captain indicated. Well, it won't be right now if he's letting me sit.

'So Exeter said, and left chemical formulae for future reference. Good idea, that. Fleet Command keeps sending us bursts of information but it's not always what we need, or what we can profitably use. I dare say you'd be able to explain it.'

'My pleasure, I assure you,' Thian said, steeling himself against the inevitable storm.

'You'd have no objections to sharing explanations?'

'Me? No, why would I, sir? The 'Dinis are open in their admiration of human achievements, and I think they've a few we could profit from.'

'Do you now?'

Thian rebuked himself for being so cocksure but nervousness, the knowledge that he'd already bungled his first moments aboard, made him babble so inanely. If only he knew whether or not the captain was pro or anti Talent. Or 'Dini.

'Such as?'

Well, go for broke, Thi boy, he told himself. 'Such as their air purification systems.'

'Really?' And the captain's heavily marked eyebrows rose.

Just then Thian felt something soft brush his hand. As unexpected as it was, the touch was so familiar that he automatically put his hand down to caress the animal that had somehow got in the captain's ready room.

'Hello there,' Thian said in another almost automatic response to the presence of a known and friendly entity. Then he blinked in utter astonishment. 'You've got a barque-cat!' he exclaimed in surprise and awe, his hand poised to complete a stroke.

The cat raised her front paws off the ground, imperiously butting her head at his hand to continue the caress which he hastily completed. She was a magnificently marked tri-colour with a white muzzle, white socks all round and a tiny puff of white on the tip of her tail. She was also very pregnant and nearly overbalanced. He put a deft hand under her barrel to support her and felt a rumbling purr vibrating through her gravid body.

'What's her lineage, Captain? She's gorgeous. I've only

seen one other tri-colour and little Zsa Zsa isn't a patch on this one.'

'Princess Zsa Zsa of the *Trebizond*?' Ashiant asked, watching as the cat continued to push herself against Thian's leg and hand.

'That's the one. She never threw any tri-colours that I heard about.'

'No, she hasn't, but not for want of the *Treb*'s crew trying,' the captain said with a snort. 'They even asked for the service of our tom. They got marmalades and even a tabby but no tri-colours, or females for that matter.'

'Who is your beauty? Whoops, easy there, missus,' Thian said when the cat, despite her bulkiness, leaped into his lap and began circling to settle.

'I've never seen Tab do that before,' and the captain sounded slightly offended.

That's all I needed, Thian thought, closing his eyes briefly, not only against the sudden kneading of Tab's claws in his leg but also because no crew liked to see their barque-cat display affection to, or even interest in, newcomers.

'I'm sorry about this, too, sir,' Thian said, lifting his hands up and down, wanting to pet her because one was always polite to a barque-cat but not wanting to further offend the captain of her ship.

'You do seem to have a way of relieving the tedium of a long voyage, Prime!' And when Thian stared at him in surprise, he added, 'Oh, pet her before she makes ribbons of your leg. She's insatiable for attention when she's gravid. Now, where were we?'

'I think you were about to tell me off for my antics today . . .'

'I was?' The captain's eyebrows once again raised up in feigned surprise. 'You know that for certain . . . Prime?' There was a delicate pause before the last word.

'Sir, you must know that with a shield as tight as yours

88

I couldn't get a trace of your feelings about my . . . unorthodox behaviour. Which,' and Thian lifted a hand in apology, 'is as good as admitting that I tried, I know, though ethics do inhibit me from reading past the public mind unless given explicit permission. But with so much at stake . . .'

'Indeed there is, young Lyon,' Ashiant said, leaning back in his chair as he watched the cat lower her head to her paws on Thian's lap, 'which is why I will ask you from now on to stick to the normal procedures whenever possible. You acted with promptness – if in a most unusual manner – in a situation that could have had tragic results. I see, however, that your . . . ah . . . skills will be more extensive than I had been led to believe. I feel much better about communications already after your exercise of 'Dini today.

'First I'll discuss with you the duties which Earth Prime felt you would be able to perform to ease the discomforts of this long voyage.' He held up strong thick fingers, ticking off the responsibilities one by one. 'All interracial ship communications which, in all honesty, have been damned sparse and misunderstood so far; all necessary transportation between ships in this squadron; receipt and despatch of all capsules, drone and personnel; instruction for all officers in basic 'Dini. Among us we've only enough to express "stop, go, port, starboard and attack imminent: yellow and red alert".' His eyebrows did a roller-coaster effect of disgusted dismay at such paucity. He waited significantly until Thian nodded hurriedly in acceptance. 'I've a list— ' and he passed over a comreader pencil file, 'of all those on board who've tested Talented. Not many but I'm told that their abilities can augment yours in an emergency . . .' Ashiant paused again, eyebrows raised at Thian.

'I'll try to announce emergencies whenever possible, Captain,' he said meekly.

'Emergencies never announce themselves beforehand,

89

Prime,' Ashiant said, his sentence a long sigh of resignation. 'However, you *will* discuss what might be demanded of them, preferably singly as what you have in your hand is exceedingly top secret,' and Thian quickly shoved the file into his breast pocket, pressing the closing tab tight. 'We have, unfortunately, found that those with minor Talent are disadvantaged by it so, unless those on board have discovered each other by chance, they're unknown to each other. But it's nice to have a back-up system . . . ' Thian thought his parents and grandparents would have strangled at being termed 'back-up' system but Ashiant was only repeating what was a common attitude among non-Talented. 'Introduce yourself so you can be tuned, or primed or whatever for whatever code or method you use to do whatever it is you Primes do.' He made circles with one hand to indicate either indifference or ignorance. Then he leaned forward and lowered his voice. 'Thian Lyon, I'm the only one on board who knows your chronological age. That white lock doesn't wash out, does it? No?' The captain nodded when Thian murmured that it was a genetic attribute. 'But Jeff Raven assured me that you've had excellent training and sufficient solo operations to handle your various duties. After today's exhibition, I think you do, too.'

Astounded, Thian stared back at the captain.

'Now, what's this about air purification? We've been sucking this smog so long we don't smell it any more, even if half the time we can almost chew it. Small wonder your 'Dini couldn't breathe.'

Still stroking Tab, Thian hitched himself more upright in the chair and began to explain about the 'Dini vegetation used to purify the air on their long-voyage ships. Although human life-support systems were more than adequate for the usual duration of voyages, even those not assisted by Talent thrusts, this long cruise had obviously taxed the system.

'Now I understand,' Ashiant said, leaning back and

swivelling idly in his chair. 'The *KLTL* 'Dini offered me some plants after our last conference. Didn't realize how significant that offer was.'

'How would you know? You didn't, by any chance, *dream* about plants the next couple of nights?'

Ashiant stared at him, his brows nearly meeting over the bridge of his fleshy nose. 'I did! Thought it odd because I dreamed there were these big leaved pots all over the ship, and everyone was smiling like loons.'

Thian grinned. 'You did know that 'Dinis use dreams as communications?'

'Yes, I'd heard that, but dreaming plants? C'mon now, Prime, that's too exotic for this mother's son.'

'I also interpret 'Dini dreams – if you get any more, sir. Strictly top secret,' Thian said, hoping he hadn't misjudged the captain's humour.

He hadn't, for Ashiant roared with laughter. 'Never thought I'd have a 'Dini dream. Not that sort of temperament.'

'Temperament has little to do with receipt of 'Dini dreams, sir. You learn to respect repetitions because that's what they want you to ask about.'

'Oh, do they so? Hmmm.'

The upshot of that interview was that Thian made a second contact with the *KLTL*, conversing this time with their life-support systems officer and discovering that yes, there were available *sgit* plant shoots that could be spared and possibly more from their sister ship in the squadron, the *KLTS*. An improvement would not be immediately noticeable, depending on how long the over-use of the oxygen had been but a gradual betterment would occur. *Sgit* plants grew rapidly and had to be constantly separated, which was all to the good for an air-improvement system. If there were sufficient shoots, pots of them could also be put in cabins or larger facilities to assist local improvements. Leaves and stalks of young plants were edible.

'Some of their vegetables are quite tasty, Captain,' Thian ventured and then grinned at his expression.

'I only eat enough greens to keep balance,' Ashiant said and then, after a pause, added, 'but I think I'd be willing to try them. For good will, you know. Ha! Glad you're aboard, Prime. You'll sort out a lot of this kind of misunderstanding. And I think I'll do some discreet enquiring and find out if any officers or ratings have had odd dreams. I'll tell Exeter – you've met him – in case he's had incidents reported to him.'

Then he took Thian to the bridge to introduce him to those on duty. If the bridge crew had any private thoughts about the congenial attitude of their captain for the newest arrival, they kept so tight a lid on them that Thian couldn't sense a thing. Thian was invited to the captain's mess at 2000 hours and provided with an escort – until he learned his way about the ship – to return him to his cabin.

Wearier than he had ever been before – even after helping his parents push big-daddies – Thian was grateful to close the panel on his tiny cabin. Dad had warned him that it would be different working totally on his own. Thian had been dismissive then, but now, with no other Talent as back-up, it *was* different. Slumping down on the bunk, he had only to extend his hand to the terminal and contact sick-bay.

'He's fine,' the medic said. 'No, *it's* fine. Read somewhere that these creatures don't have any sex.'

'They do but they don't discuss that aspect of their biology. In 'Dini culture, "It" is always preferable to either gender designation, Doctor.'

'Why?'

'Doctor, that requires a very long explanation.' And a yawn surprised him.

'I'll catch you later,' the medic said with a chuckle.

Thian was almost asleep before his head hit the bolster.

Dinner at the captain's mess was not an obvious ordeal.

Drinks were offered as well as hot finger-foods which Thian decided were not the standard fare to judge by the pleasure of their reception.

The captain cleared his throat and the wardroom had his immediate attention.

'In case you haven't guessed, the extras served tonight are thanks to the supply drones brought in by Prime Thian Lyon,' and Thian tried to demur as he'd been as much a passenger as the food. 'Whatever, Prime,' the captain went on, 'we have it and intend to enjoy it and it came with you. As most of you already know,' now Ashiant grinned as he glanced about, 'the Prime has demonstrated some of his potential use to the Fleet by what I hear— ' he cleared his throat, 'are termed his antics today. "Antics" if you will, but they saved the life of one of our allies and have given us the opportunity to forge stronger links with them. So welcome aboard, Prime Thian Lyon.' He held his glass up, looking about to see that his toast was being recognized by everyone, and drank to Thian.

Thian cleared his throat several times, bombarded by far too many reactions emanating from all sides of him: one outright black thrust of suspicion and distaste, several sceptical ones, but more were curious, with tinges of amusement and slightly malicious anticipation. To counteract the negative feelings, Thian began to project serenity and compassion.

'Considering the havoc I played today with navy protocol, sir,' he said, grinning sheepishly, 'I can only say I'm infinitely relieved to be here and not in the brig or sent back where I came from.'

That reply generated a few honest laughs but also a second shaft of malicious amusement at his self-deprecation.

Cloudhead's smarming the audience, is he? was the verbalized thought.

On the pretext of lifting his own glass to toast his company, Thian looked around, trying to spot the source.

Oho! Could he have heard me?

The thought was all too ephemeral and there were too many people who could have thought it. Thian hadn't been quick enough to catch that second unexpected lapse. He let his glance slide quickly from Commander Tikele to the chunky sallow-skinned woman beside him: a security officer by her shoulder-tabs – Vander-something – and around the immediate circle. The com officer, Eki Wasiq, a very gaunt man with soft brown eyes that made him the least likely suspect of the group; the exe, Jaskell-Germys, a few centimetres shorter than Thian, with a carefully controlled face that gave away nothing of his thoughts. Lieutenant Sedallia, the only one he already knew by name, exhibited polite attention, while the gunnery officer, an older man Fardo Ah Min with the squint that had become a programmer's trait, had been so abstracted that he was late lifting his glass and more irritated by that lapse than shooting snide thoughts at the newcomer. The two juniors present, because it was their off-duty time, were laughably easy to read: they hadn't expected the chance to dine well tonight.

Thian tipped his glass to his lips and drank. The malevolence was as startling in its absence as in its brief flare.

As he was seated opposite the security officer, Lieutenant-Commander Ailsah Vandermeer, he had a chance to put her to the most adroit mental probe he could summon: the kind he got away with using on his cousin Roddie. He could read no more than her public mind without breaching the most stringent injunction of his training but, if she was dissembling, she was making an extremely skilful job of it. Her thoughts were clearly centred on enjoyment of the excellent meal: such comments as she directed at him were about learning Mrdini.

He was astonished at how many were willing to learn Mrdini, including Lieutenant Sedallia. In answer to a direct query from Commander Tikele, Thian – again sensing only genuine interest – agreed to produce 'Dini engineering terms and their phonetic equivalents for the engineering officer to study. Tikele already had plans of the 'Dini engines but was unable to decipher some of the special terms for a full understanding of the intricacies of the 'Dini drive: a system that had some advantages over the type which the humans used. Tikele was hoping to draft some refinements, using the 'Dini method, that would improve the *Vadim*'s drive. Sedallia was his design assistant.

On a chase assignment like this, as on exploratory vessels, crew and officers were encouraged in off-duty studies and occupations, interspersed with emergency drills for any contingency the devious mind of their captain could envisage. As Thian later heard a chief petty officer proudly remark, 'Cap'n Ash-i-ant can sure think up some dillies! Ain't caught us out yet, neither.'

The wine that was drunk that evening was not part of the supplies which arrived with Thian and his 'Dinis. But it was the last of the dry white the mess steward had and he advised all to make the most of it. Thian liked wine, perhaps too well, for he seemed unwilling to refuse a refill of his glass, yet he didn't think he'd ever been what others might call drunk. This evening, probably due to the cumulative effects of the day's busy-ness, he did find himself a little light-headed. That's when he began to 'hear' the snicking little taunts. As these came through in the form of mental commentary, he couldn't even identify the sex of the source. Whoever it was did *not* like Talent, of any degree, though Thian suspected the person was unaware that he or she possessed some: the person was 'sending' on a telepathic level which, to Thian, indicated a latent Talent of some degree. The content of those little barbs was much like the sort his cousin Roddie would verbally throw out. At least with Roddie, you knew who you were fighting.

The time – when Mur would be released from its treatment – saved him from both too much wine and too much stress under the continued barrage of malicious jibes. He excused himself to the captain, thanking him again for the meal, and once again repeating his wish to be of service to

95

the *Vadim* in any way he could.

'D'you know your way to sick-bay?' Commander Tikele asked as Thian had his hand on the wardroom door release.

'I think so, sir,' Thian said with a smile at the medics in intense conversation and left. There'd been no over- or undertones to that remark and yet . . .

Thian had lied. He'd had enough wine so that he didn't know if he should turn left or right – port or starboard. He'd better get accustomed to thinking all the time in nautical terms. He looked up and down the passageway, closed his eyes and 'ported himself into the main corridor outside sick-bay. At this hour, as he'd hoped, there was no-one about and he went in.

Mur was out of its bath, colour bright and pelt shining, poll eye sparkling. On the other hand, Dip looked exhausted.

THIAN HAS COME FOR US, Mur said in its clipped staccato fashion and a nurse looked around the curtains separating the cubicles.

'Oh, Prime, you're very punctual,' she said and then smiled broadly. 'Mur is quite recovered but I don't think Dip has stood the gaff as well. I offered . . . you do call them "its", don't you . . . ?' When Thian nodded, she went on, 'But all it took was some enhanced broth. Dr Exeter looked up what additives would be sustaining for a 'Dini. He was really frightfully pleased to meet such a distinguished 'Dini physician, too.'

Despite his fatigue and the blurring caused by the wine, Thian couldn't help but note that she regarded him with keen interest, tilting her head and smiling at him. She was pretty, he thought, and certainly gave off a reassuring aura. She'd be a comfort to the sick.

'Thank you, Lieutenant . . . ' All navy nurses were at least lieutenants, weren't they?

'Greevy, Alison-Anne Greevy,' she said. 'Most people call me Gravy, though,' she added with a rueful grin.

'Oh,' was all Thian could think to say at first, then he added, 'most people call me Thian.'

'But you're a Prime,' she said, surprised.

'Primes are people, too . . . Gr . . . Gravy,' he said, annoyed that he was stuttering. There was something wrong and he didn't know what it was. His mind seemed gluey.

WE MAY GO NOW, Mur said at its firmest and folded its digits about Thian's hand. COME DPL.

Gravy looked down at them with the sweetest smile on her face. 'They are the darlingest creatures. I'm so glad Mur recovered.'

He gulped. 'Where are the two from the other ship?'

She smiled again. She seemed to have quite a vocabulary of smiles. This one was slightly condescending, as if he should have known. 'They're asleep. They were tireless in their care of Mur. And they speak very good Basic. They will contact you when they have refreshed themselves – their words – and are ready to return.'

'Oh, good. Yes, that's fine.' Thian was excessively relieved that he didn't have to 'port anyone anyplace tonight.

Dip was swaying.

'Ah . . . um, Gravy, how do I get back to my cabin? Eight Deck, cabin C80N?'

'Very simple,' and it was, when he took the directions from her mind and paid no attention to what she said, for she had a habit of using her right hand when she said 'port', and her left hand when she meant him to turn to 'starboard'.

That they got back to his cabin at all was due to Mur's attention.

WINE, TH? Mur asked once on their way.

WINE, MRG, Thian admitted. NO GREAT QUANTITY INGESTED. FATIGUE ASSISTS EFFECTS.

TH WORKED HARD THIS DAY. REST COMES.

DREAMS, TOO, GOOD DREAMS WITH MRG RECOVERED. And Thian was overwhelmingly grateful that this was so, and hugged the silky body to his side. He helped the 'Dinis into their hammocks and then stretched out, once more, on his own bunk.

And there were dreams, but not 'Dini inspired. Gravy seemed to be flowing all over him while something black hissed out of the walls of his cabin which compressed and expanded with no warning.

Over the next few weeks, Thian was so tightly scheduled that mental exhaustion made him sleep deeply and dreamlessly. Gradually, as he became accustomed to the new routines, he did enjoy dream-time, with his 'Dinis and with the other new 'Dini personalities he met, either physically, as he 'ported them to the *Vadim* or took Captain Ashiant and other officers to the *KLTL* and the *KLTS*, or by communications. These dreamers were different to any he had previously encountered: older and considerably more active so their dreams were projected on many levels: some which he couldn't understand. Mur and Dip, as juvenile in experience as himself, were unable to give him any help; as much because they were more in awe of these contacts than anything else.

His classes were surprisingly crowded. In the first morning slot, which held the most officers, was Malice and Thian began to narrow down the possibilities: Tikele was one, though that surprised Thian; Ailsah Vandermeer was the second; the weapons officer, Far Ah Min, a Terran ectomorph with black hair, a sallow skin and high cheekbones, was the third, and the fourth was one of the surgeons, Lacee Mban, a round-faced man, pale haired and eyed, with the smallest hands Thian had ever seen on an adult. Lieutenant Sedallia had initially been a strong contender for the honour but he worked so hard at learning 'Dini that Thian scratched him off the list. Innocently Thian was hoping that this antagonist would lose the edge of his distaste for Talents when Thian proved himself on this level but the malice hovered expectantly:

but expecting what, Thian didn't know. Still, it kept him constantly on the alert, hoping to penetrate the identity or reduce the resentment.

He had three hours of classes in the morning. Mur and Dip acted as his assistants which speeded instruction considerably for they could conduct pronunciation lessons with those struggling with crucial words and phrases while he explained grammar and syntax and increased vocabulary, written and spoken. These were techniques which his sister had found useful teaching 'Dinis and which he could adopt for human students. The adults of both species had trouble getting their tongues to accept such contortions. Only now could Thian appreciate the manner of his own learning from childhood onward. None of the humans would know how often Mur and Dip were convulsed in 'Dini laughter and sometimes he too found it difficult not to join in: 'Dini laughter being infectious – for him, at least.

By 1200 hours, he grabbed a quick lunch with Mur and Dip and performed any 'portation duties. Sometimes he was awakened by an urgent request to 'catch' a supply drone for the *Vadim*: usually a medium-sized affair. He didn't mind such awakenings for he had a chance to exchange greetings with the sender, often his grandfather or grandmother, and sometimes – when he 'caught' for the 'Dini ships – Laria.

To her alone could he mention Malice.

Poor Thian, and on your first assignment, too, Laria had said with full sympathy. *And you can't identify him, her? It may just be sour grapes, you know, since the person is projecting. Sometimes Talents are too nebulous to be directed or refined and the person is naturally resentful. But aren't you meeting with the listed Talents on the ship?*

Yes, but it's slow, what with all the other duties I seem to have acquired. Thian didn't exactly feel abused but he also didn't seem to have time for anything but his duties, eating and sleeping.

Don't worry, Thi, his sister said encouragingly, *it does* seem that way at first. *You'll have more time once everything's settled down – to mere boredom.*

They've a barque-cat, Lar, and she had kittens, he told her the morning after Queen Tabitha Many-Coats produced six: three of them tri-coloured females. The entire crew had rejoiced! *She likes me,* he added rather smugly, adding glimpses of the several times Tab had sought his company.

Don't antagonize the crew over their cat, Thian, she warned him urgently in a fashion that would have irritated him from his sister if he hadn't also 'seen' her genuine concern. *They're not Coonies, you know, who are notoriously fickle! Be careful not to let one of the kittens decide you're his, or hers.*

Thian sent her a patronizing grin. *Yeah, sis, I know!*

Thian, about the other problem. Trap Malice into revealing himself. Remember the way you got Roddie into trouble?

Thian chuckled out loud. *Thanks, Lar. Surprised I didn't think of it myself.*

It's not as if you haven't had a lot to think about, Thi! Love ya! She sent a mental hug that was almost as palpable as a physical one.

Trap my Malice, huh? he thought, still reclining in the couch and becoming aware of the normal bridge activity around him. The way I did Roddie! He'd have to go about it cleverly: his antagonist was an adult, not a petulant boy.

And Laria might be right about a sour-Talent. None of his suspects were on the list Captain Ashiant had handed him. So far, none of those he had interviewed privately – and that had taken time and effort – were more than minimally Talented. He'd three 12s, the lowest weight, two 10s and a 9. He was saving Alison-Anne Greevy – whose appearance on the list wasn't that big a surprise since she was a T-5 Empath – until the last as he'd already had enough contact with her to access her mind in an emergency. The 10s and the 9 were mechanically inclined which could be helpful in special emergencies and one was a chief petty officer. The three 12s, ratings all, would be makeweights, none of them having any other special aptitudes. The captain's name was not on the list either, although Ashiant's ability to shield his thoughts indicated some latent gift: maybe just to shield. Some people had that and no other aptitude.

He was also assembling a thesaurus of specifically technical terms, using the Rondomanski technique. Over his lifetime, since the 'Dinis approached his mother and father on Deneb, drafters and scientists had been correlating technical data, drawings, equations, theories for translation. 'Dini and Terran science had been exchanged on all levels in every aspect of space travel and exploration: the 'Dinis and Terrans alike using conflicting terms to describe the apparatus used in the same manner or the same end. One had to be careful not to confuse terminology. Having been raised on a mining planet, Thian was already familiar with technological terms – and the technological mentalities – but he also needed specific naval applications and asked Commander Tikele to suggest personnel to assist him.

'I'd best do the engineering,' Tikele told him gruffly and he went on to recommend officers in the other disciplines. 'Sedallia can help, too.'

Thian was both surprised and pleased by such co-operation: this could be a chance to probe two suspects. Both engineers were so enthusiastic and involved in the task that he found it hard to consider either of them as his private 'Malice': that personality was much too negative about so many aspects that were raised in the language lessons. Malice was negative in all comments so far.

Then, just as he was beginning to be easy with the established routine, several incidents occurred. The first happened in sick-bay. Or rather the aftermath of it came to his notice in sick-bay. Although the air on the *Vadim* was slowly improving, Mur occasionally had bouts with dehydration hiccups which were eased by immersion. On instructions from Sbl, Commander Exeter had kept the treatment water from the first bath and, when needed, Thian took Mur down to sick-bay for another session. They arrived at the facility to find shore police on guard, looking exceedingly stern. Sick-bay itself was packed with personnel. The bruisings, black eyes, broken noses, split lips and skulls and several men nursing damaged hands, arms and fingers left no doubt in Thian's mind that there had been a major brawl. In his surprise, he let down his shields and was bombarded by active hatred and such negative emanations that he was nearly ill. But he couldn't ignore Mur's condition.

Chopping off all natural empathy, he worked his way towards Gravy who was cleaning the blood from a burly gunner's face. Her public mind was vivid with disgust for the stupidity which led grown men to beat each other to pulp for the sheer exercise of brute force, and an earnest wish that head wounds didn't bleed so profusely. Thian 'put' a finger on the artery that was producing the flood so he could find out from her where Mur's water-cask was stored.

'Thian, you don't know anything about first aid, do you?' she asked, giving him a distraught smile, her expression anxious.

'Enough to help out, I think,' he said, 'but only after I've got Mur in the bath again.'

She rolled her very expressive pale green eyes. 'We've no place to put him – it, not with all these here and, honest, Thian,' she said in agitation, 'you don't want your friend anywhere near these clods.'

'No, I don't.' Just to be sure his 'friends' might not be part of whatever argument occasioned the brawl, he shot a quick look behind her public mind. She had such a genuine caring personality that it was not an intrusion. To his relief, the mêlée had started over some perfectly innocuous statement which was taken up wrongly by men too long in each other's company with no relief. 'We can just manage the bath in my cabin, I think. Show

102

me where it is,' he added, dropping his lips close to her ear.

She blinked, squidged her eyes shut in an effort to concentrate on its position in the storeroom and he chuckled.

'Gotcha, and thanks,' he said, moving away.

Foremost in Gravy's mind was the wish for an extra pair of hands right now to stop bleeding, check for skull depressions or other less obvious and internal results of the fierce, if short, confrontation.

Thian knew that he could be of some assistance, even if no-one would ever be aware of it – which was probably the best way to handle his intervention.

First Mur had to be taken care of so he 'grabbed' the cask and the bath and shoved them up to his cabin. He collected Mur and Dip who had waited in the corridor with the statuesque SPs, and urged them on to the next empty passage.

I MUST HELP MEDICS. DPL, BATH AND TANK ARE NOW IN CABIN, CAN DPL MANAGE NECESSARY ARRANGEMENTS FOR MRG?

HAVING OBSERVED THEM, IT IS EASILY DONE.

I SEND YOU THERE.

MRG NEEDS BATH. DPL MANAGES. TH NEEDED MORE HERE TO BLOT HUMAN FACES STITCH HUMAN WOUNDS SET HUMAN ARMS. And Dip made shooing gestures with its upper extremities.

'Dini humour was usually unexpected and Thian grinned appreciatively. Then, very carefully, he 'ported his friends to the now tight confines of his cabin where Mur could bathe in peace.

Next he let himself into an empty cabin adjacent to sick-bay and started to scan the waiting patients, keeping a light contact with Gravy. His great-grandmother, for whom he was named, had made certain all her descendants understood basic initial medical treatment and its mental signs. Thian had never thought he'd be putting that training to use on such a wholesale basis. When he

sensed internal bleeding in one young rating, he directed
Gravy away from the next man in line to him, suggesting
to Gravy that the boy's colour was wrong. He 'pressed'
on any number of arteries to curtail bleeding and eased as
much pain as he could. He also 'heard' many grievances
of men and women cooped for an unconscionable time
in each other's company with no respite for months, and
none in sight . . . unless the bleeding planet of the bleeding
Hive was found and even action would be preferable to
sitting in this bucket ploughing who knows how many
years away from a decent port.

When he heard the legitimate occupant of the room
returning, he 'ported back to his cabin. Mur had just
finished the bath and Dip was drying its pelt. The cabin
had a medicinal smell to it: not too unpleasant. Tired
as he was, Thian decanted the bath into the cask, and
replaced both in the storeroom.

The next day the second incident occurred when he
received a request from Sblipk for him to despatch a
personnel carrier from the *KLTL* with young 'Dinis to
be returned to the homeworld. They were the result of
that latest hibernation of 'Dinis on board.

That, in itself, surprised Thian. He knew, from a remark
of Gravy's that strict contraception was practised by the
mixed crews of the human ships. But 'Dinis were not
human and their procreative drives did not respond to any
contraception that he'd ever heard of. He wondered why
it hadn't occurred to anyone that there would inevitably
be young on board long-haul 'Dini vessels. How they
had solved the problem before he didn't ask. It wasn't
his business. Not only did the 'portation of sixteen young
'Dinis give him a chance to have a few words with Laria,
but it also gave him a very good idea.

D'you get many nursery shipments, Laria? he asked in the
process of despatching the carrier.

*More than you'd guess, considering how long the various
elements of the Search have been going on.* He could see the

grin she must be wearing. *You'd think they had nothing else to do on board.*

Laria! He was surprised by the overtones.

They've a far more acute problem than humans do, although that is hard to believe.

Humans have another problem the 'Dinis don't have – short fuses.

What? Oh! A bad brawl? On shipboard? Isn't that dangerous?

There were twenty-five in sick-bay, and not all with just black eyes and bruises.

Ready when you are, Thian, Laria said in her professional tone and he pressed in on the *KLTL's* engines to 'port her the precious young 'Dinis.

Apart from protesting the journey, they're safely here and such a to-do from the Nursery! Laria's tone was amused. *Inform Sblipk that all have safely arrived and will be settled with appropriate fosters of the same colour.*

THIS IS WELL DONE! HUMAN HELP WAS NEVER MORE NEEDED. THESE WILL NOT BE WASTED, Sblipk said, bowing with more than formal courtesy to Thian.

As Thian returned to the *Vadim*, he suddenly realized what happened to 'Dinis born on long journeys and was almost overcome with a wave of painful regret. Small wonder human help in transporting their young back to the homeworld was so well received.

That was what gave him the idea. It wasn't only young lives that could be lost on a long voyage, no matter how well conditioned men and women might be to such confinement. He asked for, and received, an immediate appointment with Captain Ashiant.

'Sir, I was down in sick–bay yesterday . . . '

The captain regarded him with a blank expression.

'Sir, why do I have to send *empty* drones back to the supplying planets?'

Ashiant cocked his head slightly, and without even trying to, Thian could hear him mentally repeating his question. A smile began to bloom on the captain's face

105

and he regarded Thian with overt approval.

'I don't know why drones have to be sent back empty to the supplying planets, Prime Thian, but if you don't mind the extra mass, I think we can equip them with temporary oxygen, and obtain temporary relief from a problem that is becoming more and more urgent! This cruise has already set records in modern naval annals.' The captain rose from his desk and extended his hand to Thian who managed to dampen his own thoughts sufficiently in order to complete the handshaking. The captain was a deep rich brown, clever, astringent. 'I beg your pardon, Prime,' he added, suddenly realizing that he had been extremely personal with a Talent.

'My pleasure, sir,' Thian replied, bowing slightly from the waist. The captain was very definitely his friend.

'I'll make up a shore leave list immediately. The very fact that shore leave is possible is going to have an excellent effect on morale. How many can a drone take?'

'Comfortably and safely, ten.'

'How many uncomfortably?' Ashiant grinned.

'Twelve to fourteen depending on size.'

'Give me weights . . . '

'Mass and volume, sir,' Thian said, and made rapid mental calculations which he jotted down on the captain's desk pad. Ashiant watched, washing his hands together with great satisfaction.

'Yes, this'll make all the difference.' Then he let out a gusty sigh. 'Of course, we'll have to avail our sister ships of the courtesy, too. That'll cut down on the numbers the *Vadim* can send. Nevertheless,' and he grinned at Thian, 'I appreciate it, young Lyon. With two and three drones coming in every seven days . . . ' and his grin broadened without the need for words. 'Wonder why I never thought of it before.'

'I should have, if you didn't, sir,' Thian said, more than a little ashamed he hadn't.

'Yes, well, I'll scarcely fault you on that, Thian!'

Why Thian should feel as if the captain had paid him a great honour by using his first name, he didn't know, but somehow that was the feeling he left with.

THN HAS DONE SOMETHING SPECIALLY GOOD? Mur asked.

THN HAS FINALLY THOUGHT OF SOMETHING HE SHOULD HAVE THOUGHT OF THREE MONTHS AGO, Thian replied. And explained circumstance and idea. His 'Dini friends were oddly silent when he finished and he wondered.

THN GO HOME SOON? Dip asked in such a curious tone that Thian knew something was wrong.

TROUBLE, FRIENDS? And he put his arms about them, drawing them closer, radiating comfort.

Mur and Dip exchanged such rapid sentences that even he, well accustomed to such a pace, missed half the words. As, he suspected, they intended.

WHAT IS THE TROUBLE? THN DEMANDS KNOWLEDGE.

Together Dip and Mur sighed and leaned into him.

MUST GO SOON.

WHY MUST THN GO SOON?

MRG AND DPL MUST GO SOON SO THN MUST GO SOON, TOO.

The coin dropped and Thian hugged his friends. IT IS NECESSARY FOR MRG AND DPL TO HIBERNATE, IS THAT NOT IT? When their pliant bodies gave assent, he hugged them firmly again. MRG AND DPL MUST GO WHEN THIS IS NECESSARY.

BUT THN WILL BE ALONE AMONG STRANGERS AND THIS HAS NOT BEEN GOOD.

ON THE CONTRARY, DPL, THIS HAS BEEN VERY GOOD FOR THN. MRG AND DPL MUST GO TO RETURN REFRESHED. TIME WILL GO FAST FOR YOU AND FAST ENOUGH FOR THN. THN HAD NO PROBLEMS WHEN THIS WAS NECESSARY ON AURIGAE. NO DIFFERENCE NOW ON SHIP.

IF MATTERS WERE PROPERLY ADJUSTED *KLTL* COULD HAVE BEEN USED BUT IT IS OVER AND THE *KLTS* WILL BE TOO LATE.

HOW SOON MUST MRG AND DPL LEAVE?

107

WITHIN MONTH.

SOONER IF REQUIRED? Thian could sense a reluctance in them to leave him, which was gratifying, but he was also well aware of how much they would suffer by prolonging the essential hibernation. MRG AND DPL RETURN TO AURIGAE WITHIN WEEK!

HOMEWORLD WILL DO AS WELL. There was something about Dip's manner that made Thian laugh.

'You are irrepressible!' he said, crowing at Dip's cunning. The pair could have been accommodated at the Aurigaean installation but there was a certain cachet to going through the process on the homeworld which the two had not yet enjoyed. Even the Mrdini understood the subtleties of status. AND MRG AND DPL WOULD FORFEIT THE COMPANY OF FRIENDS AND RELATIVES AT THIS TIME TO BE ALONE ON THEIR HOMEWORLD?

THN WOULD BE ALONE HERE. IT IS ONLY FAIR THAT MRG AND DPL BE DEPRIVED IN SOME WAY AT THE SAME TIME.

Thian rocked with laughter, falling backwards on his bunk and cracking his head on the wall. As if they had caused his bump, the 'Dinis were all over him with tender digits and soothing caresses.

THN WILL MISS HIS FRIENDS. THN ALWAYS DOES, he told them when they quieted and he could hold them against him.

The next day when he appeared for his morning classes, there was an excited buzz in the air and many smiles for him. Except, of course, from Malice. Thian could feel dark brooding discontent from that source, as if Malice resented him doing this service to his shipmates. Or perhaps had small hope of being one of those on a shore leave roster. What amused him was the fact that there had been no official announcement of shore leave by means of Talent-assisted personnel capsule. In fact Captain Ashiant's bulletin was anticlimactic: everyone on all four human ships knew about it.

Three days later Thian sent the first three drones back:

two to Earth as requested by the personnel and one to Betelgeuse.

You've made more work for yourself, the Rowan told her grandson as she 'caught' the first of the three. But he sensed that she approved.

There's been a significant improvement in morale, he said diffidently.

That is very important on a search mission such as this. Your grandfather says you ought to have warned Fleet so Earth could be warned.

That's not my responsibility, he began and then realized that he was being teased. *Think of the money they'll be spending!*

6

Ten days after the first shore leaves were 'ported, the long-range sensors discovered an object moving at a very slow speed in the general direction of the squadron: a very large object to have been picked up at such a distance. Too far as yet to be identified, its presence livened all discussions on the *Vadim* and the other ships of the squadron. Thian 'ported all captains aboard the flagship and attended the meeting as recording interpreter. He was proud of his 'students': even after only four months intensive study they were able to discuss much in 'Dini, a fact which certainly pleased the 'Dini captains. Nothing could be done until identification was made, of course, but several courses of action were discussed.

The 'Dini reluctantly allowed the possibility that the object might be a wandering planet, blown out of its native solar system by a nova – several had been noted in this quadrant. Such phenomena had been noted by both human and 'Dini in the course of space explorations: the planets or asteroid fragments sterile and lifeless but occasionally worth prospecting. Thian knew by their language that the 'Dini captains were convinced beyond doubt that this was more likely another Hive ship. It was travelling from the general spatial direction of the ion trail they had been following, hoping it would lead them, at last, to the Hive Home System. The ion trail had been getting weaker as its traces dissipated during the months of the search but was still discernible on the highly sensitive equipment the 'Dinis had developed. Space being the immensity it was, even a general direction for search was a plus.

The 'Dinis wanted to go on yellow alert and to implement intensive drill in the strategy of penetrating and destroying a Hive ship. As these tactics were of a suicidal nature, the humans, understandably, temporized, suggesting careful surveillance and reconnaissance in order to make the most effective use of the new weaponry with which the squadron was equipped. Untried against a Hive ship, to be sure, but theoretically more sophisticated than known Hive ordnance, delivering a paralytic shock of purportedly lethal proportions. Even glancing touches could inhibit movement for hours.

This was where the 'Dinis and humans diverged in their mutual war against the Hive World. Technically speaking, the squadron's orders were to seek and identify the Hive World, and return for further orders. A single fast scout might have accomplished the same mission but a single fast scout could neither carry the armament needed in case it encountered Hive ships – which was a distinct possibility given the unusual Hive activity that had created this emergency – nor the supplies to last an indefinite search period. So a squadron was committed to the task, with orders that one ship must survive to report.

In the 'Dini view, coming across a Hive vessel meant it *must* be destroyed. It could not be permitted to exist, no matter what cost the destruction. It could be heading for *their* homeworld and must not be allowed to proceed once intercepted. Whereas 'Dini soldiery was quite willing to die to achieve that end, humans, not having had wars in several centuries, were not disposed to commit themselves with such fervent dedication. To be sure, naval units met with disasters of all kinds, causing the death of many or all those aboard the stricken vessel. But no human warship *sought* deliberate attack, nor considered it the logical conclusion of sighting an alien vessel. Cowardice had nothing to do with this: common sense did.

'He who fights and runs away, lives to fight another day,' might be a human sentiment but it was, unfortunately, an intolerable concept to the 'Dinis.

As translator – and someone more familiar with the nuances of 'Dini speech than any of the others at the conference – Thian was doing his best to tone down the challenging language from the 'Dini while injecting vehemence into the almost diffident human responses. To the 'Dini warrior ethos, this was put up or shut up time, while the humans seemed more interested in discussing alternatives that did not, in 'Dini terms, exist. The on-coming object *must* be a Hive ship. It *must* be destroyed.

When Ashiant, for one, realized that 'destruction' was the preferred 'Dini tactic, he cast a meaningful glance at Thian. Thian gave his head a quick shake, wishing the captain hadn't such a tight natural shield so he could immediately explain that there was no way he, with twelve minor Talents – even augmented by the generators of six big warships – could do what, two and a half decades ago, had required several hundred Talents in the Denebian Penetration.

The human captains vigorously insisted on discussing alternative identities for the wayfarer, the favoured one – which the 'Dinis repudiated as soon as it was mentioned – was the possibility of meeting yet another sentient species in space. Thian privately agreed with the 'Dinis on that score. 'Dinis had explored enough over the centuries of their space travel capability to be cynical about that prospect: especially in view of the fact that they had already found humans.

Politely, Captains Spktm and Plr listened to the humans but Thian could see that they were convinced this was Hive and it couldn't be anything else.

In the face of that unalterable opinion, Ashiant and the other human captains wisely initiated intensive drill procedures but an actual discharge of the new weapons system, of course, was out of the question. The surprise of such new weapons might even have an effect on the implacable Hivers. The Hive was also known to have acutely sensitive scanning devices – as some unfortunate 'Dini scouts had discovered. Biologists had suggested that the Hive members probably had more acute hearing than vision. What few fragments of Hive ships were left after a 'Dini suicide penetration gave little evidence of internal lighting systems.

Fortunately, none of the humans even mentioned evasion tactics though it was no secret to Thian that each human captain was reviewing how to preserve ship and crew even if the 'Dinis were quite willing to spend lives and ships to destroy a Hiver.

Privately, Thian wondered how many escape pods he could fling to safety with or without the impetus of generators in the event the *Vadim* was badly struck. There was also the ethical and moral problem of should he also contrive to save himself, the Prime, if it was at the expense of fellow shipmates? He decided that avenue of thought was depressing and self-defeating.

This squadron had six of the newest, best-equipped and best-armoured vessels of their respective navies, and powerful new weapons. Contemplation of defeat and/or suicide was self-destructive. Even thoughts of evasion could be defeatist. He started emanating stern resolve and optimism.

Somewhat to his astonishment, his efforts began to produce results in the discussions as humans and 'Dinis both began to talk themselves into more positive thinking.

HIVE SHIPS FOLLOW TRADITIONAL PATTERN NO MATTER WHAT

SIZE AND NEVER DEVIATE, Captain Spktm said, slipping a pencil file into the ready room reader and bringing up the enhanced image on the main screen. WEAKNESS REMAINS WEAKNESS, STRENGTH STRENGTH WITH THE QUEENS ALWAYS IN THE MOST PROTECTED SPOT, EGGS NEXT AND EXPENDABLE WORKERS DRONES AUXILIARIES IN OUTER SHELL. The spherical shape of the Hive had been opened in one arc to show the levels. Much was extrapolation since Hive ships had to be blown apart to be stopped, fragmenting both attacker and attacked. The 'Dinis had gathered their information – painfully – over the centuries. SCOUTS ARE ALWAYS IN EXTERIOR BAYS. WEAPON SYSTEMS CONTROLLED FROM QUEENS' LEVELS BY SPECIAL DRONES. BELIEF IS HELD THAT THERE ARE SPECIAL REINFORCEMENTS TO PERMIT QUEENS AND MOST VALUABLE EGGS TO SURVIVE EVEN THE TOTAL DESTRUCTION OF THE SHIP. 'DINI ATTACK GROUPS HAVE LEARNED TO RESERVE AT LEAST ONE SHIP TO CHASE AND DESTROY THESE SPECIAL INTERIOR CONTAINERS WHICH HAVE ON OCCASION CONTAINED SMALLER UNITS LIKE HUMAN ESCAPE PODS. (Mrdini ships had no comparable unit.) THE SURVIVAL OF AT LEAST ONE QUEEN ONE ATTENDANT DRONE MEANS THE HIVE SURVIVES. SUCH SURVIVAL UNITS HAVE ACHIEVED ESCAPE VELOCITIES THAT, UNTIL RECENTLY, EXCEEDED THE BEST SPEED OF CHASE VESSELS. QUEENS AND EGGS SURVIVE IN CONDITIONS FATAL TO MRDINI AND HUMAN.

Then the 'Dini captain activated an animated reconstruction of the phases of attack and dissolution of a Hive ship. As often as Thian had seen this vid, it never failed to give him nightmares. The average Hive ship had between twelve and thirty Queens. Tear-drop-shaped vessels spurted from the exploding wreckage of the demonstration Hive ship. They travelled at incredible speeds, disappearing so rapidly in all directions from sensor range that a fix could not be taken, making pursuit difficult – especially if only one 'Dini ship remained operational at the conclusion of the battle.

For just this Hive manoeuvre, every ship in the squadron

had been provided with eight high-speed pursuit craft cradled in the shuttle bays.

Optimism spread and defeatism dissolved as the humans began to psych themselves up for their encounter with this implacable enemy and destroyer. The fatalism which always motivated a 'Dini soldier began to seep into their human allies as Sblpk pointed out primary targets for the initial assault. Then the human captains began to embrace the actual, not the theoretical, aspects of the possibility of their first space battle in generations.

Finally, Thian was asked to inform both homeworlds of the discovery of an as yet unidentified object. Thian decided he'd tell Jeff Raven, as Earth Prime, first.

Shouldn't we wait to find out if the thing's really dangerous? Jeff asked.

I'm following orders, sir.

As indeed you should, even with news as momentous as this, Jeff replied equably. *It does add a little spice to an otherwise dull day. I'm passing the word to the High Council so you can expect to be on call now for messages. Are you a hard sleeper?*

No, sir.

Well, get what you can when you can. That's the downside of this job. Ah, yes, High Council is calling an emergency session. Have you apprised the Mrdinis yet? Do so immediately. It is only proper you would inform your own species first.

When Thian 'pathed Laria, she erupted with what he felt was unprofessional excitement; more nearly exultation of a bloodthirsty variety.

I'm not blood-lusting, Laria replied with some indignation, *I'm practising 'Dini hurrahs. They've waited so long for a breakthrough like this.*

We don't know if it is a breakthrough, sis.

Go find out! Like Mother did! The suspense would kill me.

Mother didn't know what was out there, then, or I'll bet she wouldn't have gone.

But how long before we know? Laria demanded, her mind

115

sparkling with excitement. She was positively blood-thirsty, Thian thought.

Even at the speeds we're travelling, it'll take several days to close the distance between us.

What about probes?

We're not even close enough for a probe, even those new hypersensitive ones.

But Laria had planted the notion in his head of a 'portational reconnaissance and he couldn't shake it out. It might redress the impression the 'Dinis had that humans were unnecessarily cautious. Even among his own kind, he'd accrue considerable prestige from such a daring action. And, speaking of suspense, establishing a definite ID would improve morale considerably. Waiting was always the worst part of any ordeal. Also, if Thian could prove himself, he might even get rid of Malice. Most of that person's dislike centred around him being a *civilian* on a naval mission, a weasel-lover on a human-crewed ship, a snot-nosed kid who'd been pampered all his life because of a lucky genetic break.

When they got somewhat closer – for even his mother had not risked going too far from her power base – he might just mention it to Captain Ashiant. Thian knew his strengths but he also knew his own limitations. Lucky he knew himself to be: but not snot-nosed.

Busy as he became, hauling in more supplies, retrieving crewmates from their home planets, for all shore leave was cancelled, Thian also quickly found a way to answer the pressing need of his 'Dinis. Hibernation was not considered a dereliction of duty for usually only immature or post-mature 'Dinis went on long-distance duty. As it happened, several 'Dini observers from the High Council on Clarf required transport to the *KLTL* and *KLTS* so Thian arranged that Mur and Dip would have space on the return trip. Mur and Dip had the dubious pleasure of accompanying four of the largest 'Dinis Thian had ever seen.

He missed his life-long friends almost as soon as he lost

their 'touch' as Laria took control of their capsule at the change-over point. This was not like their yearly retreat on Iota Aurigae: they weren't a matter of kilometres away in a hillside he could see from his bedroom window. Their companionship had also afforded him relief from his anomalous position on the *Vadim*. He missed them more as his workload increased and tensions rose, in him and throughout the ship and squadron.

Two days after the sighting, he had an unusual interview with Captain Ashiant.

'You've handled yourself extremely well, young Lyon,' Ashiant began, steepling his fingers and staring so hard at him that Thian began to worry about what the man was leading up to. 'I gather that our 'Dini allies find our attitudes towards a possible engagement at odds with theirs.'

'They've fought the Hivers for centuries, with considerably more direct experience than humans have had.'

'They also consider there's only one way to promulgate this war.'

'They've only found one that's successful in destroying the enemy. Any other outcome is unacceptable considering what this enemy does unchecked.'

'Well, at the risk of appearing cowardly, humans have usually,' and Ashiant stressed the adverb, 'found that retreat can often result in significant victory.'

'Humans have only been up against a Hive ship once,' Thian was obliged to remind him. 'The scout ships don't, apparently, count.'

'That's not what I wish to discuss with you. If we come up against a viable Hive ship this time, young Lyon, you will act upon these special orders should the special circumstances arise,' and Ashiant handed over a transparent pencil file. 'You have an eidetic memory. This destructs after one reading and leaves no trace in your terminal.'

Carefully Thian inserted the file in his breast pocket.

'You will memorize the contents, and then forget them until you are required to implement the orders.' Ashiant

117

rose to pace the long side of his ready room. 'I intend to commit the *Vadim* as thoroughly as our Mrdini allies will commit their ships. In the event the *Vadim is* committed past the point of return and orders are given to abandon ship . . . ' Thian held his breath, fear trickling down his arms and legs at such a contingency, ' . . . you will ensure that the nine people on that pencil file are 'ported to safety. And that *you*,' Ashiant swung about to point his forefinger at Thian, 'leave with them. Are you clear on that point?'

'Yes, sir.'

'How many of the Talents on board have you contacted?'

'Only six so far.'

'Well, do what is necessary so that, in the event the generators can't assist you, you can effect the removal of the persons in your orders. They do *not* have the option of remaining. Are you clear on that?'

'Yes, sir.'

'Are nine too many for you to cope with?'

'No, sir.'

'We'll be holding pod drills frequently over the next few days so you're to familiarize yourself with the equipment and those in your pod. Each lifeboat has an engine as well as the initial break-away thruster. I'm not certain how much power that will give you, which is why you must use the other Talents as boosters. If the order to abandon ship is given, you are *first*—' and again the index finger jabbed in his direction, '—to get in your own escape pod, then make sure that the others get in, too. If the worst possible circumstances ensue, and you are the only survivor, you leave! You cannot be jeopardized.'

'Because I'm a *civilian*?' Thian asked, indignant with hurt pride even as he recognized that to be an immature reaction.

'No, sirree sir, because you're a Prime . . . and because you'll have had access to most of the information other captains and experts would need to combat the next Hive ship we encounter.' Ashiant waited a full beat and then added

118

with a rueful smile, 'You're much more valuable alive, young Lyon. Before that blip appeared on our screens, this was not a dangerous assignment. It is now and you are not to be endangered. Do I make myself clear?'

'Crystal clear, sir.'

'Good lad,' and the captain gave Thian an approving thump on his shoulder. That comradely gesture reduced the resentment he'd been feeling. 'Now, implement your orders, Lyon.'

The orders were signed by the High Council Coordinator and, although several of the names surprised Thian, he had them memorized long before the pencil file disintegrated. As he made necessary, but discreet, contact with the other Talents, he also began to meet some odd resistance and reactions from crew members, men and women who had been at least polite to him. He found the answer to that hostility from Gravy. They'd met from time to time in the officers' mess and in the corridors, but he hadn't been able to find a time when they were both off-shift and he could outline what might be expected of her as a Talent. But it had become necessary for him to seek her out and he found her alone in the gym, working out on the rowing apparatus.

'I'm glad to see you, too, Thian,' she said, mopping her brow and resting her arms on the oars. 'I've heard some spaceflot that I don't really want to report to the captain . . . ' She cocked her head at him and he sensed her hesitation. 'You know I've got a little Talent?'

'Yes,' he said, sliding on to the apparatus next to her, 'in fact, I'm glad I've a chance to talk to you because I'm supposed to touch bases with all Talents on the ship.'

'Hmmm, in case of emergency, yes, I sort of figured you'd get around to me on that score,' she said equably. 'I'm not sure what good I'll be. I'm only an empath . . . '

Thian grinned at her. 'Don't knock it, Gravy. *Only an empath* is much more helpful than *only* a receiving or sending 'path.'

'But what good would I be?'

'It's like this, Gravy,' and he found himself more easy with her than with anyone else on the *Vadim*, the very reason why her empathy was so valuable, especially as a nurse. 'Should an emergency arise when I'd have to tap into all the Talent on board, your empathic strength is added to the pool. You're down as a T-5 which is the highest, bar me, on the *Vadim*. You'd be more help than you might realize. Now, what's this spaceflot?'

She frowned. 'It's talk but it's nothing . . . good.'

Thian wondered if Malice was showing his hand. 'Don't worry about my feelings, Gravy.'

She gave him a very direct look. 'You may think you're fooling others, and you are, actually, since you're so good at what you do, but I happen to know you're not as old, despite that sexy silver streak of yours, as you'd want others to think you are. Especially when you're teaching,' and she grinned at him, to take the sting from her message, 'you sound exactly like our Professional Ethics prof, so stuffy and precise . . . Of course, speaking 'Dini makes you *be* precise or you garble everything . . . '

'Gravy, you're hedging,' he said, not prying but recognizing a delaying tactic.

'Partly because I think the rumour's so stupid,' she said with some heat, and then rushed on to say, 'but there's some think you're a glory-grabber.'

'What?' Thian laughed in surprise, more relieved than he could ever let Gravy realize. He couldn't imagine how anyone could have overheard his interview with the captain, or known of the special preservation list, but if that was what Gravy had heard, such orders were already compromised.

'They seem to think that you'll reach out with your Talent and somehow do what the Fleet ought to be doing.'

Thian laughed more heartily then. 'Gravy, that's not very likely. Not to mention impossible.'

'But you Talents did that at Deneb. Twice!'

'Talents, plural, Gravy. In fact every Talent available

120

down to kids of ten and twelve. Not singular, me, with a dozen minor Talents to assist. There's no way I could or would grab any glory. 'Sides which, I do know my limitations. Heroism is not indicated.'

She gave a sniff. 'Heroes happen. Generally,' and now she grinned rakishly at him, 'when it's *not* indicated.' Then her expression altered to earnestness. 'However wrong the thinking is, it's there and it's not good. Folks are odd. I mean, here you got a lot of 'em home for shore leave – even if it got cancelled – and you'd think they'd be at least grateful. But no, they're out to find something . . . something . . . '

'Negative?' Thian suggested, knowing exactly what people could find to disparage the Talented.

'That'll do,' she said. Then, in a rush of empathy, she put her hand on his arm. 'You're a nice guy, Thian, and I'll do what I can to offset the flot. D'you want me to report it to Ashiant?'

'Only if you have something specific that has an adverse effect on morale as a whole,' he managed to say, more distracted by the warm hand on his arm, and her very feminine presence, the delicate floral taste of her, than he thought possible.

She caught his response, though, because he was lax in reining in his thoughts, because he hadn't felt the need to shield in Gravy's company, and because he was missing the company of Mur and Dip.

'Sometimes it's better to squash a rumour as flat as possible – especially right now when we might be heading into action,' she said, keeping her hand on his arm so that he couldn't help but 'read' her which, he also realized, was exactly her intention. Her very expressive eyes confirmed it.

'I thought,' he began in a sort of daze, 'that's when rumours would multiply, a sort of combat-readiness reaction.'

'Hmmm,' she said, leaning into him, clearly no longer

121

interested in the previous subject of conversation. 'D'you know where I got my nickname?' she asked.

Thian rather thought he did but he hedged in a sudden fit of shyness. He had had that dream involving her, and he'd dreamed long enough with 'Dinis to know that there were true ones.

'Can we get to your cabin without being seen?' she asked him, her eyes sparkling with anticipation. He was suddenly deluged by intense sensuality which he was unable, and unwilling, to deflect. Her smile challenged him to seize the moment.

'Yes, ma'am.' And grasping her in his arms, he 'ported them neatly on to the floor space beside his bunk. But he had slightly misjudged their mass and, offbalance, they tilted on to his bunk. That took care of his residual reserve.

Thian had never truly appreciated the company of an empath such as Alison-Anne Greevy and he didn't care where she acquired her nickname. He hadn't had so much experience that he was confident of his ability to perform but Gravy made it all easy, natural and rather special.

'How long are your friends away?' she asked at one point.

'Two months.' He suppressed a speculative spurt as to where he'd be in two months' time.

'What did they have to go for?' she asked and he realized that she honestly didn't know. 'I mean, all crew have been recalled, haven't they?'

''Dinis in need of hibernation would be no good in an attack. No blame is attached to their absence . . . at least from 'Dinis.'

'I'd heard about this hibernation business. What exactly happens?'

Thian chuckled, stroking her fine blonde hair. It was softer and silkier than a 'Dini pelt. 'Something like this.'

'You don't know?' She was surprised.

'There are some things species should do for themselves to themselves in absolute privacy.'

'I couldn't agree more,' she sighed with a mischievous glint in her eyes as she pulled his head down to her again.

The intercom buzz roused them and, for a split second, Thian was disoriented by the feel of a body against his.

'Mr Lyon?' was the query.

'Here,' Thian said quickly.

'Captain's compliments and can you come to the ready room?' was the voice message.

'Whoops!' Gravy murmured into her hand, instantly awake and rather charmingly rumpled by sleep, her fair hair standing out in wisps from her head while one errant curl pressed into her cheek. He smoothed it back, not quite wishing to relinquish their physical contact. 'And look at the time!' She drew her breath in a hiss, at the same time smoothing her hair back.

'You don't share a cabin, do you?'

'Thank the gods, no,' she said.

'I'll just put you back unseen then,' he said.

'Hey, that'd be tops!' she said, hurriedly pulling on her exercise gear and swinging her legs off the bunk to stand up. 'This right?'

'Thanks, Alison,' he said.

'Catch me any ol' time, Thian love,' she said, her grin mischievous, her eyes dancing, and her mind exuding the genuine pleasure she had received and given. And the position of her cabin, two decks below.

Thian 'ported her there and then took time to use the dry shower and dress appropriately for the day.

'We've more information on that object, Mr Lyon,' Captain Ashiant said. Tikele, the security chief and the com duty officer, this time, Steena Blaz, were also present.

Thian seated himself comfortably, ready to 'path messages but the captain continued to pace the length of the conference table.

'We have first established that there are no emissions of

123

any space drive known to exist, human, 'Dini or Hive,' he said.

That was a surprise and Thian restrained his amusement. No glory at all to grab. And no lives to be wasted in an attack to the death. But he maintained an alert interest as the captain continued.

'It would appear to be a derelict of some sort.'

'An unusually large derelict,' the com officer said softly, evidently not comfortable with what she'd seen on the sensors.

'That's a pity,' Thian said, since that was their feeling. Odd how brave people could feel *after* an emergency had passed.

The captain flicked one heavy eyebrow in dismissal. '*If* our readings are correct. And I'd like you to check with the 'Dinis on this. There's been enough time for them to have analysed the same readings.'

Captain Plr agreed with Ashiant but Captain Spktm, who was the senior naval commander, was not totally convinced.

'It says that the lack of emissions is not conclusive evidence that this is a derelict. It advises great caution.'

'Hmmm.' Ashiant paced one more length. 'The *KLTS* has had more contact with Hive vessels than anyone else in this squadron. Hmmm.'

'It wants to send a probe.'

'Of course,' and Ashiant paused, fingers over the terminal station. 'Theirs or ours?'

Thian enquired and replied that the 'Dinis believed human probes to be more efficient. Thian did not add the 'Dini qualification that human probes were more efficient because they employed gadgets to do what personal observations could do better. The 'Dinis were not precisely calling humans cowards, but certainly overcautious.

'So they approve of our hardware, huh? Well, they're right as well as honest,' Ashiant replied and gave the necessary orders for a probe. 'It'll be at least twenty-three

124

hours before it gets there and starts reporting. Carry on, gentlemen, and rejoin me at 0800 tomorrow. A moment, if you will, Thian.'

'Captain?'

Ashiant nodded for him to keep his seat as the others filed out.

'I read somewhere that your family can identify Hive materials by the . . . ah . . . sound of them?'

As this question wasn't at all what Thian had expected, he laughed as much in relief as surprise.

'That's true enough, sir. On Deneb they're still turning up buried pieces of the first scout vessels. There's a naval research facility investigating the composition of the material. I was on only one successful expedition with my cousins: we got an interior panel about,' he encompassed the size with his hands, 'this big. It did give off a distinctive emanation, I guess you'd say. Family called it a sting-pzzt. Other sensitives agree.' He shrugged, searching for another way of describing the sensation. 'It comes across as an actinic smell in the back of your throat, a sharp pinch in your nasal passages and an unpleasant smell.'

Ashiant grunted. 'But you would know it?'

'Anywhere, sir.' Thian waited, respectfully silent while the captain continued to ruminate. He made no attempt to plumb those thoughts.

'A probe can bring back only mechanical information, Thian,' Ashiant said at length and suddenly Thian knew what he might be asked to do.

He couldn't help but react and the captain caught his grin.

'Yes, Thian?' He raised his eyebrows, expecting an answer.

'I'd heard, Captain . . . well, there's some spaceflot about Talents grabbing all the glory . . . '

'Oh, that,' and a gesture dismissed the rumour. 'As you're already aware, I am under orders not to put you at risk – which is where glory is usually grabbed – but I

125

will ask how far you can propel yourself in a capsule.'

'To the derelict-planetoid-whatever?'

The captain held up his hand, 'But well outside the known range of Hive weaponry . . . with which our allies are so familiar.'

'If it would help, sir, I'm willing.'

'I'm just thinking aloud, Thian. Wanted to get the straight of that . . . ah . . . trick. You are of great assistance to us in many other capacities.'

'I appreciate that, Captain. In the event such a service is required, it is entirely within my scope of abilities and the position I was asked to fill . . . if that's what's bothering you.'

'Thank you, Thian. That's all now, I think, until we've the probe report. Damned thing could be just lying doggo.'

'That isn't what Senior Captain Spktm believes.'

'Oh?'

'But it is adamant about approaching with great caution. Even Hiver wrecks have had nasty surprises for boarding parties.'

'So I'd read in those exhaustive 'Dini reports they furnished us. You'll be informed when the probe starts transmitting.'

'Aye, sir . . . '

'And Thian, I wouldn't let the spaceflot bother you. Nerves talking, not common sense. We're still on yellow alert, of course, but some of the urgency has dissipated now we know the thing's inactive.'

'Thank you, sir.'

As Thian left the ready room, he wondered if he had missed an opportunity to mention Malice. Though he hadn't heard any barbs from that direction since the blip had come up. Hopefully too occupied with more urgent duties. The crew of the *Vadim* were busy preparing for action. He was nearly at his quarters when another pod drill was called by the hooting of the siren.

With a grunt, he 'ported himself to his designated escape pod and counted in the nine others assigned to it. By now he knew all of them well enough to have 'saved' them no matter where they were on the *Vadim* should the abandon ship order be given. He wondered if any of them knew of these orders but all he ever sensed was annoyance that their current task had once again been interrupted by a geedee drill.

A circumnavigation by the probe produced very interesting results. The derelict was undeniably Hive designed which excited the 'Dinis who were generous in their rectitude.

'Captain Spktm says it's bigger than any they've encountered, with certain design features that are new and it's very glad the vessel's non-functional,' Thian reported to the specialists assembled in the ready room.

'Measurements indicate it's a third again as large as previously encountered vessels,' Commander Vandermeer said. 'A small planet!'

'Readings indicate the ship was bombarded with intense heat. Radiation is still present as well as some very odd traces of other elements that are being spectro-analysed. There's no known weapon that devastating, or one that could have left such traces.'

'Something blew two-thirds of that ship to hellingone.' Then Vandermeer shrugged. 'And it's nothing the 'Dinis have ever encountered. Nor us.'

'I'd hate to meet what has that kind of fire-power,' Ashiant said.

'That's precisely Captain Spktm's sentiment,' Thian reported and then grinned. 'It would like whoever it was to be on our side.'

Ashiant laughed out loud and there were other smiles about the table. 'I didn't know the wee . . . ahem . . . our allies had a sense of humour.'

'They do, sir, believe me!'

Ashiant steepled his fingers, rubbing the end of his nose,

before he laced his fingers together and leaned forward on his elbows. 'Gentlemen, this artefact requires our earnest investigation. First time there've been big enough pieces to work with, I understand.' He cast a sly sideways glance at Thian, quirking one of his eloquent eyebrows. 'Do our allies agree?' He turned to Thian.

'Indeed, sir, they're forming a volunteer squad to investigate. Do we wish to send representatives?'

Several hands immediately went up.

'Thank you, gentlemen. I will want volunteers from communications, engineering, mechanical, security. Mr Lyon has to be included as interpreter . . . '

Vandermeer cleared her throat. 'Sir, I believe that won't be necessary now.'

'Yes, Ailsah, I know you've become quite fluent in 'Dini but Mr Lyon goes in several capacities. How soon are the 'Dinis assembling, mister?'

Thian queried Spktm. 'Right now. They're asking for a pre-boarding conference with our teams. They are appointing fifteen specialists from each of their ships: we should supply as many from ours. This will be a big undertaking.'

'It's also an immense ship, even with two-thirds of it blown away,' Ashiant interposed.

'Captain Spktm strongly recommends that we halt at forty spatials to be sure there is no reaction to our presence.'

'That's well beyond maximum Hive weapon range,' Ashiant said, surprised.

'Beyond range of *known* Hive weapons. Captain Spktm reminds you that this is a new, unknown design.'

'But it's dead.'

'Captain Spktm may be overcautious, sir, but . . . ' Thian wasn't sure how to phrase the exact wording of the 'Dini's statement.

'Yes, yes, I appreciate that this is an unknown quantity but the probe read no life signs and no viable life-support systems working.'

'As far as the probe could tell.' Thian kept his voice neutral, being merely an intermediary but he could sense that Spktm's cautionaries were not being well received by the *Vadim*'s officers.

'Since Captain Spktm is around to caution us, we will not be rash,' Ashiant said before turning to the security officer. 'Strange that they're so cautious on an approach course when they're quite willing to suicide to destroy a Hiver. Whatever! Commander Vandermeer, you'll lead the human contingent. Pick a boarding party of fifteen, with all necessary specialists represented. Declan, get me channels through to Captains Smelkoff, Sutra and Chesemen. They're to send teams, too. We won't be close enough to launch the shuttles for another six hours even at our present speed. That gives us plenty of time for an interspecies, intership conference.'

'Indeed, sir,' Vandermeer said, well pleased with her assignment but, as her glance slid over Thian, he caught a brief flare of resentment from the woman. However, it didn't have the tone of Malice: she simply did not like having to be responsible for a *civilian*.

Briskly she gave orders, picking from the *Vadim*'s crew and then accessing the other ships to discover whom they were sending.

Thian had to sit heavily on an increasing excitement as he listened to Vandermeer with growing respect. She ordered the big shuttle to be ready for launch in six hours. Full radiation suits must be put on board, full medical and emergency packs. From communications, she wanted additional printout of all the probe's data for the briefing. All officers were to be armed with the new stunners, developed from the one hand-weapon the 'Dinis had found effective against Hive drone warriors. The boarding party was to join her in shuttle bay in exactly one hour from now, ready to go.

'Have you been issued any ex-vehicular gear, Mr Lyon?' she asked, finally turning to him.

'No, ma'am.'

'Then get some.' With that she rose from the table and strode out of the ready room.

'Well, you heard her,' Ashiant said, smiling.

'I also heard you say that I'm going along in several capacities, sir. Which?'

'Interpreter, observer, and . . . lastly, but most important, the Talent to whip someone out of trouble if necessary.'

Thian got himself a full-radiation suit, and the requisite stunner which Lieutenant Sedallia handed him with a supercilious expression on his face.

'I don't imagine you've needed to handle a weapon before . . .'

'On the contrary, I've hunted for the family table since I was old enough to pull the trigger of a rifle.' At the surprised look, Thian added. 'And we always ate well.' He sighted along the thick barrel. 'But this is a spread weapon anyway. I certainly ought to be able to hit a shuttle-bay door with this.' He slapped it back into its clip and, with a nod to the ratings handing out equipment, left. He could 'hear' the comments and most were complimentary. Sedallia wasn't that popular.

Thian was prompt at the intergroup meeting, held in the ready room, with screens linking the six ships of the squadron. Ashiant introduced Commander Vandermeer as the human leader and she quite ably greeted her 'Dini counterpart. Thian kept his expression neutral but he was rather pleased with his student. Her sentences were, of course, brief and there were pauses while she accessed words from her vocabulary but Plr, the leader of the 'Dini boarding parties, understood her perfectly.

The 'Dini showed her a chart of the vessel and identified certain of the remaining portions as the part of the main propulsion unit, fuel storage, resting cubicles, nesting and work quarters. The Queens' accommodations had been blown away for they were usually in the centre: some peripheral weapons were still in place as well as several arsenals and storage areas. Plr then drew longitudinal lines, separating the wreck into six sections and assigned a boarding team to each. Vandermeer agreed with the assignments even when Plr preempted the sector holding the remaining weapons.

'It's more familiar to them than any of us,' she said to her own group.

The meeting was concluded and final preparations made which, Vandermeer said, would begin with a good high-protein meal.

'Leviathan,' Thian murmured more to himself than Lieutenant Ridvan Auster-Kiely sitting beside him.

'Say what?' Ridvan asked, bending his ear towards Thian.

'That thing is not just big, it's a Leviathan,' he repeated, struggling not to hunch his shoulders away from the immensity of the damaged space vessel. Thian remembered that 'Leviathan' was what his grandmother had called the Hive ship that had been destroyed beyond Deneb over forty years before.

The shuttle was obediently waiting at the forty spatials to see if there was any reaction from the vessel. The 'Dinis had said that a Hive ship would automatically open fire on anything that approached even though it was out of range.

'What's a Leviathan?'

'Something as big as this.'

'This is not the time to be funny.'

'The best time.'

'Be serious, Thian. Say, couldn't it be a planetoid? I mean, it could have been hollowed out . . . '

'And then metal coated and levels dug out?' Thian chuckled. 'No, Ridvan, it's a ship and not as big as say, Callisto, either.'

'That doesn't reassure me.'

131

Ridvan was nervous and didn't bother to hide it. Thian was neither nervous nor scared and wondered if this was wrong. Excitement was the prevailing sentiment within the shuttle, certainly. He knew his senses were all heightened and he wondered that he didn't feel – even through the vacuum of space – the sting-pzzt of proximity to a Hive artefact. No-one else in this boarding party had ever been so close to a Hive artefact. Admittedly, he had only helped dig up a panel on Deneb, exciting enough in itself when you're only ten, and help sling it into the 'copter scoop. That still doesn't make you an expert, he told himself firmly.

They waited, getting bored with the view of what Thian began to describe as a semi- demi- hemisphere. The northern pole was intact all around to about the tenth latitude in the east where damage began. The western hemisphere extended almost to a tropic of Cancer in places but the southern pole cap had been totally blown away. As if something, incredibly mammoth, had taken a massive bite out of the Hive sphere, leaving pits, pith and intestines behind.

Finally the 'Dinis judged it safe to approach: slowly but surely. Their shuttle, the one from the *Beijing*, and one 'Dini angled to starboard, closed on the wreck. The third human shuttle followed at a discreet distance. They passed around the outer skin of the wreck and immediately Thian was conscious – even inside the shuttle – of the sting-pzzt effect of Hive metal on Talented perceptions. He ran his tongue around his mouth but the actinic taste was in the back of his mouth, far stronger than it had been when he was in direct contact with the Hive panel. Was it because this was a newer construction? Louder or more potent in its emanations? He wished he could contact his grandmother or grandfather right now.

The captains had decided to wait until there were concrete details to report before publicizing this expedition: Thian had had to report that the discovery of the ship had caused wide panic on every inhabited world. So he was as glad not to have to add to it. Nor to say anything about his participation in further close investigations.

But should he report to Commander Vandermeer the intensity of the Hive aura? Captain Ashiant had known of it. Such information was not really of use, he thought, except that it verified the origin of the ship. As if there was much doubt about that.

The shuttle wended its way through immense shards of outer hulls, inner skins, deck levels, past structural members as thick as the *Vadim*. Big as that star-class ship was, she, and a hundred of her sister ships, could have docked in a quadrant of this one.

Everyone reacted as the shuttle's exterior lights began to illuminate details of the innards they were traversing.

'Storage area?' one of the engineers suggested, pointing to odd-shaped containers partially fused against bulkheads. They passed much smaller divisions the size of the *Vadim*'s adequately large shuttle bay. Bent tubing several metres across dangled pendulously into emptiness.

On the forward screen, they saw the 'Dini shuttle veer to port, heading towards its appointed landing spot. Thian, being nearest the porthole, looked back as long as he could, to see the 'Dini disembarking in their space gear.

Then all too soon their shuttle landed on its designated site. Helmets clicking into place were the only sounds. Then they were on suit air.

'Set your watches, gentlemen,' Commander Vandermeer said, her voice muffled on the intercom, 'you have exactly three hours and twenty minutes' oxygen.'

'I thought we had four hours' air, sir?' Auster-Kiely said.

'We do, but for practical purposes we'll all assemble back here in three hours and twenty minutes. Clear?'

'Yes, sir.'

Someone in the group let out a snide bark of a laugh which Vandermeer instantly silenced.

'Enough of that! Let's move out. Mertz, Jimenez, Kaldi,

go as far up as you can in this segment, then work down. Sedallia, see if those mangled coils might be drive components. Kes, you go with Sedallia. All of you: call out if you spot something one of the specialists should examine. Take all the snaps you can but remember to light 'em. It's darker in here than the devil's belly.' She went on assigning search areas. 'Remember to keep one hand for yourself and don't drift off. We can't waste time hauling you back in from outer space. Lyon, you stick on this level with Kiely. There seem to be undamaged compartments along this corridor. Let's move it.'

As soon as the others had dispersed in their appointed directions, Kiely pulled Thian close enough for them to touch helmets and Thian could see the furious expression on the lieutenant's face. He resented being treated like a liability.

Thian grinned back at him, gesturing towards the dark interior and mentally trying to soothe the young man. He found that the sting-pzzt dampened his Talent, muffled it, so he gave up trying to project. He started forward, his boots locking on the plates of the deck so that each step required effort. Then he saw Kiely floating ahead of him, grabbing handholds where he could to propel himself forward, his helmet light illuminating the way. Thian lifted one foot free, grabbed hold of a solid spar and yanked the other boot loose and followed Kiely's aerial example.

Great heat had certainly seared and boiled any organic substances away, leaving only burst containers that had exploded and some that had apparently imploded. Depending on how long ago the catastrophe had occurred, some traces of the contained substances might be found for analysis. They could do that on their return to the shuttle. As he and Kiely made steady progress into the interior, Thian saw nothing very promising, except that the Hive had been transporting an unimaginable amount of cargo or stores. For an hour, they poked, prodded, peered, squeezing carefully into compartments on either side of

134

this broad but squat-ceilinged avenue.

According to his understanding of Hive ship construction, this corridor might be just above the doubly shielded quarters where, traditionally, the Queens were sequestered, constantly laying the eggs that would be stored for use in setting up the next colony. But, look as hard as he could, he could find no access to the lower level. When he saw the first of the tubes, he wondered what function it had performed. Then he came upon a cluster and the sting-pzzt that had been constantly with him increased in intensity. That alone was unusual enough to make him call to Kiely to come back a moment.

'Whatcha find, Thian?'

'Don't know but here's a service door, or something, and – whaddya know, it opens,' and Thian was as surprised as Kiely when his jerk pulled the panel free and it slowly drifted out. Thian pressed his foot against the upper half and it settled to the deck.

Kiely, floating above him, poked his head down the opening, the light narrowing as it pierced the blackness of the tunnel.

'Up and down,' and Kiely experimented with lighting. 'Long way up and not so long a way down. Down's it.' And before Thian could caution the young lieutenant, he had pushed off down the tunnel.

'Commander,' Thian said, dialling more power to his helmet comunit, 'Kiely and I are investigating some conduits or tunnels that appear to be intact and lead to a lower level. We've found nothing else of note.'

'Proceed with caution. Much of this wreck is just waiting to fall apart. Kaldi had a lucky escape when a bulkhead started to go.'

Thian did not go head first: he stepped off the deck and let that impulsion and his own weight carry him slowly down. Consequently he saw what Kiely had missed: regular openings off the tunnel, compartments that appeared to be sealed with a semi-transparent material which had not boiled, seared, ex- or imploded, and which gave off the most virulent sting-pzzt he'd ever felt. Wincing in discomfort, he slowed his descent by one of the apertures and let his helmet light pierce the gloom. What he made out of the occluded interior made him gasp.

'Commander, I've found something,' he said though his mouth and throat were dry with the actinic flavour.

'What, Lyon?' and the commander sounded annoyed by his vagueness.

'I think it may be Hive larvae, sir.'

Kiely's helmet bumped into his feet, pushing him out of alignment with the opening.

'You what?'

'Belay that, Kiely!' Thian roared back, grabbing at the smooth sides to try and halt his upward progress.

'I think you're right,' Kiely murmured in a subdued tone and shot past Thian to their point of entry.

7

There was such a babble over the helmet coms that it took Vandermeer minutes to get the noise level down to where individual orders could be understood.

'Just how can that be, Mr Lyon?' she demanded. 'The probe registered no life readings.'

'Yes, ma'am, but larvae aren't alive – yet. Besides which, I don't think the probe's sensors were programmed to pick up that sort of . . . of unborn things.'

'Point!' Her admission was not exactly grudging. 'What's your position?'

He gave it while Kiely jostled him about as the lieutenant tried to see into one or another of the larvae tunnels.

'Are you sure, Thian?' he asked, touching helmets and turning down his com. His face was worried.

'As sure as I can be, never have seen Hive larvae but whatever it is in there isn't damaged and this is also the general area on a Hive ship where eggs were stored.'

Kiely still wasn't sure. 'Fardles, but there's acres of 'em. How many d'you suppose are in each tube? tunnel? comb?

And how are we going to blast 'em in such a confined position?'

'Blast them?' Thian was stunned. 'They shouldn't be blasted, Ridvan. They should be studied.'

'HUH?' Now it was the lieutenant's turn to be stunned. 'You don't know what you're saying, Thian. Here we have hundreds of our enemy . . . '

'Helpless and vulnerable! Great targets for warriors!'

'No need to come on like that! But you certainly don't expect us to leave all these . . . these things alive?'

'Considering how little we actually know about Hivers, this is a find of unparalleled magnitude. Even more important than the ship itself.'

'I can't believe you! Let 'em live?'

'I think you'll find that the 'Dinis will insist on it.'

To make certain of that, Thian turned his helmet comunit up to full and crisply informed Plr of the find.

'Lyon!' roared Vandermeer. 'I heard that!'

'Of course, sir. The 'Dinis expect to be informed of any unusual discovery,' Thian said, deliberately misinterpreting her.

'What'd you expect from a goddamned weasel-lover!'

Despite distance and com distortion there was no mistaking Malice's tone nor an implicit promise of retribution. That chilled Thian more than the prospect of someone trying to destroy the most important alien artefact – if one could so term the larvae – that had yet been found.

So far the xenobiologists had had to extrapolate mock-ups of Hive Queens, drones, workers and other specialized forms from fragments of corpses strewn in space after encounters, or charred remains on destroyed ships. Though much had been learned even from such imperfect material, they were still guessing about the true form and nature of the types of Hiver which made up a ship's crew.

'Belay that!' Vandermeer bellowed again to quell the vociferous protests. She went on in an icy voice. 'You've exceeded your authority, Lyon.'

138

'No, ma'am, I haven't.'

'You're in for it now, for sure, Lyon,' Kiely said and his voice was harshly accusing.

'I operate under directives of higher authority than yours, hers or even Captain Ashiant's,' Thian said as stoutly as he could but the objections had shaken him. 'Get back up and lead them here.'

'Me? Go? Why you'll . . .'

'*I* won't do anything to them. I can't trust you not to.' And, grabbing Kiely by the arm, he thrust him upward in the tube while the lieutenant sputtered in indignation.

Thian watched as Kiely continued upward, and then propelled himself out of the shaft. Thian waited until he could hear Kiely's angry mental noise diminishing. Then he, too, exited the tube and propelled himself to one of the few chambers that opened on to space itself. The hole wasn't large but it also wasn't shielded by the ship's hull material.

He had never tried such an unpowered stretch of his mind before. It would have been better to use the shuttle's engines but he didn't have time enough to go that far – and make certain the larvae would not be summarily destroyed by those coming to see what he'd found. The larvae must be saved! The information that could be revealed far out-weighed any momentary destructive satisfaction.

Grandfather! Jeff Raven! Earth Prime! Listen to me? He put the energy of every cell of his body in that call.

An unpowered send? I'll tan your hide, boy!

Later! Larvae have been discovered intact. Must be preserved.

Of course they must! What incredible luck!

I'm the only one who thinks so.

Not at all, my boy. You've done well. I'm already forward-ing the news where it must be known. Now, shut up and save your strength! The very idea of an unpowered call that far. He's worse than his mother.

Thian had to grin at that tag or perhaps that was why Jeff Raven had allowed it to be heard. He felt depleted but not as bad as he might have. The elation of discovery seemed to have buffered him. Though that dwindled away as he thought of facing the anger and resentment of his shipmates. And Malice was in the boarding party. That was an unfortunate circumstance. But that was the goad that stimulated Thian to action now. If Malice got here first, before the commander . . . He pushed off the deck and floated beyond the target tunnel, catching a thin pipe and halting his drift, slowly pulling his body slightly into the next tube opening. That was all that saved him.

GOTCHA! That was all the warning he had.

Out of nowhere, for no helmet lights heralded the approach, the shock wave of a stunner blast shoved him with crushing force against the back curve of the tube.

That single mental shout, with its ferociously triumphant tone, gave him the nanosecond required for him to tap reserves he didn't know he had. Reflexes he had never had to use were triggered to form a shield, not as strong as it would have been if he hadn't lost energy calling his grandfather. Even so, he blocked the worst of the blast effect and struggled to retain the consciousness needed to keep the protection in force in case Malice came to inspect his victim. He tried very, very hard to project a Mayday, and was mildly amused that his attempt came out in 'Dini. He felt himself slipping. Here goes the captain's bright plan to evacuate his chosen few, he thought, amused that he could be amused as he wilted completely.

A buzzing in his ear was irritating but it could not be ignored. It was a warning. Why did every nerve in his body scream? He tried for mental control of pain synapses but his head was indulging in a monumental ache. His brain lining felt far too full to be contained by his skull. He was panting with effort. He opened his aching eyes a slit, coughed in the foul air he was breathing and vaguely realized he was wearing a helmet. The buzzing continued.

He tried to focus his eyes. His vision was blurred but he seemed to be inside an escape pod.

There had been an emergency, hadn't there? The buzzing meant it was over. Good! He could get out of the space suit. He fumbled strengthless gloved fingers on the helmet release and knew he'd succeeded only because he felt cooler air brushing across his sweaty throat. He couldn't do more than twist the helmet once but more fresh air relieved the necessity to pant. He lay where he was and willed himself away from the pain of his body.

'HE *IS* HERE! I'VE FOUND HIM!'

The glad cry came through Thian's mind physically and mentally. It was the mental identification that re-assured him and he opened his eyes, smiling weakly up at Gravy's anxious, tear-streaked face.

'Oh, however did you get here, Thian? Oh, thank all the gods that you're safe! If you knew . . . '

I have an enemy, Gravy. Guard me! he said.

Her eyes bugged out. 'I heard that,' she said, sensibly whispering. *An enemy?* she added with reasonable tele-pathic strength. *Who'd want to hurt you? You're a Prime.*

Tell only the captain but guard me.

Even that brief exchange took what energy he had.

'Stungun. Bolt. Got me. Hurt,' he whispered, too weak to writhe with the pulsing agony still throbbing along nerves and blood.

'Stungun? On you?'

He couldn't have missed the outrage, horror and fury she broadcast had he been a 12. Returning consciousness reminded him that there was something much more im-portant he had to know and he struggled with words to form the question.

'This is only standard, but it might help,' Gravy was saying and her hands were pulling at the neck closures of his suit: it hurt even to be moved about. He was relieved that he'd still been out when she'd removed the helmet.

Then he felt the blessed coolness of a hypospray and tried to speed its dose through his system. He couldn't manage much on that front either. 'Who did this?' she demanded.

He managed a helpless grunt in answer. Even that sent a spasm of pain through him. 'Larvae? Safe?'

'Oh, Thian love,' she cried and bent to kiss his forehead, a loving gesture which Thian knew oughtn't to hurt as much as that one did, 'you're amazing! Worrying about those damned things when you're in bits . . . '

'Saaafffe?' he repeated urgently, trying to raise one hand to emphasize his need to know.

'Yes, of course they are. The most important find ever! The 'Dinis are triumphant. Mind you,' she added swiftly, with a glance over her shoulder, 'there're some who were for blasting 'em to space dust but the captain stopped 'em. Well, it took you guys long enough!' she added in a brisk critical tone.

There was movement beyond him, movement and noise and his head began to throb painfully in reaction.

'Gotta get his suit off 'im first,' a male voice said. 'How'd he get through the port with it on?'

'Never mind. Is Commander Exeter there?' Gravy asked in a no-nonsense tone. 'The man's badly injured and will need heavy sedation before he can be moved. Here, Commander,' and Thian felt in every nerve of his mangled body the reverberation of heavy feet as the medic entered the pod. Gravy dropped her voice. 'He's been stunned, Ted, with one of the Hiver weapons.'

Exeter inhaled sharply. 'That's criminal!'

A second cool spray on Thian's throat and he thankfully dissolved into a painless world.

He regained consciousness a number of times for very short periods, finding himself immersed in a thick liquid, his head resting on a cradle. Mostly it was pain that woke him but he was immediately medicated and was sent back to sleep. The third, or maybe it was the fourth time, he

142

awoke, the pain wasn't so intense. And his mother was sitting beside him.

'Ah, Thian, back with us for a bit?' she asked, her expression loving and yet oddly stern. She smoothed his hair, the silver streak that matched hers, back from his forehead, and, with that tender gesture, the pain was also smoothed from his body.

'Mother?'

'Didn't you *know* I'd come if you were hurt?' Absently, she gathered the long hair that had fallen forward across her shoulder and flicked it to her back. 'You're improving. No brain damage, no lasting physical damage, though you may twitch occasionally. The worst discomfort will disappear very soon now. You were lucky to get only the fringes of that blast . . . the tunnel as well as the suit protected you from a direct hit. Which you wouldn't have survived.'

'D'you know who, yet?'

'Lieutenant Greevy said you mentioned an enemy.' Her lips thinned briefly with displeasure. 'Do you know who?'

'I had suspicions only. I got resentful sendings, malicious ones, but I could never identify who. I had choice.'

'I must see what I can discover then.'

Thian's reaction was ambivalent.

'The punishment should fit the crime?' his mother asked, wryly amused at the dominant thought in his mind.

'Well, I know Primes aren't supposed to be vindictive but . . . ' he began in a rueful tone, 'but I'd sure like to pay back in kind for something like this.'

'Natural enough,' Damia replied neutrally.

'Oh well,' and Thian found himself forced to rationalize. 'He or she was only spouting the usual anti-Talent privileged-position nonsense we've all heard from time to time,' he said, having thought better of inflicting that degree of agony on another human, however misguided. 'I suppose me wanting to save the larvae was the last straw!'

'Something like that,' Damia agreed easily.

The 'Dinis were right, Thian mused, humans were soft. 'How long have you been here?'

'Three days now. I had to push your father out of the way to come,' she added with a grin. 'But I am your mother and the stronger Talent. He had to admit that I have a special touch for easing pain.' Her smile was extremely tender but Thian knew she wasn't thinking of him just then. She stroked his face again, her fingers marvellously gentle and reassuring as she moved down to gently knead muscles in his neck and shoulders. 'You were very wise to have contacted Dad. He had me in a capsule and on my way with Fok and Tri before the boarding parties had assembled at the larval combs. I made it eminently clear that no larvae were to be destroyed. That was my first priority. That was, of course, before I realized I couldn't "feel" you on the wreck. I *could* sense you near by which confused everyone but you wouldn't – then I realized – couldn't respond.' Her face mirrored the anxiety she had endured.

'But the larvae weren't touched?'

'Indeed not! Their discovery will provide inestimable data on Hivers. Incalculably valuable. However, not as valuable as you are to us. Your life would not have been a fair exchange for that data. And I was horrified not to be able to locate you: you were there and you weren't. You couldn't be located here on the *Vadim* but I knew approximately where your body should be. It was Alison who thought of the pods. Why ever did you go there?'

'Abandon ship drills,' Thian said, managing a slight grin which surprisingly didn't hurt, though his face muscles still ached. 'Are you great-grandmothering me?' he asked, realizing that her subtle soothing strokes were purposeful and he was feeling drowsy again.

'A bit of,' she said with a grin. 'Glad you can feel it working. Isthia swears it brought Dad back to life. And you're in need of more healing.'

★   ★   ★

Gravy was his attendant the next time he surfaced. Testing his mental health, he found it sufficiently cured so that a light mental cast located his mother, fast asleep near by.

'Gravy?'

'So you're awake, are you?' And she moved to the side of whatever sort of a tank they had him floating in. 'By any chance, would you be hungry?'

'You must be reading my mind.'

Her smile was radiant. 'Nah, you should be hungry about now, if the treatment's working.'

His first meal was only broth but it was more delicious than any he remembered.

'That's because you're hungry,' she said.

'I didn't say anything,' he replied, giving her a long look.

She grinned, wrinkling her nose at him. 'That's something, isn't it? I'm picking up more than ever I did before. Only short-range but that's fine by me! Damia says sometimes fright triggers or expands Talent. And I won't lie that I wasn't terrified when they reported you couldn't be found at the wreck. Lieutenant Kiely set up an awful stink. Then your mother arrives in an unscheduled capsule, knocking a drone out of its cradle. The watch in the shuttle bay thought they were being invaded by Hivers and she'd have been charred if she hadn't paralysed their hands so they couldn't fire on her. Then she compliments the captain on such an alert crew and insists that the larvae be preserved . . . Which is the first Captain Ashiant had heard about *that*! But he got Vandermeer on the blower which was smart, because they were having quite a time, keeping the 'Dinis off 'em while they planted charges because they thought destroying the things,' and Gravy shuddered, 'was the right thing to do.' Then she grinned. 'I think your mother made herself known to Vandermeer and that was that! End of problem! I heard Vandermeer say she found herself removing the charges before she knew what she was doing. Can Talents do that? Make someone *do* something?'

145

'It's not considered good manners,' Thian began, enjoying the vision of his mother manipulating the sturdy and strong-minded security commander as easily as she'd have controlled an errant child. 'It's an invasion of privacy and *not* something Talent would consider except under very unusual circumstances.'

'Which those were! Crims, Thian,' and Gravy's eyes sparkled with excitement, clearing her mobile face of more solemn considerations, 'even the guys who were for charring the larvae are now patting themselves on the back for being in on such a find. But the glory's all yours!'

'Mine?' Thian hesitated only one brief moment before he said as earnestly as he could. 'But Kiely was first down the tube, not me,' he said in perfect truth.

'Kiely?' Gravy was astonished.

Thian nodded once emphatically. 'Kiely was first down that tube.'

She stared at him, puzzled. 'But I thought . . . '

'Kiely deserves the glory for being first. I wasn't even sure what the things were. I called Commander Vandermeer because I thought she should see what Kiely'd found.'

'And here Kiely's been down-playing his part . . . ' Gravy trailed off and then her grin was smug. 'Well, we'll just see about that!'

Thian was well pleased.

I am, too, son of mine, said Damia. *That will go a long way to discredit rumours.*

You've heard some?

He heard his mother's sigh flutter in his mind. *No more than usual.*

Have you found my assailant?

I shall perhaps have better luck now. Your touch is much surer today. Everyone will be overjoyed to hear my report of your return to health – with one notable exception. I'll be 'listening' for that!

'Considering the trauma to nerve, bone and tissue, you've

recovered amazingly, young man,' Exeter told him when Thian was allowed out of the restorative fluid. 'I thought that stunner was supposed to work as effectively in vacuum as in atmosphere, but maybe not. Can't think how else you could have survived.'

'Oh, I was raised hardy on Aurigae, you know,' Thian said easily.

Exeter scratched his close-shaven pate and grinned wryly. 'So I'm led to believe. Amazing woman, your mother. Ah, here's the orderly to escort you to your quarters. Now, you're still on sick leave, Thian. My orders are for you to take it easy: report to Lieutenant Clark for physiotherapy to get those muscles toned up. You'll be on the special diet for a while but that's not going to hurt anyone's feelings the way your mother's been hauling in provender for us.'

Thian thanked Exeter for his attendance and followed the orderly into the passageway. To his surprise, Flk was waiting and rubbed its silky furred arm up and down his in affectionate greeting.

FLK MOST WELCOME OF OLD FRIENDS. HOW GOOD TO BE SO GREETED.

DAMIA ASKS. FLK AGREES. THN WALKS SAFELY.

Thian gave the orderly a quick glance and smile but the man seemed unconcerned by their quick 'Dini exchange.

DAMIA SAYS ENEMY HERE? Thian asked, swinging his voice upward in query.

ENEMY EXISTS UNTIL REVELATION. CLEVER ONE. HIDES IN CROWDS. TIGHT MINDED. FIRST SON CANNOT BE VULNERABLE IN PRESENT WEAKNESS.

NONSENSE! Thian said with such angry authority that Flk skipped a step and tipped its poll eye down to Thian's face. SORRY! DAMIA HAS UNNECESSARY ANXIETY. THN WELL ABLE TO CARE FOR THN.

THAT WILL BE SEEN. And the downward note of the last sound was the end of that discussion.

To his surprise, Thian was escorted up to officer country.

'Your gear's all stowed here, Mr Lyon,' the orderly said, pulling back the door into one of the visitors' cabins, far more spacious affairs than his previous quarters.

'Thank you very much indeed, Tedwars,' he said, peering in, but he gestured for Flk to precede him.

'Checked the place out myself, Ambassador Flk,' Tedwars said in mild reprimand.

Thian laughed. 'I guess I'd better get used to being treated like eggs.'

'No, sir, the eggs get treated much better'n you,' Tedwars said in an aggrieved tone but closed the door before Thian could recover from his surprise.

He did shoot a quick probe at the orderly whose mind he had found to be open and honest. Tedwars privately thought all the trouble about the beetle eggs was vastly overdone. Eggs as could survive a bloody nova wouldn't be harmed by much else.

'Ah!' Thian turned excitedly to Flk. THE SAILOR SAYS THE WRECK WAS DAMAGED BY STAR NOVA?

Flk gestured for Thian to seat himself which he was quite willing to do for even the short walk up from sick-bay proved tiring. 'Dini seating had been included in the furnishings of this stateroom and Flk made itself comfortable on the padded stool.

ANALYSIS SUPPORTS NOVA THEORY. ONE RECENT NOVA IS IN ESTIMATED TRAJECTORY OF WRECK. SIZE OF VESSEL SUGGESTS FINAL MASS EXODUS. UNUSUAL AMOUNT OF STORAGE SPACE ON VESSEL PLUS EXTRA SHIELDING AROUND EGG REPOSITORIES AND QUEENS' QUARTERS. TWO QUEEN QUARTERS WERE NOT TOTALLY DESTROYED BUT BODIES REDUCED TO RUBBLE. VALUABLE STILL. BIGGEST QUEENS EVER NOTED. THEORY IS THAT VESSEL WAS ESCAPING WHEN STAR ABRUPTLY EXPANDED. THEORY IS THAT PREVIOUS THREE SHIPS WERE ALSO FLEEING, IN TIME, FROM NOVA.

ESCAPE PODS? Thian asked, having such facilities much in the fore of his mind.

Flk gave the rasping noise of 'Dini amusement. SOME

ESCAPE PODS RELEASED ON OUTWARD SIDE. TWO QUEEN SKELETONS FOUND IN PODS ADJACENT TO QUARTERS. FOUR MORE PODS WERE NOT OCCUPIED AND HAD NOT BEEN ACTIVATED. THREE WERE GONE.

ALWAYS SAVE THE WORST NEWS FOR THE LAST, MMMM, FLK?

Flk shrugged its upper limbs and bent its poll eye on him. NOT WORST NEWS BUT REQUIRES ALTERATION OF CURRENT PLANS.

IN WHAT WAY?

Flk tapped its feet, which included the toe wriggling that had fascinated Thian since he was a child and found his toes could not duplicate the motion.

SPKTM VOTES TO CONTINUE VOYAGE TO INVESTIGATE NOVA, DISCOVER WHAT DEBRIS MIGHT EXIST OF THAT STAR SYSTEM . . .

Thian grinned. TO BE ABSOLUTELY POSITIVE THAT THE HIVE WORLD WAS VICTIM OF NOVA?

EXACTLY.

THN CAN HARDLY FAULT THAT.

THN WOULD NOT.

AND THE HUMANS VOTE?

THEY WISH TO PICK UP TRACE OF ESCAPE PODS AND FOLLOW.

THAT COULD TAKE A LONG TIME AND A WIDE AREA TO SEARCH.

NOT SO WIDE. TRACES ALREADY FOUND. THREE PODS, THREE HUMAN SHIPS. GOOD CHASE. NO REAL DANGER BUT MUCH LEARNING AND MUCH GLORY.

SO LONG AS IT IS THE HUMANS WHO ACQUIRE GLORY. Thian heard a trace of bitterness in his tone and corrected his thinking.

IF GLORY IS GOAL. Flk shrugged.

THAT LEAVES ONE HUMAN ONE DINI SHIP?

WRECK MUST BE BROUGHT BACK FOR INTENSIVE INVESTIGATION.

THAT COULD BE DONE ON SITE, Thian said, thinking of the monumental salvage operation that would mean.

CAN ALSO BE STARTED NOW AND CONTINUED UNTIL FINISHED.

149

THAT WILL TAKE TIME. THIS VESSEL SALVAGES WRECK. THN REST NOW. ORDERS.

WHOSE? Thian asked even as he swung his legs around to the bed. And it was a bed, not a bunk, and a double one at that.

FROM THIS TRP, DMA, MEDIC, CAPTAIN, SECURITY PERSON, ENGINEER . . .

AGREED. ACQUIESCE. GRATITUDE. DREAM WELL.

TRP STAYS. THN MAY SAFELY DREAM.

BODYGUARD? Thian half-rose from the comfortable bed, disgusted but oddly reassured. That triumphantly hateful 'GOTCHA' lingered in his mind like a glowing canker.

REST GUARD SO SLEEP WILL RESTORE STRENGTH, THN. And Flk spoke as gently as to a 'Dini pup.

Sleep, Thian, or shall I assist? his mother said.

Oh, very well, he said and drew the cover over him.

Over the next few days, Thian learned more of what had been done and discovered during his convalescence. Once the yellow alert was cancelled, shore leaves were granted and, when Damia 'ported them to their various destinations, she 'ported in specialists, civilian and naval, who were excited to be able to examine a more or less intact Hive facility. There were many new faces in the officers' mess and he realized how very lucky he was to have such a fine stateroom to himself. Two ensigns had shift usage of his old cabin while scientists bunked in theirs.

The six ships had taken up positions for easy access to the wreck. It was ablaze with lights, in every corridor, tunnel and chamber, colour coded by area so that the ship blazed like a minor galaxy. Big drones had been 'ported in to transport sections as well as the invaluable larvae, the charcoal and dust and anything else that could be detached from the shell.

Three distinctly separate types of Hive larvae had been identified and sufficient numbers of each so that, as his mother dryly remarked, the diverse theories on how to

150

stimulate and mature the life forms could be tried. Scientific debates raged more fiercely than any armed encounter.

'A full-scale war would probably be quieter,' Damia remarked, 'and with fewer battles.'

'It's all bloodless,' Captain Ashiant said.

'There are nevertheless casualties, bloodless or not,' Damia added.

'"And no discharge in the war",' Thian put in, not quite sure what he was quoting.

THE MRDINI PO-ET KPLNG, Flk said, THN IS WELL VERSED IN CLASSICAL STUDIES.

Captain Ashiant blinked in surprise at that for he was now able to follow most 'Dini conversations. 'Kplng? It means Kipling!'

'Whoever,' Damia said, smiling. Then she turned to Thian. 'You go back to work tomorrow, Thn!' And she used the affectionate 'Dini of his name.

'I'll be bloody glad to, too.'

Damia tsk-tsked at his language but she approved his attitude.

'We've a lot to 'port back and team-work will reduce the load for me and ease you back into the job. As soon as I'm certain you're fully operational, I've got to go back. Your father can NOT handle big-daddies with just Rojer.'

'Zara's old enough, isn't she?'

Damia wrinkled her nose. *She's too inattentive to be of any real assistance. Heaving big-daddies requires full concentration.*

'But surely the mines will be slowing down if the Hive sun went nova,' Thian said.

The captain snorted and his mother regarded him oddly.

'The sun may have gone down on the Hive homeworld but there're all those hundreds of Hive ships and Hive-dominated worlds out there! Oh, no, Thian, this is just a brief chapter even if a very illuminating one,' his mother said.

'The other squadrons, lad,' Captain Ashiant took up, for evidently the subject had been much under discussion, 'that are in pursuit of the three outward-bound ones, will need support. And then there's mopping up . . . all the worlds that the Hive ships have already . . . ah . . . appropriated. They must be discovered and . . . cleared.'

'Aren't we then doing exactly what the Hivers tried to do to the 'Dinis and us?'

'Which would you rather have? Them on the loose or contained?' the captain asked.

Damia leaned forward. 'That's another bloodless war that's being raged in the High Council. Total destruction or planetary containment.'

'That's species suppression which is against the finest principles of both human and 'Dini morality,' Thian said, beginning to be annoyed with their intransigence. What had happened to his mother? Where were the values she had instilled in him and his sisters and brothers?

THN VIEWS BLACK AND WHITE. GREY IS A VERY GOOD COLOUR, Flk said, surprising the three humans by entering the conversation.

But its remark caused Thian and Damia to burst out laughing. Which required a rather long explanation to Captain Ashiant because Flk had been unusually witty; 'grey' was one of the most prestigious pelt shades for 'Dinis.

'Flk is grey!' Ashiant exclaimed, slightly more puzzled than enlightened. 'What would be called battleship grey – if that matters.'

VERY GOOD GREY AS TRP HAS SAID, was the rejoinder and Flk, in an excess of camaraderie, bobbed its head up and down, blinking several lids.

'We'd better stop,' Damia said, struggling with her laughter, 'or Flk'll be impossible.'

'By the way, where's Tri?' Thian asked his mother. 'I thought it'd join us for dinner.'

TRP IS NEEDED ON THE KLTL, Flk replied. TRP WILL BE PLEASED TO BE MISSED.

When Thian returned to his stateroom that evening, he realized that somehow he had been subtly diverted from what might have been a fierce debate over the morality of the courses open to humans and 'Dinis on how to end the Hive menace. Or did you just apply your ethics to your own species?

His intercom buzzed. He hesitated before answering. Very few people knew where he was now billeted. He might have very little pre-cog, though turning into that tube might have been in response to a subliminal fore-warning. He didn't 'feel' any premonition and depressed the acknowledge toggle.

'Lieutenant Greevy speaking . . . '

'Gravy!' he said and pressed full visual.

'Am I glad to find you! Look, you should know this: one of the ensigns in your old quarters is in here with a knife wound. He got attacked as he was opening the door. Knife just missed his lung. You being careful? Who knows where you are now?'

'Very few. How'd you get through?'

'Ted Exeter told me to warn you. He's still operating.' Anxiety kept flickering across her expressive face.

'I'm fine. I've a 'Dini guard out front and, with so many important experts on board, this deck's well patrolled.' Seeing Gravy reminded him that such vigilance could also be a disadvantage. 'Are you on duty, Gravy?'

'No,' she began with a frown and then her face bright-ened into a broad, happy and eager smile. 'No, Thian, I'm not. I just ended my watch.'

He was also exceedingly well pleased with his 'portation of her. Though he felt an uncomfortable surge of awk-wardness when she was amazed by the luxurious amenities of his stateroom, it was hard to stay tense in Gravy's company. She had him laughing over her queries about some of the unusual items in one locker. In the next she found the bottles of exotic spirits, and couldn't make up her mind which to try first, so she poured judicious levels of each one into a big glass, careful not to disrupt the lower layers, finishing up with a remarkably colourful 'lethal cocktail' which she made him sample, too. By the time he fell asleep with his arms about her, he decided that the most exotic spirit in the room wasn't bottled!

It was great to be working again, and with his mother. They accomplished a great deal before their 'day' ended: auxiliary engines, propulsion units, thrusters and communications gear were 'ported from Earth, Betelgeuse, Altair and Procyon for installation on the wreck for its outbound journey.

The impetus given the vessel by the searing wave of nova force was nearly spent and, even on tow, it would need some independent impulsion. One of the large shuttles had been altered and then anchored to the most stable level to serve as bridge and quarters for the watch.

Once the wreck was close enough for a 'portation, it would be 'lifted' to its final destination, at the moment a point equidistant between the 'Dini homeworld and Earth was being discussed though, as all the Primes pointed out, its exact location was relatively unimportant. Scientists could be transported from anywhere. There was also controversy that the very presence of the hulk might somehow attract other Hive ships to its position – therefore it should be as far away from either homeworld as possible. This was a theory more voiced on human worlds than 'Dini.

'Perhaps,' Thian had remarked when the subject was discussed in the wardroom where he was lunching, 'because 'Dinis have already had Hive ships in their skies and survived. But then, so have we!'

There was a moment of stunned silence, broken by such a whispered curse from Malice that Thian wondered if he had imagined it. He took himself heavily to task for being so lax, and slow. He ought to have followed that whisper as quickly as thought. But he hadn't. He should have been ready, especially since the attack on the ensign who was recovering slowly. Thian hoped that Malice had had a shock over that miscalculation. With his mother, he'd gone over the names of the boarding party in the hope that some clue might be triggered. Except that twelve of the other fourteen members had attended his language classes, there was nothing to trigger identity.

Although there were still deliveries of equipment, most of what Damia and Thian 'ported now was food and water to provision the three human ships that were to pursue the three Queen pods, and the *KLTL* which was continuing on to the suspect nova. Spectroscopic analysis said that the flaring star contained all the elements which had permeated the wreck. The 'Dinis would not accept that evidence as proof positive that the Hive world had been involved in, and not survived, the holocaustic disaster.

Thian wondered if his tour of duty would soon be over and was almost relieved when he had a summons to appear in the captain's ready room.

'Come in, young Lyon, and be seated.' The captain steepled his fingers, once again rubbing the fleshy end of his nose before speaking. Today Thian sensed that the hard mind shield was not so firmly in place and the captain was not certain how his next words would be taken. 'I'm given to understand that you've an illwisher on board the *Vadim*.'

Thian nodded.

'Your mother has not been able to apprehend your assailant and, although the gunnery officer discovered one of the weapons had been discharged, unfortunately no record was kept of which weapon was issued to which member of the boarding party. Do *you* know who the party is?'

Thian shook his head.

'Well, then, you'll not be staying on board the *Vadim*, lad. I'm not risking a Prime's life.'

'Sir . . . the *KLTL*'s continuing. She's not going to make the entire trip on the provisions she's been taking on: not even if she stuffed every spare cabin. Not unless she has . . . me on board. If I could volunteer for the duty . . .'

155

'But you'd be the only human on board . . . for well over a year . . . '

Thian grinned at Ashiant's expression. 'Sir, I'm too young for a year to matter that much.'

'Claptrap! A year's a long time at your age.'

'Captain Ashiant, it's like this. I can't finger my enemy. I won't give whoever it is the satisfaction of thinking that he or she has forced me to retreat. I'm too 'Dini for that. I can and will continue this voyage. That was what I was asked to do and what I intend to do – with your permission – continue on until we reach the Hive system. That makes me very human, Captain, living to fight another day.'

'Well, well! Well! Hmmm, yes, well,' and Ashiant steepled his fingers again, the slow grin on his lips echoed in his eyes. 'Yes, well, that would serve both causes admirably because, to be aboveboard with you, Thian Lyon, Spktm asked me if you'd consider transferring to the *KLTL*. It's been impressed with you, as interpreter, teacher and crewmate. It sees this voyage as a marvellous chance to make its crew learn sufficient Basic to get along with humans anywhere.'

'What did my mother say?' Thian asked, knowing perfectly well that she'd been asked.

Ashiant chuckled. 'She left it up to you. Says you're a grown man now.' He chuckled again. 'I think she's proud of you.'

'Then I'll transfer to the *KLTL*, if I may.'

'And Spktm also wished me to say that it'll be happy to receive your 'Dinis back when they can return. Said that'll make you happier aboard a 'Dini vessel.'

'Oh, I will be happy on board the *KLTL*!'

Alison-Anne was not happy that he was continuing on-ward when he could just as honourably have returned home on the *Vadim*. With her. She had been a regular evening guest as she was fortunately doing the day watches.

156

'How'll you ever find out who nearly killed you? And nearly killed Ensign Kalickmo! You'll be well guarded up here and we'll find the bastard sooner or later.' Gravy could look exceedingly fierce and determined for all she was a sensitive empath.

'It's more knowing where I could be of real service, Gravy,' he said, smoothing her silky blonde hair. It had enough static so that the fine stuff clung to his hand, leaping out from the pillow to caress his skin. Her skin was silky soft, too, but he needed to catch his breath a bit. 'I *know* the 'Dinis will be on pretty slim rations until they can reach a pick-up point. Young 'Dinis need proper nutrients or they will never reach any significant height. And the older 'Dinis need just as much to keep healthy. If I stay with them, they won't have to go on hard rations. And they'll feel freer to investigate every aspect of the nova position without losing any crew.'

'Whaddya mean? Losing crew?' She propped herself on an elbow to stare accusingly down at him. More of her hair tangled about his wrist.

''Dinis hold slightly different views about life and living. 'Dinis are taught to revere their elders . . . '

'And we aren't?'

'Not in the same way. A 'Dini will starve itself to give food to an elder . . . '

'Huh! They are backward.'

'Not really. 'Dini elders possess great wisdom and experience and must be preserved for their knowledge. An inexperienced young 'Dini considers it honourable to die lest those assets be lost to the race.'

'So – couldn't they just ration food?'

He tried to do this tactfully. 'Ah, they . . . well, they not only give up their lives . . . '

She drew in her breath in horror. 'You mean . . . ' When he nodded, she gulped. 'Gossake! Didn't think they'd have that in 'em!' She was more awed at that final sacrifice than appalled. Thian was oddly pleased by her attitude

157

especially when she added, 'Knowing that, you've got to go. I like the 'Dinis. I miss your two. But, say, Thian, that trip's projected for a whole year, Standard. How'll you get along? I mean . . . ' and to Thian's delight and amusement, Gravy blushed.

He hugged her to him and her hair clung to his face like a gossamer veil. He'd miss this right enough and said so. 'I'll be fine though. I'll miss you, I really will. It's much better this way but well, you've heard of 'Dini dreams?'

She nodded and he had to carefully remove clinging filaments from his mouth, chuckling as he did so.

'Well, 'Dini dreams are very . . . very . . . well, they do the trick.'

'NO!' She was up on her elbows again. 'That, too?'

'If Mur or Dip were here, I'd get them to show you.'

'Now just a living minute, Thian Raven-Lyon, Mr Prime . . . ' He turned off her threats with a deep kiss because he knew she'd withdraw any objections once he got the 'Dinis to dream with her. And that he did plan to do some day when he was back.

The unsolved problem of Malice continued to niggle at him. Unfinished as well as unsolved which, despite his strategic retreat, did not set well with him. And there was the matter that it was no longer Malice's hatred of him that had to be addressed but the iniquitous attack on Kalickmo. Yet how to identify Malice when that mistake had obviously resulted in this current total silence. Then Thian remembered his sister's suggestion and mentioned this to Damia.

'I'll spring the trap, Mother. The two of us ought to be able to close on him.'

'Him? You're sure of that?'

'After the knife attack, yes.'

'Humph. Really,' was his mother's cryptic response. 'Very well. When?'

'Tonight you're being given a special dinner. I know

158

Malice was part of both my language classes and the boarding team. I'll have the wardroom steward put all of us at the same table. That won't look particularly contrived. We often chow down together.'

'All?'

'Uhuh. That's why I'm so puzzled as to who it really is. I mean, he's got stomach enough to eat with me, hating me as he does?'

'So? When this evening? I'll want to know so I can be wide open, which is not exactly comfortable for any length of time around here.'

Thian smothered a guffaw because his mother had been admired by every male officer of the human squadron and one of the like-sex lieutenants. Regarding his mother objectively, she certainly didn't appear 'old': she'd married his father at eighteen and had only recently celebrated her fourth decade. She certainly didn't look the mother of eight and she was unquestionably the most beautiful female on board.

'Clean up that laugh, son of mine,' she said, but there was an amused sparkle in her eyes.

'Since it's my last night aboard, I have to give a farewell speech. I'll spring the trap then.'

'When you stand, I'll snap!' And she brought her teeth together with an audible click, then went off to finish her day report.

THAT IS WELL DOWN, THN, Flk said, appearing at his side from nowhere. TRP WILL WATCH AS WELL.

Several times during what seemed an inordinately long dinner, Thian had to rub his sweaty palms on his trouser legs. He hoped that he gave no other outward sign of tension. At one point, he asked his mother's opinion but she assured him that he wasn't laughing too loudly at Kiely's jokes or looking bored by Eki Wasiq's long-winded yarns.

In fact, you look quite handsome and confident.

159

Shakes don't show?

Only a mother would notice the shakes, and tonight I'm playing belle of the ball.

He grinned absently as someone on his left finished a joke but he knew she'd know it was for her.

Dinner ended almost too abruptly and it was time for him to spring his trap. He rose, glass in hand, stepping slightly back from the table so that he had a good view of the faces on both sides, politely turned in his direction. Then, while everyone was gathering themselves to stand to join the toast, he said mentally as loud as he could: *GOTCHA!*

Down the table – and it was only then that Thian realized the man had never sat close to him – Lieutenant Sedallia doubled up, slamming his face against the table edge, hands to his skull.

'Oh, do something about the wretched man, Flk,' Damia said and, with the startling speed which 'Dinis could show on occasion, Flk and Trp moved to bracket the lieutenant. Smoothly, they lifted him from his seat and as smoothly, carried him from the wardroom. 'I do believe he's had a seizure,' she said to Commander Exeter who excused himself immediately and followed.

Captain Ashiant frowned, looking at her composed expression and then at Thian.

I never once suspected Sedallia, Mother, Thian said, shaken by the surprise.

He's an inhibited Talent from what I could probe. Ugh! I didn't care to go very deeply. Get the toast over with. Everyone's waiting and it's the best wine Afra could get for us on short notice.

'I guess Lieutenant Sedallia will be sorry to see me go, gentlemen and ladies,' Thian began and saw expressions that suggested Sedallia's departure had caused the mildest ripple of surprise and no curiosity.

Thian, you're as cool as your father! And no, no-one thinks anything of it. The man was just taken ill and decorously

160

removed. We can explain to the captain later. His mother's comment almost rattled him but he went on.

'For I must leave the *Vadim* tomorrow—' His announcement provoked murmurs of genuine regret, though some were tinged with envy. '—to serve on board the Mrdini vessel, the *KLTL*.' That produced more reactions and surprise exclamations. 'I did, after all, sign on as a civilian—' and the reaction to that made him grin, '—Prime to assist a search for the Hive Home System. My 'Dini colleagues say we have not ended that search—'

'They're nuts,' Kiely said stoutly, glowering at Thian. 'A waste of time!'

'Your Talents are needed elsewhere, Lyon!'

'Stay with us! We need you, too.'

'Captain Ashiant . . . I protest . . . '

When Thian raised his hand for silence, it was politely restored. 'You all must know by now that my family is deeply involved with our Mrdini allies. I know that those on board the *KLTL* will suffer considerable hardship and loss if an FT&T Prime does not accompany them. Look at it this way, mates, I finally learned human naval customs: now I've got to learn 'Dini ones!' That brought a sprinkle of chuckles. 'I shall miss you. I've learned more these last few months than stevedoring and I'm grateful for your patience and your understanding. Good luck and a safe journey back.' Then he raised his glass, surveyed the messroom and knocked back the last of his drink.

He sat down to raucous cheers and banging of cutlery on glasses and the mess' good porcelain.

'Now hear this,' and the captain's stentorian voice could have been heard from stem to stern with no amplification. 'I think I speak for the entire crew, Mr Lyon, when I say that it has been a pleasure to have you on board and it is *our* right to wish *you* good luck and a safe, and speedy, journey home, lad!'

'And so say all of us,' Kiely leaped to his feet, glass in hand, and all in the messroom were not a second behind in joining him as Kiely led the traditional three cheers for Thian, a jolly good fellow!

Your father and I are very proud of you, Thian! his mother said. *Your grandfather and grandmother have decided that you are eminently worthy of being in the Clan Gwyn-Raven!*

8

A Year Later

'Xexo?' Afra called. *XEXO?* he added with more volume in the mental call. The Tower engineer had enough Talent to hear that. *Rojer!*

Afra could now locate both minds in the machine shop where Xexo in his capacity as chief mechanic – and lately his truant son – were most often found. When Afra 'felt' Rojer's mind, it was bristling with such vivid calculations, theories and excitement that small wonder the boy hadn't answered his shouts or telepathic query. Rojer's fascination with and attention to all things mechanical – preferably with moving parts – was absolute. Not a bad area of concentration, but only in the proper place and time.

'Yeah, watcha want, Dad?' was the muffled but incurious-sounding acknowledgement.

Rojer's mental tone held neither apology nor anxiety: more an impatience at being interrupted just then for any reason.

It seemed undignified to Afra to summarily 'port his son away as he had frequently had to do when the boy was younger. But fifteen-year-olds can be extremely concerned

163

with dignity – even if they are concerned with little else except the project at hand.

While Afra and Damia approved of the boy's keenness – Xexo said he was a very good mechanical apprentice – a Prime had to be well rounded and versed in more than just the generators which augmented his mental abilities. Afra muttered to himself and proceeded to the oil- and grease-redolent chamber that was his wayward son's heaven. When he reached the doorway, he stood for a moment, surveying the scene.

Xexo and Rojer were peering at a screen which showed an enlargement of many parts, some obviously twisted out of their original shape, others broken, with assortments of likely missing bits arranged like satellites about them, indicating possible appropriate matches. On the table were scale-accurate plastic facsimiles of all these pieces, arranged almost exactly as the screen display.

Xexo was a master mechanic, often inspired, considering how he managed to keep the elderly generators of the Iota Aurigaean Tower working. He adored machines, contraptions, gadgets, any device, far more than he liked humans. In that he had found a soulmate in Rojer Raven-Lyon – up to the point where said fifteen year old skived out of regular duties – and Rojer was definitely delinquent in these right now.

Furthermore, his 'Dinis, as much satellites of Rojer as the boy was of Xexo, were also engaged in trying to assemble anomalous parts into a whole. Sprawled belly-down on the grease-stained floor, they were clicking and clacking as their clever finger digits patiently pushed bits around the periphery of larger pieces, trying to make a fit.

'Rojer . . . oh, Rojer,' and Afra added a mental poke.

'Huh?' His son looked over his shoulder, widened his eyes in semi-horror as he also saw the digital clock on the wall, clapped an oily hand to his mouth, leaving a black four-fingered imprint on an already grease-smeared skin, and broadcast apology, dismay, guilt and self-reproach all at once. 'Gee, Dad, I'm sorry. I didn't realize it was getting so late . . . Did anyone else go out hunting?'

Hunting had been an immediate need and, his parents having dismissed Rojer from the Tower to handle it, they had gone on to other business. Afra tapped his foot and sighed heavily to indicate his displeasure. Lately, since the Joint High Councils had released data on every bit of the salvage so far recovered, as well as schematics, drawings, approximations and deductions concerning the Hive wreck, there wasn't an engineer anywhere that wasn't trying his or her hand at putting just a tiny portion of the puzzle together.

The 'Dini ship, the *KLTL*, which had continued its search for the Hive homeworld and/or the space debris thereof, had collected more bits and pieces which had been strewn by the injured Hive ship as its nova-driven path hurtled it outward. Afra thought that Thian's affinity for the odd sting-pzzt of Hive artefacts must be on overdrive, considering how much he had located in the vastness of space. There was no telling how much more would be found but each discovery was carefully documented in the absurd (Afra felt) hope that perhaps enough of the enigmatic Hive engines could be reconstructed to give the Allies some clue as to how their space drive had operated, and what fuel it used.

In the centuries of their lone battle against the Hivers, the 'Dinis had twice managed to pierce a Hive ship with projectiles and, they thought, punched through to the drive unit but each time the torpedo had failed to explode and 'Dinis wished to know why. The firing mechanism on their projectiles was *designed* to explode. The fuel Hivers used would at least give the Allies an idea of how to explode it the next time. The monetary award offered to any one or any group who solved even part of the immense problem was secondary to the prestige such a feat would accrue.

'You're lucky tonight,' Afra said severely because Rojer's

165

mind exhibited his singular concentration. 'Zara and Morag went out by themselves.' He noted that Rojer was chagrined by that. 'Zara and the 'Dinis picked enough greens to last a week and Morag stumbled across a warren. But *you* were to have led the hunt and preferably bring back enough to provide several days' protein. You know that Zara and Morag are much too young to go far on their own.'

'But they did it, didn't they?'

'That's not the point, Rojer, and you should know and appreciate the difference by now.'

Rojer sniffed and hung his head, mentally sorting which excuses might propitiate his parent. 'I just didn't happen to look towards the digital.' That was genuine enough.

'Not with your nose pushing plastic about,' Afra said, trying to keep his tone severe.

'It's my fault as well, Afra,' Xexo said, wiping his hands. 'He was helping me with the alternators, and then we both thought we recognized how these pieces,' and Xexo pointed with the fine-tip driver to what was strewn on the table, 'might link up. I should have reminded him that he had chores.'

'Xexo, every one of my children has a well-developed and perfectly adequate time sense. You only needed to trigger an alert, Rojer. From now on, if you don't do so, you will be sequestered. Do you understand that clearly?'

'Yes, sir.' Rojer's head was down and he tried to shield his thoughts but Afra wasn't a T-2, as well as a practised parent by now, to be diverted. In any event, he was faster at reading than Rojer was at shielding. 'I'll have none of that sass, either, young man.'

Rojer shot his father a guilty, but still slightly impenitent, look and sniffed again. Clear blue eyes met orange and began to glitter: the intent now carefully hidden from Afra's sight.

'If Xexo and me *did* get a piece together, you'd be awful proud of us, wouldn't you, Dad,' Rojer said, smiling with the charismatic brilliance that this son had inherited

166

in far too generous a measure from his mother and grand-father to suit Afra. Even so, the Raven charm melted his severity.

'Your mother and I would be immensely proud, of course, but we'd be prouder if you could – at least once a week – remember you are needed for mundane duties.'

'I do my Tower duty like everyone else.'

'Few would consider those hours mundanely spent,' Afra said, gesturing for Rojer to clean up his work-space and himself and hurry back to the house.

'Leave it, Roj,' Xexo said, rubbing greasy fingers along his jaw. 'Not the pieces. I want to puzzle this a bit longer. It'll be here for you tomorrow – if you're free.' The engineer shot a quick glance at Afra and received a nod.

'And do remember to feed yourself sometime today, Xexo,' Afra said, although he sent word to Damia at the house to see that some sort of hot meal appeared near enough to Xexo for him to see, and eat, it.

'Sure, sure,' Xexo agreed but he was already brooding over the artefacts.

DINNER TIME IS NOW, GRL, KTG, Afra added to the 'Dinis who hadn't looked up from their shoving and shifting.

HUNGER NOT IMPORTANT. MUST FIT PIECES. GAIN MUCH RESPECT AND ENLARGE THIS PAIR, Gil said but it jumped upright in the sudden way of 'Dinis shifting position. Sometimes Afra thought they must have some latent kin-etic Talent to execute such rapid displacements. And there was still the conundrum of how 'Dini dreams could pen-etrate human subconscious.

In deference to their 'Dini companions, for Afra's friend, Tri, was waiting outside, enjoying the fresh air, the Primes walked up the slope to their home. Lights were coming up as dusk was well settled on Iota Aurigae. The ever-present dim noise from the mines and smelting works which were active on an uninterrupted schedule reached their ears, punctuated by occasional loud rattles, like distant avalanches.

More big-daddies to shift tomorrow then, Rojer thought with a resignation which he quickly depressed where his father couldn't sense it. But involuntarily a sigh escaped his lips.

It's good practice for a developing Prime, his father said, permitting a little pride to be read in the thought. *Linking minds as well as 'porting masses.*

'Porting all the time is boooooring. As soon as the thought crossed his mind, Rojer regretted it.

And spending hours contemplating bits and pieces is not? Afra gave a good-natured snort.

Rojer answered that with a sniff. *Not the same thing at all, Dad. Link, grip, lift, push!* That's *boring. We're never allowed to hang about and listen to what the other Primes tell you because*, and here Rojer allowed his disgust to colour his tone, *we're too young!*

The time of being too young is so short, my son.

The wistful tone in his father's mind surprised Rojer and he glanced at Afra. Suddenly his father smiled and Rojer answered because they both realized that he didn't have to look so far *up* any longer. They were nearly of a height.

Yes, Rojer, the time of being young is very short. There are very few months left when you may indulge your enthusiasms.

But, Dad, haven't there been engineering Primes?

The critical need for FT&T right now is for Talents able to handle the responsibilities of a Tower.

Or a ship? Like Thian? That prospect did excite Rojer. *Dad, couldn't I at least ship out?*

Because Thian has? Afra smiled without rancour, for Rojer adored his older brother and, most of the time, chose to emulate his example. *That is not up to either your mother or me.*

Wouldn't you at least ask Grandfather?

Afra placed his arm gently across his son's shoulders: broad enough already and certainly strongly muscled.

Your grandfather is aware of every facet of your training, abilities, and yes, your wishes. I will not say we have to

168

transcend personal preferences right now . . .

You just said it anyway, but Rojer grinned at his father. *And I know my duty!*

Afra heard the resignation in that and wished that Rojer were as pliant as his older sister and brother, as enthusiastic about the shape of his future as they had been. He also remembered how rebellious he had been at Rojer's age but, he devoutly hoped, without the same cause. As much as they could within the framework of their contracts with Federal Transport and Telepath, they tried to prevent their children from feeling trapped by their Talent. They'd sent their children to other planets – Deneb, Earth, Altair, and once even Capella though that was not a successful visit – to broaden their outlooks and perspectives. The service of FT&T was not without its prerogatives which – most of the time – made up for the responsibilities. He must have a few words with Jeff, to be sure that the head of FT&T was fully aware of Rojer's mechanical aptitude and interest. Or perhaps a word with Gollee Gren – who was head of Placement and Training – might be more fruitful.

Aromatic odours wafted on the soft evening breeze and both men and 'Dini increased the speed of their strides.

'I'll tell you this but once, Rojer,' Afra said sternly as they hurried up the terrace steps to the house, 'you hunt next, by yourself, on Thursday, and if you forget, you'll not only get no supper of any kind, but you're sequestered!'

'Yes, Dad,' Rojer agreed meekly because that was fair. Zara hated to hunt – she was really so sensitive an empath that she could not accept the necessity of killing for food. Good thing she had gone with Morag who had no such compunctions and had developed into the best shot in the household. But she shouldn't have to do all the hunting: that wasn't fair either. But he had been so sure that he'd find the match the very next minute . . .

WE ALL GO. WE FIND MUCH TO EAT, Gil said earnestly, tugging on Afra's fingers.

Afra squeezed once in acknowledgement and then pushed

169

open the door into his home, always aware of his great satisfaction in being *here!*

You're in good time! 'Wash!' Damia said, scowling at the state of her third child and his 'Dinis and pointing a slender but firm finger towards the washroom.

Zara was coming down the backstairs as Rojer entered the washroom and she gave him a look of such deep reproach that he knew his hunch had been right. Morag, not at all sensitive when the quantity of food on her daily plate might be reduced, came clattering down and grinned when she saw him.

You're in deep kimchee. I called! I called good and loud!

'From where? The hillside?' Rojer asked because he knew how fond Morag was of hunting. And to be out as hunt-leader would have pleased her no end.

He ignored both sisters then and scrubbed diligently at his greasy hands and arms, right up to the elbow. No sense being sent back for another scrub like Ewain always was: not when dinner smelled as good as that. Then he helped Gil and Kat get their arm pelts dry. They didn't like to have their fur back-rubbed but it was the only way to blot the moisture sufficiently to stop itch.

It was a good supper: a stir-fry with the greens chopped fine and cooked crisp in fat. There were enough greens to satisfy him and Gil who were particularly fond of them done that way.

Mother was just about to serve the sweet course when she jerked erect and the 'look' crossed her face. She whirled, gesturing for all of them to link with her. It was now such a reflex action that they were linked before the second word in Damia's mind.

Recognizing his grandfather's voice, and the tone in which the news was couched, Rojer's eyes widened in reaction.

. . . best possible news has come through from the Beijing *of its pursuit of the Hive escape pod: it has been found with its occupants alive.*

Soundlessly Rojer mouthed 'wow': a sentiment which certainly his parents shared, judging by their jubilant expressions.

Jeff Raven's mind-touch relaxed as he continued. *Evidently very much alive and the* Beijing *captain says that he has grave doubts of how to contain the occupants if they break through the seal they managed to affix to the main hatch of the pod. He recommends immediate transfer to reinforced accommodations. That means Talented help on the spot. The mass is such that I'd not risk collecting it myself.*

You wouldn't do it by yourself, Jeff Raven, said the unmistakable voice of the Rowan.

Rojer noticed Morag's grin and signalled her to clear her expression. Grandmother wasn't being funny.

Where's the pod right now? Damia asked.

When Smelkoff realized that the hatch might be opened, he put the pod off the ship, on tow. He couldn't risk it staying on the Beijing, *even if they evacuated the air in the shuttle bay. Damned awkward that Thian's so far away, on board the* KLTL. *Ah . . .* Jeff began.

Rojer saw his mother's eyes flash.

Father!

Actually, my dear, I was wondering if I could borrow Afra and young Rojer . . .

Rojer's only fifteen . . .

Dad and I fling big-daddies about all the time, Mom, Rojer cried, though he knew he oughtn't to interrupt.

Dad . . . Damia began again.

They all heard Jeff's sigh. Rojer thought his grandfather had a real good repertoire of expressive sighs, though he daren't think that very loudly.

Afra and Rojer have already teamed up on many occasions when you were unavailable, Damia. This is a one-shot affair. We'll get them out to the Beijing. *They've the experience required from shifting so many drones from the mine yards so the pod being on tow won't be a problem, once they can see it. Captain Smelkoff has estimated the mass and volume involved*

171

which is no more than both have handled easily. Afra will handle the focus, if that's what's bothering you. But we've got to get that thing in a secure installation as soon as possible.

Then Rojer saw his mother narrow her eyes in a way he knew would exclude him from hearing what she said on a very tight personal mental shaft to his grandfather and he *knew* he was going to be left out of the fun things. *Why* hadn't he remembered to hunt today? It wasn't fair, because he *was* a T-1, just too young for Tower responsibility as yet even if he *could* do everything on his own . . . especially with his father. They really linked well, even better than he could with his mother, or even with both parents during very sustained heavy 'ports.

Afra leaned forward across the table, lightly tapping his wife's hand and she turned to make eye contact. Rojer held his breath, wanting to be bold enough to 'peek' at what was being said, but knowing that would be the death of any chance he had. Surely his father was arguing that he ought to have this chance . . .

In the hour, then, and thank you, Damia. Once again, you're decorating the family crown with the jewels of your womb!

DAD!

Rojer couldn't help grinning because his grandfather had meant him to *know* that he'd get this splendid chance to see some action! Then he caught how thin his mother's lips were and saw the anger in her eyes.

Oh, pleeeeeeassssse, he said, shutting his eyes so he wouldn't see any other negative signs.

Oh, open your eyes, Rojer. Wiser heads than mine have prevailed, his mother said, her tone caustic, but when he dared look in her direction, she had just the slightest hint of a smile. *I think you're too young but my father and yours believe you're not!* She cocked one eyebrow up – in challenge – and he grinned back at her.

'In an hour, Mother?' Rojer was so excited he could barely enunciate the words.

'You're going to let Roj go?' Zara asked, incredulous with eyes wide as saucers.

Damia cleared her throat. 'He won't be gone *long*, Zara,' she said firmly and shot Rojer a reproving glance for he was jumping up and down in his chair.

WE GO TO THE *BEIJING*, TO THE SHIP, TO SEE THE QUEEN, he told his 'Dinis who began hooting and whistling. That set off all the rest of the young 'Dinis – with the exception of Gil and Kat who were so astonished at their good fortune that they had covered their poll eyes.

It took all the adults, and some loud crackling from Flk and Tri to reduce the noise level. Then Damia called her dinner table to order.

'You'll need all your dinner for a stunt like this,' she said and served Rojer first.

It happened to be his favourite fruit pie. He'd finished up his portion when Zara dumped half hers on his plate: her manner was so mournful that she must think he was going to his death or something.

Sweetie, don't be sad! I want *to go*, he said, cuddling his sister because he could never bear for Zara to be anything but happy and carefree. She never whined but oh, could she look pathetic! Not even Mother could withstand a truly unhappy Zara.

Morag, on the other hand, was frankly envious of his assignment and Rojer hoped that this would settle her down when she had to be in a Tower link. Kaltia, Ewain and Petra were still much too young to do more than exercise around the house and grounds. But Morag was twelve and a good strong Talent, probably Prime stuff – if she'd ever work at it.

Who was he to talk?

That's right, son, his father said unexpectedly and Rojer grimaced, hoping Dad hadn't 'heard' much. Dad just didn't violate privacy. He had wanted to get his attention. *If you've finished eating, we've some details to go over, and listen for. They're still deciding where to plonk the pod down.*

I'll just bet they are! Rojer still couldn't believe his good fortune. Going on such a trip and with his dad! Then he saw his mother's unqualified smile of approval and grinned back. *You'll see, Mom. We'll make 'em all notice Iota Aurigae!*

Damia was still smiling but she said, *I'd rather the operation went so smoothly, no-one noticed!*

Damia, love, he's fifteen and this is glory!

You got it, Dad! And Rojer gave the all-ahead-go signal. 'You'll need ship suits and they're packed away,' Damia said, leaving the table to go to the storeroom.

Is she really angry? Rojer asked his father as softly as he could while he pretended to finish scraping his dessert plate.

Not angry, son, not angry at you. You're all growing up too fast for her. The proud look Afra gave his son made him feel as if he could lick a Hiver Queen single-handedly.

I don't believe that will be necessary, his grandfather's voice said gently in his head. *Please listen, Rojer!*

Right and tight, sir!

Then his parents added their touch to his and he knew this was a *Talent business.* He sat up straight on his chair and, putting a hand on each of his 'Dinis, made them stop their wriggling.

An old installation of Earth's moon is available as security quarters for the Queen and whatever else occupies that pod. I've just lifted a probe with all necessary placement pictures to the Beijing *and Captain Smelkoff will be fully briefed and is expecting you. Your grandmother and I will 'port your carrier to the* Beijing . . .

The very best handling, added his grandmother's unmistakable voice at its dryest.

Rojer didn't dare even say 'hello' – this was business.

This is where you'll be setting the pod down, and Rojer's mind was flooded with details that instantly organized themselves into a coherent vision of moonscape, a dome, with blocky buildings under secondary domes. The place slightly resembled Callisto Tower compound in that it was protected from the vacuum by main and auxiliary domes. It was bleak, whereas Callisto was bright and colourful. The viewpoint altered while his grandfather continued to explain the internment site.

Food will be provided: Hivers are vegetarians and an ample selection is being installed. The Rowan's working on that right now with both human and 'Dini biologists and botanists. If no indication is shown of tending the crops, it's easy enough to resupply. They can make what they like of the buildings: they're all empty and all exit locks are being sealed. The only way in or out will be by 'portation. Fortunately Hivers are also dependent on oxygen and it's doubtful if there'd be the Hiver equivalent of spacesuits aboard a pod.

Aren't there going to be guards, or scientists or something? Rojer couldn't help but ask.

Not in situ, Rojer, his grandfather said just when Rojer thought he'd get a scolding from his mother for blurting that out. *Remote sensors are all over the facility. That's one reason it was chosen. The 'Dinis have nothing comparable anywhere and we can provide their experts with laboratories, scanners and whatever diagnostic or screening instrumentation they need. Our science has not been on the defensive mode as long as the 'Dinis' has.*

The images faded.

Sir, what if that pod has comunits 'n' things?

Jeff Raven chuckled. *Quick lad. It took the High Council a lot longer to ask that. Truth is, Rojer, where would a com signal go now that their homeworld's rubble. The 'Dinis assure us that there are no nearby Hive worlds. They aren't a species that clubs together for protection as we and the 'Dinis do. Each Hive world is apparently autonomous. The only suitable planets they won't attack are ones already colonized by their species. Unless – which the best of the experts agree is unlikely – they have some sort of integral communication . . .*

They couldn't be telepaths, could they?

Don't *interrupt your grandfather,* his mother said sternly.

He's a member of the mission, Damia, he has the right to ask questions. They've been good ones. No, Rojer, *there is no evidence of telepathy beyond what your grandmother and other Denebian women 'felt' which many say was a mass precognition or premonition of tremendous danger. More that, than a thought transference. I think it's reasonably safe to say that no interstellar communication was ever developed. However, the monitors about the compound are extremely sensitive and will record the most minor variations. The underground units have clocked solar winds and monitored even the slightest coronal flares. I think the creatures will be safely contained.*

There's also a very handy and hot sun in case of emergency, his grandmother said in a voice that sent shivers down Rojer's spine.

Any other questions? Jeff asked.

Rojer shook his head, mentally as well as physically.

We'll be ready as soon as we've changed, Jeff, Afra said and paused. *Xexo's got the generators up.*

Rojer remembered his manners and wished his grandparents a good day.

That's a few hours off right now, lad, but I accept the thought.

Rojer wondered if his grandfather had really meant *that*.

Father loves to pun, his mother said, her tone amused so Rojer realized that he hadn't embarrassed her.

Then he, Gil and Kat made a dash for the bathroom and made a very thorough job of cleansing themselves. Afra came in just as Rojer had finished, with a single suit of navy blue over his arm. He was dressed in a similar outfit, and there was an unusual twinkle in his eyes. It occurred to Rojer that his father was going to enjoy this break from routine just as much as he was and he grinned at that perception.

It is sometimes very beneficial to do something different. Afra tossed the single suit at him. *Wear your Tower shoes. The navy gets annoyed if you scar their planking or decking or whatever the term is for their floors.*

When they came back into the living room, Zara was

176

cheerful, too, as she and Morag were clearing the dining table with their 'Dinis. Rojer rather thought Morag was trying very hard *not* to look envious or resentful.

'I'll ride Saki while you're gone. She needs the exercise,' Morag said, watching to see his reaction.

'I appreciate the offer, Morrie,' he said with great dignity, 'but we're not going to be gone more than a day.'

'You didn't ride her yesterday, you know.' Trust Morag to keep track.

'So you'll ride her first thing tomorrow morning,' his mother said and Morag rolled her eyes and turned to her chore, '*then* you'll do Tower duty. With my top Talents off gallivanting about the galaxy, we gals have to prove we can stand in with no trouble at all.'

Zara looked as if she'd been offered a summer on Deneb with that silly cousin she adored, but Morag tossed Rojer a 'so-who-needs-you' look. He didn't need his mother's quick glance to know he'd better not react to that blatant challenge.

Then in the next breath, it was time to go. Gil had lost its favourite belt and when that was found, Kat started drinking bowls of water until Flk stopped that, and hauled Kat off to drain.

They got to the Tower and into the capsule well before the end of the hour. Rojer settled himself, strapping Gil and Kat in on either side, both squirming like eels, as the generators built. His father was last in and then Keylarion herself closed the hatch.

Ready? His mother sounded so cool and businesslike. *Just remember,* and suddenly her voice wasn't so sure: to his astonishment, she seemed to catch herself back, but continued, *just remember that your father links first, Rojer.*

He knew what she meant and why her voice had suddenly altered.

You've drilled me well enough in that protocol, Mother. Have no fear!

Even through the stout metal walls of the personnel

carrier, he heard the exact moment when the generators reached the peak note. He didn't feel motion – but then he never did when his mother or father 'ported. He did feel a subtle alteration in the pressure of 'portation.

He's clever, this one, Jeff, said his grandmother and Rojer realized that his mother had handed over the 'port to Callisto Prime.

The pressure increased and he felt his father's fingers squeeze his hand. He turned his head and grinned, saw his father grin back and then the pressure went away. Outside the capsule were distinct noises, metallic clangings, shouts, orders.

Someone politely rapped on the hatch. 'You all right in there, sirs?'

'Indeed we are.'

The hatch opened and an older man looked in, then braced himself and saluted. 'Chief Petty Officer Godowlning, Mr Lyon sir! Captain Smelkoff's compliments. He's on his way here but you sure made it in a hurry,' he added in a less formal tone.

Rojer tried not to gawk and turned to release the straps on his 'Dinis who began to snicker.

GOOD DAY. GOOD DREAMS, Godowlning said in understandable but oddly accented 'Dini and that set both of them clittering and clattering.

'Thank you!' Rojer said, not knowing the proper way to address a chief petty officer. He should have listened to Thian's maunderings about naval protocol and stuff.

'T'ank oo,' Gil replied in its best Basic.

Godowlning's broad pinkish face was graced by a jovial smile, showing yellowish but even teeth.

THE SHIP WELCOMES MRDINI GUESTS and the chief got that sentence out with the concentration of one who has rote-learned phrases and was not really thinking in the language. But thinking in 'Dini, as Rojer well knew, was not easy to achieve.

'You don't know how pleased they are to hear 'Dini,

Chief Godowlning,' Afra said, rising up from the carrier.

'Your son was giving lessons, Prime, and I took as many as I could,' the chief said and then, hearing new voices, turned. Rojer could see his shoulders ease with relief. 'Here's the captain.' He leaned conspiratorially towards Afra, a tableau that made Rojer grin. His father was long and lean and the chief rather short – Rojer was taller – and as rotund as regulations allowed. He turned now and braced again. 'Captain, sir, the Primes have arrived.'

'For the record, chief,' Afra said in a low voice as the captain hurried to the cradle, 'I'm not the Prime. My son is. I'm T-2.'

The chief gave Rojer a worried look but Rojer smiled at him as he'd often seen his mother smile at sceptics and bent to help Gil and Kat from the carrier.

'I say, Mr Lyon . . . Messrs Lyon,' and Smelkoff corrected himself with a genial laugh that echoed in the big shuttle bay, 'you are prompt to the second. Caught me still on the bridge. But we've auxiliary screens here so you can see what we've salvaged.'

He was then close enough and extended his hand.

One shake is only polite. Shield, Afra told his son as he followed his own instructions.

Rojer complied and noticed the surprised look on the chief's face but their acquiescence to the courtesy did much to raise them in his estimation. Talents rarely allowed casual contacts but to have refused the forgetful captain would have been impolite.

Remember that, Afra said.

'So you're the Prime, are you, boy? This your first official act?'

'No, sir, I've been on Tower duty since I was twelve.' Rojer could 'feel' his father listening hard and *not* reminding him to be properly modest about his abilities. 'All of us do Tower time. But my father *is* the focus, not me. He's got to guide. I'm the grunt.'

Rojer heard someone's politely muffled guffaw but he

could also sense his father's approval, and that the captain was totally reassured.

'That wasn't how Earth Prime described your separate talents, young Mr Lyon, but whatever gets that pod where it's safe . . . ' Only the two Talents were aware of how nervous and vulnerable he felt, even with the pod towed kilometres behind the *Beijing*. Outwardly, the captain was relaxed, assured and exuding an air of authority and competence. 'This way . . . ' and he led them to the companionway leading up to the control room. 'Commander Strai, my chief engineer, is waiting for you in case you need to know anything about our engines.'

'I understand from reports sent back by Isthian Lyon on the *Vadim* that we'll have no problem gestalting the *Beijing*'s engines. More power than we'd ever need.'

'You are Mr Lyon's father, then,' the captain said conversationally.

'Yes.'

'And you're his brother, young Mr Lyon.'

'Yes sir,' and Rojer couldn't suppress how proud he was of Thian. 'We're a long-tailed clan,' he added because the captain was telling himself not to babble: there was only one Talent family named Lyon, and they were kin to the Earth and Callisto Primes. 'I've half a dozen cousins serving on Capella in various Towers.'

'Do you so?' the captain continued, feeling less gauche. Rojer couldn't help but read his public thoughts: the man's apprehension left him wide open. Rojer did ignore Smelkoff's fears that the kid didn't *look* that young, with that white streak of hair, but he couldn't be very old or he'd already be Towered somewhere, since FT&T could use a hundred Primes and still have vacancies. Couldn't the senior Lyon have handled the 'portation by himself? He had a very competent, experienced look, the sort a man could trust, even if he was Talented. T-2? That wasn't much under a Prime. Oh, well, FT&T knew what it was doing. He hoped.

'Messrs Lyon,' and the captain gave his engineering officer a broad and genial grin as they entered the control room, 'meet Commander Strai. He rigged the tow in jig time! Neatest job I've ever seen.'

Commander Strai, a keen-eyed man with rusty-red hair, gave the two Talents a crisp and respectful bow, and then swung round to the two conformable seats that looked out of place in the room. 'Thought these might help.'

'Very kind of you, Commander,' Afra said and motioned for the 'Dinis to stand in one corner.

MAY DREAMS BE DEEP, the commander said to them, again surprising the Lyons.

'Does everyone speak some 'Dini on the *Beijing*?' Afra asked, smiling his surprise.

'Seemed silly not to take advantage of the opportunity, Mr Lyon,' Strai said as he keyed codes and the screens above the console lit up.

At the sight of the Hiver sphere, apparently just sitting in space, Rojer caught his breath but then so did his father so he didn't feel he had betrayed too much surprise.

'Any idea what the hull is made of?' Afra asked after a moment's pause.

'Still analysing. It's a highly sophisticated alloy but with an ingredient we can't identify,' Smelkoff said.

'One of my lieutenants thinks it's a coating of some kind, maybe even something the Hivers secrete from their bodies,' Strai said. 'Doesn't even pit, so it's remarkable the other pod was destroyed.'

'I wonder they released the pods at all,' Afra said, 'if they knew the nova was about to happen.' Then he added more briskly, 'We'll need your mass and volume figures, gentlemen. I think everyone will feel easier once this package is secured elsewhere.'

'Amen to that,' the captain said, trying to sound more jovial than relieved by the prospect.

'How can I assist you, Mr Lyon?' And Strai looked from

Afra to Rojer who were both reclining on the chairs and settling themselves.

'Please tell your helmsman not to deviate from the present speed. Our drain will not affect the ship's speed or direction but you will hear a change in the generators.'

The captain gave the appropriate orders. Rojer had been listening to them with half his mind while the rest of his attention was on the pod. The upper hemisphere was bathed in the *Beijing*'s external lights and glowed, slickly metallic. It didn't *look* all that big, Rojer thought until he glanced for verification at the mass and volume.

'About as big as the Trefoil carriers, wouldn't you say, Dad?' Rojer said, flexing his mental muscles.

That's not necessary, son, but his father's tone was amused. 'Yes, I do believe you're right. Almost to the gram, I'd say.'

'We had a batch of them to go to Clarf only last week.'

'So we did.'

Rojer did not dare look at his father but the fact that Afra was keeping up the conversation indicated that his instinct to natter was valid. The tension in the control room abated a few degrees. They were two specialists, organizing their thoughts, making idle technical comparisons.

Seen enough? his father asked. His parents were always making sure that the visual had been properly scanned before a 'portation. You had to *know* what you were lobbing before you 'lifted'. Casual thrusts could cause uncasual damage.

Of the pod, yes. I just push you, right? Rojer eyed the barren moonscape and the lighted domes of their placement photos.

That's right. Now, pick up the power. Good lad.

Rojer was also aware of the generator gauge swinging up and over, almost to the overload position.

Link!

As he had so often done, Rojer opened his mind and 'placed' it at his father's disposal. One day, others would

182

pay *him* that courtesy. Right now he was subsumed by the deep and ruddy brown of his father's mental touch, comfortable and comforted. He felt power, directed it to the brown: brown expanded and, as if he had put his shoulder to the mental brown, he heaved forward and was suddenly the envelope that contained the pod. Wincing at the sudden sting-pzzt, he did not flinch from his thrusting.

For the first time in his life, he heard his father let out a string of spaceman's curses. *Forgot we'd get that with this effing great ball of spit!* Afra said and Rojer knew his father was feeling, *tasting* the revolting smell/touch/flavour of Hive. In the next second they had reached their destination and inserted the pod neatly inside the second dome.

Relief made Rojer light-headed. He wondered if they should have tapped on the pod door and cried, 'ollay, ollay in free' or some other, more formal, invitation to exit the vehicle.

I thought of that, too, Afra said, his mind equally lightened by success. *You took no harm,* he added, less as a question than a statement of what he knew to be fact. Rojer had felt him 'brush' deeply to reassure himself.

A snap, Dad. I can understand now why we've all had to push big-daddies.

'All safe and secure at the Heinlein installation,' Afra said, swinging his legs off the couch and rising. *I knew you'd appreciate all those boring Tower exercises. You've an enviable shove in you, Rojer. Most commendable.* 'I think you can safely say that Operation Bounce went off very well. We thank you for your courtesies.'

'Then join us for dinner, won't you? Surely you don't have to go right back?'

Rojer didn't dare breathe how much he wanted to *not* to have to go meekly back to Aurigae. Surely, they deserved a meal. He might have had dinner only three hours ago, but he was monstrously hungry suddenly.

'Thank you kindly, Captain, we'd be delighted but only—' and, to Rojer's dismay, Afra held up his hand,

'—if we're not depriving you of much needed stores?'

'No, indeed you're not, Mr Lyon. Wouldn't matter anyway, considering the service you've done the *Beijing*, but not only do we have orders to return now but your son provisioned us for a much longer journey. As soon as we're in 'portation range, six weeks at best, we'll be back to our base. We insist on celebrating with you tonight!'

It was, Rojer thought later that night as he slid down in a real navy bunk in a ship that had searched space and found live Hivers, the most glorious celebration he'd ever had. No-one had treated him like a kid. He'd been Mr Lyon this and Mr Lyon that – though he'd asked some of the officers to call him Rojer – that he would have to get his head down to size by the time they got home or his mother'd discipline him for fair. But tonight had been *his*!

Just as he drifted off to sleep, he thought he heard voices: *He's come of age, Damia. It's all there to be tapped. To delay risks more than it could possibly gain.*

Then he fell into one of the more marvellous 'Dini dreams he'd ever had: all bright colours, swirling masses, and intricate shapes and high-flying swirls and loops – a totally positive dream even if he hadn't a clue what it signified!

9

DAD!

The name was broadcast on a wide enough band to bring Rojer wide awake. It took him only a nanosecond to recognize Thian's voice. Rojer glanced at the digital's illuminated face and saw he'd been asleep a bare hour.

Hey, Thi, let a guy sleep.

Sorry, Roj . . .

That was overlapped with Afra's acknowledgement of the mental contact.

I didn't wake you, did I, Dad? I checked times and it's . . .

You didn't wake me, Thian. I've been enjoying the ship's hospitality. The captain and his officers are quite starved of news so long in this tour. Callisto and Earth are inundated with requests for transport of personnel and materiel. Mainly to Heinlein Base, and Rojer heard the amusement in his father's calm tone. *So we have been informed that we must wait in the queue.*

I can just believe that! Hoooeee! Everyone who can'll be flocking out there to gawk. Thian's voice altered. *Did you have any trouble with the sting-pzzt? I forgot to warn about that. Did Mother remember?*

I should have, and Afra's tone was unexpectedly rueful, *but your brother was superb. Not so much as a twitch, despite the force and the unexpectedness of it. You can be very proud of Rojer.*

Of course, I am. He's my brother, isn't he? That sting-pzzt, and Rojer didn't know if Thian was explaining or apologizing, *it's much heavier around live ones, though, isn't it? That's how I tumbled to the larvae. Any news on their development?*

None, and that's officially honest. Having a live Queen may speed things up . . . If it doesn't 'Dini out on us. How is your quest going?

We're still several months away from a pick-up point . . . and we'll probably have to wait our turn in the queue, too, but I've turned into a real hotdog artefact finder. Better'n a metal detector in a mine field.

But that's what you are, Rojer said, awake now and delighting in this midnight conference with his brother and father. *Hey, you haven't found any more shards like this . . .* and Rojer envisioned the group that he and Xexo had been so sure would fit: heavy bands of some ten centimetres thick, finely tooled. *They look like they should fit together, all of the same pattern.*

Yes, we did in fact. I'll copy through to you. Going for the reward, too? And the amusement in Thian's voice took the sting away. *There isn't a 'Dini on board that isn't trying to fit the puzzle pieces together. Blank your mind now and I'll send the specs through.*

They'd done this often enough with mass, weights and capsule sizes during Tower practice so Rojer thought of nothing and Thian sent him the particulars. Rojer thanked his brother as he swung out of the bunk and to the terminal where he copied down the specs. Then a yawn overcame him and he crawled back into his bunk, fitting his legs between the sleeping 'Dinis.

Say, Thian, are Mur and Dip back with you?

Have been for weeks. I didn't realize how much I'd miss them. They're larger, too. Had a good hiber . . . Dad, send me

186

a visualization of this Heinlein Base, please? It's not part of the KLTL's files and Captain Plr wants to see where the Queen's being kept. They sure are nervy about her being anywhere near Earth.

Reassure them. Heinlein Base is built in solid rock. Nothing could burrow through that. And there's nowhere to go. Certainly nowhere with oxygen.

I'll tell them.

Rojer couldn't keep awake any longer, falling asleep during the next part of the rapid mental exchanges.

A full week went by before Damia had to agitate for the return of her husband and son. There were big-daddies to transport and there was no way she could handle them *without* the mental muscle Afra and Rojer supplied.

Rojer hadn't minded. Ensign Bhuto was assigned to show him around the ship.

'Don't you mean, nursemaid me!' Rojer asked when the exec officer had completed the introduction and moved away.

Bhuto, with the darkest skin, the whitest teeth and the biggest brown eyes Rojer had ever seen, grinned broadly.

'Mr Lyon, sir, you don't need a nursemaid, not after what you did yesterday!' And he rolled his eyes. 'Eat up, Mr Lyon, sir, breakfast's the best meal of the day! Say, you couldn't haul in some fresh stuff for us, while you and your daddy are here, could you? I haven't had any fruit in yonks. I didn't get any last time your brother brought stuff in, but I figure, if I'm with you as your companion on board this ship, if supplies come in, I've a better chance now of getting a share. Wouldn't you say so?'

Just a little push at Bhuto's wide open mind and Rojer knew he was genuine. He soon learned that Bhuto talked all the time, a sort of verbal diarrhoea. But he knew the *Beijing* from turret to shuttle bay, and every single one of the access alleys. Literally he gave Rojer and the 'Dinis a tour of the ship! He also practised his 'Dini, translating what he told Rojer into their language.

'Look, why don't you just speak 'Dini?' Rojer said when they were midships and descending. 'Save your throat.'

' 'Dini saves no-one's throat. How do they manage in long speeches? That's why I speak Basic to you, give my vocal cords a rest now and then. Sure, I could just use the one language 'cos they certainly understand Basic, too, the way their eyes shine. Not stupid, 'Dinis, not like some of the A.B.s think, just because they look like weasels wearing fezes. I've never seen a weasel – live that is – but there's only a general look of a weasel about them, what with the smooth pelt and all. But 'Dinis are not the least bit weaselly, if you take the distinction.' Then he turned to help Mur through a narrow aperture into yet another access alley. KEEP HEAD DOWN SO AS NOT TO POKE OUT POLL EYE.

'Where did you get so fluent in 'Dini?' Rojer shoved the question in quickly.

'Oh, my older brother had 'Dini pairs. We were one of the first families, though I expect that you Lyons were *the* first—' and he grinned, white toothed, to show no ill-feeling, '—so to speak, what with being children of the Raven-Lyon family and each of you had pairs?'

Rojer only had time to nod before Bhuto was off again.

'All of you? Eight? Well, I suppose it's working out what with your brother first Priming the *Vadim* and now the *KLTL*. That was a really fine gesture of his, to accompany the *KLTL* to be sure they had sufficient supplies so that no 'Dini had to lay on the line.' Bhuto rolled his eyes again.

Rojer thought he must be one of the very few people who understood what that meant. He shuddered, glad that there was absolutely no chance that either Gil or Kat would have to volunteer.

'One really has to hand it to that species for per-severing against incredible odds, and suiciding to prevent a Hiver from overcoming the worlds they were pledged to protect.'

'Bhuto? Do you stop talking in your sleep?'

188

'Oh, sorry, Mr Lyon, sir. I do tend to talk a bit.'

He was silent for all of two minutes – Rojer's time sense kept track. They were in the shuttle deck by then and Rojer was quite willing to listen to the ensign's vivid description of how the Hiver pod was netted and hauled inboard.

'Tried to run from us and used up the last whiff of fuel, whatever it is they use. So the pod was just drifting. Captain thinks towards the yellow sun in 757-283. No other suitable system nearer than ten light years in this quadrant. D'you suppose the Queen knew that and had a pre-planned destination? I mean, that's awful close to their homeworld, spatially speaking. Could be there's a colony already there. Isn't one of the 'Dini-explored worlds: we had to check that. But it's not one that's tagged. Rather far out from our Hub. Even with several million planets in this arm of the Milky Way that are suitable to habitation by our three species, it's remarkable there was one near enough for the pod to reach. Of course, some think the Queen'd just go into hibernation, or suspended animation or something until such time as the instrumentation located a suitable planet. Or maybe this was always a destination. Off the wreck's trajectory but then it might not have had a chance to correct when the nova shock wave hit it.

'At that, our shuttle bay was only just large enough to haul the pod in. Biiiiiig! Six metres if a centimetre. If it were a human vehicle, could fit a whole watch on board it. Just hope there's more in there than just one Queen body. She'd be one mighty huge mother, she would. But they're saying that she'd have to bring attendants and workers and drones and suchlike because she couldn't survive without their ministrations. 'Dinis told us – when we were kids – that the Queens decide what sort of offspring the Hive needs to function and then parcel out the types among 'em to breed. That's a handy habit. Not enough deck scrubbers – make two dozen more eggs of that kind. Not enough ensigns – produce six more.' Bhuto grinned as Rojer inadvertently made eye contact. 'I do talk too much, don't I?'

189

'You talk all right,' Rojer said, projecting reassurance, 'but mostly you're interesting. Say, any of your crew interested in the puzzle?'

Bhuto drew in a delighted breath, lifted both hands in surprise and then, grinning even more broadly than usual, he beckoned Rojer to follow him towards the stern of the *Beijing*.

'We're allowed to work in Cargo Hold 3 on account of it's empty. Chief Firr programmed the engineering computer to replicate, to scale, every single one of the pieces found and he keeps up to date when new ones are brought in. I'll bet we got as good a set-up as Naval Intelligence or the High Councils of either ally.'

For a reason Rojer suspected was due to peer pressure, Bhuto did not talk non-stop in Cargo 3. In fact, he whispered only twice: once to suggest that they eat down here with the other diligent puzzle-piece workers and the second time to ask if perhaps the 'Dinis wouldn't like tripods. He knew there were some available for when Captain Smelkoff had had 'Dini experts on board.

For a short while, Rojer wrestled with his conscience: whether or not to tell Chief Firr of Thian's new finds. Wandering around the edge of the immense table on which facsimiles of the pieces were placed – much the same way Xexo had set up his display – Rojer found the ones he thought were sections of the whole he and Xexo had been working with.

He asked Bhuto to point out the chief, if he was present, and when Bhuto did, without saying a word, Rojer accosted the man, a stocky man with a big, red-veined nose.

'Sir, I'm . . . '

'And a good day to you, Mr Lyon,' was the affable reply. 'My compliments on your hoist yesterday. Glad to see the last of it. It's safe now?'

'At Heinlein Base on Earth moon.'

The chief scowled. 'Wouldn't like it in my sky, I can

tell you. What can I do for you, Mr Lyon? I perceive that you may also be a compulsive jigger or you wouldn't've hung around so long. Know that look. What do you think of our set-up? Impressive?' And the chief peered up at Rojer, projecting a wish for praise.

'It's a splendid set-up: easy access to all the main and peripheral parts,' and Rojer knew he was sounding just like Xexo but it seemed to gratify the chief. 'Ensign Bhuto—' and an odd expression flashed across the chief's face which Rojer interpreted as meaning the chief found the ensign tiresome, '—said that you've machined all these pieces.'

'I have indeed, Mr Lyon.'

'I've the specifications of some new additions . . . '

Before he could complete his sentence, the chief had him by the arm and was propelling him to an alcove where the parts programmer was installed.

'So . . . ' the chief said, turning it on and holding his fingers expectantly over the keys.

'Rounds,' Rojer said and the chief's fingers keyed the basic shape in. 'In these dimensions . . . ' and Rojer rattled them off. Like most of his family he had an eidetic memory.

When the chief had finished the programming and the items had dropped into the basket, he made a grand show of adding them to the table, announcing that these were Mr Lyon's contribution and what said they?

Rojer felt himself blushing at the cheer that issued from nearly thirty throats and hid his embarrassment by picking up the first piece to see if he could make a match.

Much later in the ship's day, his father extracted him from Cargo 3 to bring in three supply drones. Rojer remembered the ensign's comment and saved a net of assorted fruits. The young man's gratitude was touching and Rojer realized that his talk was as much nerves as anything and Bhuto really needed understanding and reassurance. Those Rojer could project whenever they were together, and not necessarily in Cargo 3. Perhaps only Rojer noticed

191

the decrease in verbiage. Or was it only because Bhuto would take Gil and Kat to one side and improve his 'Dini intonations and vocabulary. Evidently as long as Bhuto maintained silence, he could remain in the cargo hold so Rojer, too, was able to indulge his obsession.

A second compulsive Hive-oriented preoccupation had begun at Heinlein Base. All over the Alliance, viewers waited to see the Queen emerge from her escape pod. A special channel was devoted to Queen watching, with experts giving learned discussions on what she must be doing inside the pod (making sensible investigations of her new location?); when she could be expected to emerge (a matter which now involved thousands, even millions, of credits from the speculators); what she looked like – but this was based on the partial remains that had been gathered from the nova wreckage and other detritus (*large* and insectoid with useful mandibles). Some earlier estimates had to be considerably revised on the basis of the size of the escape pod. Granted, considerable space would be taken up by its life support, guidance and propulsion units. No weapon apertures had been discerned but weapons on an escape pod were considered unlikely. Of equal interest to a sight of the Queen was a look into the pod itself, to examine it inside out in minutest detail and subject the vehicle to most intense analysis. The hull sheathing was of particular interest.

Considerable debates went on about her probable companions. One block insisted that she was alone to ensure her survival if a lengthy journey to a safe haven was required. 'Dinis pondered her possible suicide rather than fall into inimical hands.

A very small group of humans wanted to greet her civilly – that being the best way to win her cooperation. How would she know, these proponents argued, that she had been rescued/retrieved by putative enemies? Human vessels had only recently taken space with their 'Dini allies and the Queen would be unaware of the Alliance. Perhaps

192

if she was met with courtesy, more could be learned.

'Dini resistance to that interpretation was solid. Denebians and any Talent interviewed refuted that attitude.

They *weren't at Deneb,* the Rowan said in an implacable tone of voice that made Rojer hope his grandmother never directed it at him. He had heard her addressing his father and he couldn't help but hear that part of the conversation. They *didn't feel the alienness that we felt, the resolution to have Deneb for their get! The Hivers cannot be allowed uncontrolled proliferation. Their depredations must be curtailed.*

I agree, Rowan, Afra said. *Risking your displeasure, I wonder if we are taking the right attitude. With the Hive homeworld destroyed, isn't it possible that the loss of their home base will limit further activities?*

Afra! Do you recall nothing of your contact with the Hivers? His grandmother's anger at his father's mildly delivered rebuttal was such that Rojer strengthened his shields. He was only on the periphery of her mental projection and the agitation was palpable. How could his father handle the full weight of her disapproval?

I recall it all in an exceedingly vivid memory, Rowan, but so far – and I haven't been against the Alliance in any way, shape or form – we've blithely accepted the Mrdini judgements as irrefutable. Would it not be the better part of wisdom – since we consider ourselves sophisticated and civilized – to see if direct contact with a representative of the Hivers is justified?

Really, Afra Lyon, only our long-standing friendship and involvement keep me from suspecting your loyalties!

Rojer scrunched down under his thermal blanket, reassured by the warmth of Gil and Kat, sleeping on either side of him. This bunk was not made for such occupancy and he woke up each morning with cramp. Not that this minor discomfort was more than that. His bed at Aurigae had always allowed for three growing bodies. He'd been having a fascinating 'Dini dream and he used this to get back to sleep, ignoring the distress that conversation had produced in him. The Rowan might be his grandmother and highly respected, a heroine for being the focus of the Denebian repulsion, but she shouldn't speak to *his* father like *that*!

When Rojer woke the next morning, he had vivid recollections of his 'Dini dream. So did Gil and Kat. They were all for rushing down to Cargo 3, for the dream had been about fitting pieces together. As sure as they were that three pieces would fit, Rojer scrambled into his clothes, remembered to depilate the fuzz from his jaw – while Gil and Kat harangued him for dawdling, jumping up and down like jacks in their excitement.

CERTAIN PERSONAL HABITS MUST BE PERFORMED TO PROJECT AUTHORITY AND PRESERVE DIGNITY, he told them so firmly that they subsided. He couldn't run ragtag about the *Beijing* as he could about Aurigae. And his father would give him one of those looks, letting Rojer know that he had dropped the family standard.

GET THERE MOST QUICKLY? Gil asked, for the first time asking to be 'ported. Usually that was Rojer's option and scrupulously observed by the 'Dinis.

GOOD IDEA THIS ONE TIME.

Rojer hunkered down, arms about his friends, and 'ported into the passageway adjacent to Cargo 3. That should be a safe enough destination. If someone spotted them miraculously appearing, well, everyone on board knew he was a Prime and why shouldn't he use the Talent he'd been given. It wasn't as if he had been indiscriminately popping in and out. And anyone who might be near Cargo 3 would know that he was also a puzzle buff.

They met no-one but they could hear the usual low murmur and occasional curse as a hoped match dissolved. Rojer was greeted by a few noddings but the attention of most was on their fittings and piecings.

Prompted by their 'Dini dreams, the three strode about the table – Gil and Kat with their heads bent so the poll eyes were fastened on their objective. Rojer scooped up one

194

piece, moved down the table, extracted a second and found the third as far to the centre of the table as he could stretch. By then, everyone was watching, sensing an Incident.

Rojer held his breath and carefully turned the one piece on its rim, for it was rounded, fitted the second to its longer side and the third to the short one. There was no question of the fit. A cheer rang out and those nearest him were slapping him on the back, nearly upsetting Gil and Kat, and rejoicing in his success. Chief Firr was roused from his bunk with the news and it percolated quickly through the ship. Rojer's piecing was registered. The fact that he was one of seventeen others in the Alliance, six 'Dini and eleven humans, to have found the same match did not reduce the jubilation on the *Beijing*.

Enjoy this moment with discretion, Rojer, his father said but did not hide his pleasure at Rojer's achievement.

Count on that, Dad, Rojer replied without bothering to dampen his private elation. After all, his dad wouldn't think badly of him if he kept the lid on a public display. *Besides which, I was not the only one.*

You are in very good company, for all the others are trained engineers. I believe that perhaps your mother and I have erred in appreciating your positive vocation. We will discuss this on our return. Your grandparents will be pleased. Ah . . .

Association had brought to the surface Rojer's inadvertent eavesdropping the previous night and his father had unerringly caught it.

Well, that can't be helped. Rowan was too distraught to narrow her thought. We are to return today. You timed your success perfectly. My compliments, Rojer.

We couldn't possibly go by way of Heinlein Base, could we? The request was out before Rojer could censor it. Everyone and his uncle's brother's cousin's grandson would be trying for a chance to visit Heinlein Base. What made him think that he had a priority on visiting?

I believe we can make a case for ourselves, his father replied.

I didn't mean that to be heard, Dad, believe me!

There was a chuckle through his father's voice. *I do. You're high from your success because, I must assure you in my turn, I was not invading your privacy.*

The significance of that mild statement capped Rojer's day. Talented parenting involved the perquisite of reading a child as deeply as possible – especially highly Talented children – to correct any psychological quirks before they became established and warped a personality. That Afra had resigned that prerogative meant he considered his son adult enough to function with no further acute surveillance.

Then his father went on. *It happens that I, too, wish to see the escape pod closer than at the end of a long tether. Screen definition is very sharp but there is a certain quality that one perceives only in the presence of the object of scrutiny. We will have the opportunity to scrutinize it.*

This exchange occurred while the general celebration was continuing, with many of the dedicated puzzlers examining the fit, doing and undoing the pieces. When Chief Firr arrived, he put the three sections under the 'scope and verified the fit. He couldn't have been more pleased than if he'd done the deed himself.

'It's up to you guys now,' Rojer said when the excitement had calmed down sufficiently for him to speak. 'Dad and I have our orders: we're to 'port back to Callisto.'

'Hell, man, why'nt you just 'port over to the Moon and get a good look at that ol' pod?' one of the mates asked.

Rojer grinned. 'Rank has some privileges . . . '

'Rank?' the chief asked, his eyes widening.

'I'm a civilian after all,' Rojer said, deceptively meek.

'You're a good . . . guy,' the chief said and Rojer knew that he'd been about to say 'kid' and Rojer grinned in appreciation.

'Wish you luck, Chief. Maybe you'll get the next match!'

'For the honour of the *Beijing*!' Firr replied with a broad grin and held out his hand to Rojer.

Without hesitation Rojer took it, and knew that the

196

chief had liked him for himself, and because he'd put a plug in that motor mouth of an ensign. He had to shake hands all round after that and did so, gathering the impression that, despite being a Talent and still downy cheeked, the crew liked him.

Almost more elated by that than the piecing, Rojer went to join his father in the messroom. Gil and Kat asked to stay in Cargo 3, just in case something else from their shared dream had results. When Rojer asked permission for the 'Dinis to stay behind, Chief Firr absently concurred: he was already collecting more rounded bits that might possibly add to Rojer's contribution.

As Rojer left, behind him was an excited buzz of folk given a positive stimulus to their avocation.

Captain Smelkoff joined them for breakfast, adding his own compliments for the join.

'On an extended mission like this, Rojer, this sort of preoccupation is invaluable and you've just added the impetus of success. Good morale booster. You two are quite a team. I liked that older boy of yours, Mr Lyon, didn't see enough of him. Real pleasure to have you aboard, and special thanks for importing those fresh supplies! Feed the crew well enough and they'll put up with a lot of privation.' Then the captain leaned towards Afra in a mock conspiratorial pose. 'You couldn't leave this one behind for a while, could you? I guarantee I'd make a sailor of him!'

Afra grinned broadly. 'Unfortunately, Captain, he's about to take up his own station.'

That was news to Rojer but, on the heels of that thought, he realized his father was courteously dissembling.

'Well, I'm sure he'll be a credit to you. A real credit.'

Rojer began to feel distinctly uncomfortable in the light of such effusive commendation. He knew he'd done a good job of what he was sent to do: he was delighted to have had a whole week on board a mission vessel; he was elated to have matched artefacts, even if he wasn't the first to do so. That was almost a relief. But he had only been doing what he was trained to do, 'porting and interpreting 'Dini dreams.

How many of the others could have shared the same dream? he asked his father, as he ate, in as self-effacing manner as he could.

That was *how it came to you then? It might be instructive to find out how many had similar dreams. The com indicated diverse origins.*

Rojer kept to himself, and from Gil and Kat, that there'd be a diversion to Callisto Station and a side trip to Heinlein Base. But that made it easier for him to say his farewells to captain, chiefs, crew and Ensign Bhuto who, for once, only grinned and let Rojer do the talking.

With the hatch closed, Rojer took a deep breath and stood behind his father's focus to push the carrier back to Callisto Station.

So my grandson has covered himself with glory, has he? said his grandmother in a mood much different from the one he had overheard in the night.

Not especially, Grandmother, Rojer said equably because he just *knew* she'd be waiting to jump on any pretensions.

Hmm. I'd say the mission did you a lot of good, young man. I hate a cocky boy!

When would one of us Lyons have a chance to learn to be cocky?

That's exactly what I meant. All right, get out of that spatial coffin and have a meal with me. I don't get the chance to see you often enough.

I'm stuffed with breakfast, thank you. Hungry as he usually was, there was a limit to Rojer's capacity.

You'll stop then while I breakfast. Then you can take yourself to Heinlein Base. I can trust you to do that, can't I?

If Dad's too tired to, Rojer said, wondering just how long last night's conversation had lasted.

I've an hour before Callisto clears.

Rojer caught his father's eye and grinned. They unstrapped, helped the 'Dinis out and took the path from the yard to the Rowan's house.

To Rojer's surprise, because he'd had no hint, Jeff Raven was also seated at the breakfast table and beckoned them enthusiastically to join him. Empty places were set for two more humans and two 'Dinis.

'I add my compliments to all the others, Rojer,' his grandfather said.

'I'd like a kiss, Rojer,' the Rowan said.

That was the ultimate accolade and Rojer nearly stumbled on his way to his grandmother's side of the table. His mother had often said that her mother shamelessly cultivated her imperious pose. It certainly scared Rojer. But, keeping the thought scrupulously private, Rojer thought she was a very beautiful grandmother, with her striking mass of silvery hair, her small but delicately featured face. She was no taller now than his shoulder. She turned her cheek to him, held up one hand to encircle his head when he appeared to hesitate, and he kissed her.

What he had expected to feel he didn't know: what he got was unqualified approval and acceptance. Her cheek was smooth as a petal and her perfume was subtly but not sweetly floral.

Thanks, Grandmother, he said gratefully.

That's the trouble with being Talented, Rojer. The ordinary human touches assume merits beyond their true status. That was a grandmotherly kiss of welcome after long absence: nothing more. But I am pleased with your performance. As deftly as ever I or your grandfather could do it. You deserve to see the thing if that's your desire.

Clearly the Rowan had no desire to view the escape pod, though that was all he sensed. No trace of her rancour and anger of last night was perceivable.

'Coffee or tea, Rojer?' she asked, gesturing him to take his place. WERE YOUR DREAMS GOOD? she asked Gil and Kat in clipped 'Dini accents as they took their stools.

VERY GOOD. WE FIT PIECES. NOT FIRST BUT FIRST FOR THE SHIP WHICH RESULTS IN MUCH EXCITEMENT AND PRAISE, Gil replied.

'Ve virr plezz'd,' Kat added not to be outdone in the courtesy department. It had never had much luck with the 'w' sound though Gil managed well enough. 'Good fun to play Uman gamez.' Kat always leaned on the plural 's'.

A USEFUL GAME, the Rowan replied though the word she employed to express game was 'well-spent free time'.

Rojer drank his coffee and found enough space for one of the delicious breakfast rolls that his grandmother said had been 'ported in only an hour before. His grandfather talked of the latest arrivals to the Denebian cousins and several recent pairings. He asked after Afra's nieces and nephews who, with Afra's adroit sponsorship, were finding positions in Talented businesses away from Capella. Rojer found the Capellan relatives dull – at least until they'd been off-world a while. Then they shed what his father called 'methody' ways but not, fortunately, their early childhood training. If his Denebian cousins were wild, outspoken to a fault, his Capellan ones were too prim and restrained.

Certainly nothing more was said about the Hive vessel or the escape pod and the Queen or other problems besetting either the Talented or the Alliance. Breakfast was conducted much as it was at his own home: pleasant, tension-free, easing into the stresses of the day.

Linking her arm through her husband's, the Rowan led the way back to the yard and the two personnel carriers cradled there. The smaller one was Jeff's and he'd 'port himself to the Blundell Tower which was the immense FT&T administrative headquarters on Earth.

Jeff and the Rowan saw Afra, Rojer and the 'Dinis settled in their capsule.

Who's making the 'port? the Rowan asked.

Rojer, Afra replied, with a solemn wink at his son.

Catch the platform bay from my mind, Rojer. This is where

you'll view that place. She apotheosized 'that place' in a dismissive tone but then he'd been forewarned of her attitude so he 'looked' deeply and 'saw' the area and the cradles available to visitors. The military police had their own docking facility.

Rojer could feel the Callisto generators picking up revolutions. He suppressed the slight nervousness he felt at performing the 'port in the presence of both grandparents but if he was able, he was able. And he'd do it. He did: the Heinlein Base vivid in his mind's eye.

Though, of course, he did not land *in* the base: he set their carrier down in the orbiting platform that was held a hundred metres above. The platform looked like a quick assembly job and Rojer remembered to check the small panel of the carrier that monitored exterior conditions. There was plenty of air and the clatter of nailed boots on metal flooring as someone rushed to check on them.

Talents Afra and Rojer Lyon as expected, his father both thought and said.

'Yes, sir, right on!' was the shouted acknowledgement. 'I'll just open the hatch for you. Ladder's in place.'

They heard the scraping and the hatch opened.

Nice of you two to come, said a second voice laughingly and Rojer recognized him as his cousin, Roddie Eagle.

His father gave him a stern look and Rojer made a grimace back, then smoothed his features. Roddie was welcome to guard duty if that's all he was good for.

Enough of that! his father said on the very tightest beam.

Rojer rose, handing his 'Dinis out first so that he'd be sure not to 'leak' his true feelings at encountering Roddie here. When he finally did make eye contact, he was rather surprised to see that scrawny, pimple-faced Roddie was a clean-shaven, fresh-faced young man of about his height, neatly dressed in an Alliance uniform and wearing the bars of a first marine lieutenant.

201

'I guess you all hadn't heard,' Roddie said, smiling a welcome. 'You've been away the past week. I can't say I like being constantly sting-pzzted all the time – not at the level that Queen is projecting – but it's the place to meet *everyone*!' And he laughed. GOOD DREAMS, GRL, KTG. RDI SHARED YOUR DREAMS BUT NO PIECES. 'Real glad you succeeded, Roj. And boy, your placement of that pod was smack on the X-mark. Good 'portation! Got a bad case of family pride, I can tell you.'

Rojer was coping with the new improved Rhodri Eagle, so unlike his disagreeable adolescent self.

'We've breakfast laid on, Uncle Afra, Roj, if you're hungry.'

'Thank you, Rhodri,' Afra said with a nod, 'but I don't think either of us could handle a third breakfast this morning.'

Roddie grinned affably. 'Yes, that's one disadvantage to 'portation. You meet yourself coming and going, so to speak. This way. Getting here before breakfast—' And Roddie chuckled. His humour, Rojer decided, had not altered all that much: still heavy-handed. '—you've avoided the crowds. And we've had them. Thank you, Sergeant,' he said to the man guarding the entrance to the main section of the platform. 'They tell me we'll have more permanent quarters shortly. These are stripped down basic but they suffice.' Roddie led them down the corridor and Rojer noticed that all his baby fat had been converted to a trim muscular shape. He was, however, a finger or two taller and that pleased him. 'I'll take you right away to the main viewer room. It's got full screens of the base. She won't be able to move anywhere without observation. That is, if she ever comes out!'

'She's still alive?' Rojer asked.

'Oh yes. We've sensors on the hull, you know, and sounds are being picked up all the time. What she's doing with all those scratching and stroking noises we can't gather. Nothing we have will penetrate the hull. We did detect that she must have sampled the atmosphere. But that happened at the end of the first day. Here we are!'

The large room they entered had a plasglas viewplate from floor to ceiling directly aligned with the escape pod, a hundred metres below, but optically the glas was altered to produce a tri-d effect that made the observer feel he was no more than a few feet from the pod. Screens gave other views and an auxiliary tier of smaller screens would be activated when the Queen exited the pod and began using the buildings.

'She appears to prefer a higher temperature than we humans like, though 'Dinis would be comfortable enough in 32 degrees Celsius. We've increased the ambient temperature in the base. Blrg, the 'Dini specialist, hypothesized two days ago that she won't make a move until the pod's oxygen is exhausted. I kinda go along with that.' Roddie smiled modestly. 'The pod would have had only so much oxygen even in that generous-sized lifeboat, for some of the cubic volume must be occupied by food and other necessities. At that you may be very lucky indeed. Three estimates for her to come out have already been passed: the experts favour her supply being exhausted some time today. Can you hang around?'

'We have time to hand,' Afra said, to Rojer's intense delight.

It'd be awful, Rojer thought, to have had the chance to see her emerge and not be able to do so.

Not that your timing's been off at all this past week, Rojer. Except for hunting, his father added privately.

Rojer 'pathed a repentant grimace. His cousin then showed them the amenities and facilities of the installation: they were sparse enough for the twenty men and three officers assigned here.

'A larger ready room's being 'ported in this week, more sanitary units, a larger kitchen though we get fresh stuff 'ported in daily. I'd put in a special order for breakfast buns. Sorry you've no appetite,' and there were traces of the young Roddie in the patronizing grin he gave Rojer.

'Maybe later, if there are any left. Wouldn't want to deprive you,' and Rojer managed to keep his tone light and pleasant.

They returned to the viewing room where more technicians were on duty, analysing tapes and discussing print-out.

'Lieutenant, we've a party of twelve asking permission for an hour's viewing about—' The corporal broke off abruptly as a loud clatter issued from the speakers. His eyes went wide, his mouth worked and he pointed frantically to the window.

Rojer and his father had been turned towards the speaker but they looked back and, as one, recoiled slightly from the view on the magnified plasglas.

The pod hatch had blown out and rattled about on the plascrete surface. First, one long spiny, oddly jointed limb appeared, slender pointed digits closed about the frame on one side, then another. The limb was a burnished deep coppery red, covered with fine hairs that Rojer thought might be sensitive: maybe he just *thought* they moved. Four more arms came forward to support the body slowly emerging. Then a 'foot' appeared on the sill. Someone had the presence of mind to alter a spotlight and catch the form framed just inside the hatch.

Rojer took firm hold of his nerves and his over-full stomach as, slowly, the tall, segmented creature emerged: its nether region a swollen tear-drop, nipping into a narrow joining to a long thin upper torso. Three sets of arms were spaced along this torso, and two sets of 'legs', one pair moving forward while the other supported the immense bulge of the lower body. A triangle with bulging eye sockets at the top of the thin upper torso had to be the head, and from the top of that multiple antennae waved furiously.

Its coloration, more than its form, captured eye, mind and attention, for the Queen was the most beautiful shades of shimmering deep coppery, burgundy red, blues and greens, like the blossom sheath of the Siberian iris his mother grew in the garden at Aurigae. The spotlight caressed undertones from her body parts, from the flat surfaces of the oddly jointed limbs, from what appeared to be the vestigial wings joined to the upper torso at what would be shoulder-height, running down to the nipped-in waist and half-opened over the bulging lower body.

'A praying mantis, that's what she's like,' his father said softly as the creature remained in the hatchway.

'Like an actress waiting for her cue,' was Roddie's unexpected comment.

'She's afraid!' Rojer blurted out, surprising himself and everyone mesmerized by her appearance.

IT SHOULD BE DESTROYED, Gil said with such fervour that Rojer had formed a sharp reprimand before he caught his father's quick head shake. IT HAS DESTROYED MANY MRDINI.

NOT THAT ONE, GRL, his father replied mildly.

It is alone and afraid, Rojer thought and shook his head to dispense with pity for this member of a dangerously predatory species.

Then, without any grace, the Queen dropped to her six upper limbs and crawled out of the pod. She showed more grace when she stood erect on the four lower limbs and turned her head slowly in a full circle. With great deliberation then, she waddled, again ungainly, towards the mounds of fresh vegetables and plants that had been replaced daily just beyond the pod. Setting back on her hind legs which Rojer thought ended in suction pads, she daintily conveyed food, hand over hand, to an orifice that opened in the triangular head. Some hands discarded samples from time to time and Roddie alerted a corporal – for the viewing room was now full of the station's personnel – to make notes of what she rejected. She ate fruits, rind, skin and pith, but carefully put aside seeds and pits. She rejected grasses, including wheat, rye and oat, though she sampled all that had been provided, ate tubers, leaf vegetables of all kinds, and sugar cane, legumes and pulses. She did not eat rice. She ate steadily through the piles and then sat.

She sat and sat and sat and did not so much as flourish an antenna or the feelers on her limbs or blink her eyes, settle her wings or give any further indication that she had moved. Rojer thought she'd stuffed herself with breakfast. How long had she been without any food, he wondered.

The twelve visitors who just missed the spectacle were horribly disappointed at such inertia and one oafish man insisted that Captain Waygella, Roddie's superior who had not missed the emergence, do something to stimulate her. The captain refused but she did set the tapes of the event to automatic replay on the main viewscreen.

When a second visitation was said to be scheduled, Afra, Rojer and the 'Dinis made a determined move to leave. The captain asked Roddie to accompany them to the bay and greet the new lot.

'Made a tape for you to take back to Aunt Damia and the others,' Roddie said, passing it to Afra as they reached the bay.

'That's very thoughtful of you, Rhodri.'

'Not at all. The corporal'll be copying that sequence all day. I've been 'porting 'em out by the dozen to Aunt Rowan to shift to everyone who needs to know,' and Roddie grinned wryly, 'and Primes need to know, don't they?' Unexpectedly he nodded at Rojer, for the first time accepting Rojer's higher rating.

'Thoughtful of you all the same, Rhodri,' Afra said.

Rojer murmured a thank you as well because the old Roddie certainly wouldn't have been so generous. Life in the Alliance Guards had certainly improved him.

They got into their carrier, made sure the 'Dinis were harnessed properly.

Generator's up, ready for your push, Roddie said.

Do it, Rojer, his father said. *If my time sense hasn't failed me, we should be home in time for breakfast.*

DAD!

206

10

You're back! Good, Damia said cheerfully. *Come have some breakfast.*

Rojer groaned as he unbuckled and his father chuckled.

Little breakfast was actually eaten that morning, and most became cold as the entire household and Tower staff watched the tape of the Queen's emergence.

'So that's what they really look like,' Damia said. 'She's rather spectacularly coloured.'

'I think she's beautiful!' Zara said, almost defensively.

Fok and Tri had been clicking softly to themselves, their pelt colours darkening with what Rojer recognized as their aggressive shade. Gil and Kat were not as bad but Zara's two, Plg and Dzl, were at first speechless: then crept close, not to Zara, but to Fok and Tri to be comforted.

After her remark, Zara watched with such a wary, scared expression on her face that Damia moved closer to her. Rojer 'heard' reassuring words which confused him since his mother wouldn't be projecting that on a wide enough band to include him.

Rojer began to wonder if Zara should watch the rest of

the tape. He found it affecting enough when the Queen adopted her static position. Zara was such a sensitive empath, lots of things that didn't bother him or the others made her fret. At the conclusion, when the Queen became stationary – and the tape wound on and on with that scene – Zara burst into tears and fled the room. Damia cast a quick anxious look at Afra and then followed her. Zara's 'Dinis did not. Fok and Tri conferred for a moment and left the room, too.

When the tape finished, Keylarion, Xexo and Herault, the station manager, wanted to see it again. So Afra keyed for a repeat.

Rojer slipped out then. He didn't quite know what to do: should he tell Zara that he had felt sadness and the Queen's loneliness, too. He doubted his mother would find that a suitable reaction: but it was genuine. But Zara might be reassured to know she wasn't alone in her sensitive response to the Queen.

As he started up the stairs, his mother was coming down and her expression told him she was very worried. But she cleared her face and smiled down at him, pausing beside him on the step. To his surprise, she touched his cheek.

'I'm very proud of you, Rojer. Now I'm glad that Father seconded you. He's very pleased, too. Even about your fussing with the pieces!' She gave him a droll grin.

'Mother, is Zara all right?'

'You're sweet, Rojer. She'll *be* all right,' and Damia gave a heavy sigh. 'She's just getting used to being womanly and is a bit . . . volatile right now.'

'Oooooh,' and Rojer drew out the soft exclamation as he understood. Then he shook his head. 'Laria wasn't!'

'Laria has an entirely different personality. A much stronger Talent. In fact,' and Damia let out a sigh, 'I'm delighted you're back. What with menstruation hitting her so hard, she's been useless in the Tower for all she's a T-1. I've never heard menstruation causing a dysfunction in Talent before, but I suppose there's always an exception.'

Damia sighed again. 'I hope you and your father are rested enough to push out some big-daddies this morning. Morag was a great help – at least with the Tower,' and Rojer didn't need a 'path to realize that Morag had probably been acting the maggot. She could be quite domineering and Zara was too pliable to resist her.

'How much is there to 'port, Mother?' Rojer asked crisply. 'I need to work off several breakfasts. Will you need me to hunt?'

'A lot and yes. We'll warm up the generators while the others have a second gawk at that raree tape you brought back.'

Aware now of her animosity towards the Hive Queen, he was glad he hadn't revealed his private reaction.

Afra joined them in the Tower and brought the rest of the Tower staff with him.

'Did you hear Xexo saying that three more pieces have been added on to your start?' Afra said as he took his couch.

'No, but I'm glad of it. And it wasn't *my* start, Dad. Seventeen other people found it, too.'

Damia grinned at her son, then nodded for them to get set for the first 'portation. There was a backlog to send so they didn't clear the loads until almost lunchtime. Rojer's stomach gave embarrassing growls as they made their way back to the house.

Morag had lunch ready, looking slightly smug and officious, Rojer thought, and decided to hunt her legs off in the afternoon; take her down a peg or two. Morag could be a pain in the neck when she tried to compete with her siblings. There was really no need for her to do that. Of Zara there was no sign, though she should have been helping. Kaltia and Ewain had fed all the Coonies, Slithers, Darbuls and horses, mucked out the stables, and evidently still had time to replay the tape for they were watching it again before lunch.

'Where's Zara?' Afra asked, glancing about.

'Leave her, Afra,' Damia replied, and obviously added a private explanation for Afra said no more about his missing daughter.

Deliberately leaving all the 'Dinis home, Rojer took Morag out with him, taking the short cut – which meant hard and careful riding – to the next valley. He knew of a couple of scurrier dens and rabbit warrens which he hoped had remained his secret. They were difficult to access, which was all to the good. At first Morag was delighted to show him how good a rider she was and kept her pony at Saki's tail on the way up. On the narrow decline trail, especially where the open side dropped hundreds of metres down to scree, she was not quite so cocky. They had to go through stiff underbrush but he'd put on his leathers and she was only in a shirt. She was definitely sweaty, branch and thorn marked, and not at all as smug when they reached the ravine at the bottom. By the time Rojer reached his destination, she was thoroughly chastened but determined to endure.

Rojer gave her credit for that on the way home, with ten braces apiece of avians, rabbits and scurriers, which had the most delicious flesh if you caught them young enough. Rojer had. He relented enough to take an easier if longer route back but he made that seem deliberate, rather than considerate, because that track passed by stands of edible greens and bushes of early plummy-fleshed rindfruits. They arrived home late afternoon laden down with provender for the next three days – unless they had unexpected guests.

Although the miners' representatives, Yugin and Mexalgo, had come to collect copies of the tape, they left after the most cursory of visits with profuse thanks. They couldn't wait to view the tape and see the enemy, they said, and on hearing that, Zara ran from the room, stifling sobs. The miners did not notice, being on their way to the door.

Zara! Easy, sis, Rojer called. *I'll help her, Mother,* he added and followed her.

210

She was in Laria's old room, having moved out of the one she had shared with her two younger sisters. Rojer noticed that neither of his 'Dinis accompanied him.

No, Rojer, leave it! she said in a voice that was broken by her mental anguish.

Sis, would it help if I told you I thought the Queen looked lonely and sad, as well as beautiful?

But you were there! You watched! And you said nothing?

He entered the room and saw her, tear-streaked face, rebellious expression, facing him in an attitude of defence.

'Aw now, Zara,' he said tenderly but she held up one hand to restrain him.

'Don't you dare "aw now, Zara" me,' and she sniffed back tears. 'I get enough of that from Mother. She just won't "see" or "feel" what I'm going through. And if you come out with some male gibberish about the time of month, I swear I'll lash you!'

Rojer hadn't any such platitudes in mind and he wasn't alarmed by her threat though it was one of the first he'd ever heard her make. She was the gentlest of his sisters and usually self-effacing and acquiescent: hardly surprising amid seven other strong sibling personalities. Rojer perched on one edge of her worktop and folded his arms, subtly projecting affection and reassurance.

'And don't try that either,' she said, rubbing tears away.

'You know, you look more like Grandmother Rowan than any of us.'

She narrowed her eyes. 'Don't try misdirection either, Rojer Lyon!'

'I'm not, actually,' he said in a brisker voice, 'but I had breakfast with Grandmother just this morning so I can see the resemblance very clearly. You *are* more like her than Laria or Morag. You haven't seen Grandmother in a while but you'd be the last one to see the likeness. I wonder if Dad would.'

But Zara was not going to be distracted. 'She'd want to kill the Queen, too, wouldn't she?'

211

'Grandmother's not . . . ' and Rojer shrugged, 'pacific at any time. You know that,' and he grinned. He got an ironic shrug from his sister. 'But I'm not talking about Grandmother's reaction to the Queen, only how much you look like her. By the way, there is a group of humans who feel that we should at least make an attempt to understand the Hiver viewpoint.'

'But you don't think much of them,' she retorted, angrily defiant, irritably pushing back her own silver wing of hair.

'I didn't say that and I don't even project it, sis. But I did want to tell you that you're not the only one to have different perceptions. *I*—' And Rojer jabbed a thumb into his breast bone. '—thought she was beautiful, too.' He couldn't quite admit that he, too, had felt she was lonely and afraid.

Zara narrowed her eyes. 'Half Aurigae City wants her publicly . . . *murdered* . . . torn apart limb from limb. Did you know that?'

'No, but it doesn't surprise me, considering the source,' and Rojer smiled condescendingly. 'Look, sis, I do respect your reactions, your feelings about the Queen. I had them myself . . . '

'But you hadn't the guts to make them *known*!' Zara flashed back at him, her eyes glinting just like Grandmother Rowan's had but with a different cause.

'Oddly enough, not all the 'Dinis want her killed. They do want to . . . '

'Probe, pry and drive that poor creature mad, finding out how she works, how she produces her young. They've already *killed* half the larvae Thian found. Oh, I wish he hadn't. Oh, how I wish he hadn't!'

'Sis, you're going off in all directions to no purpose at all,' Rojer said, becoming slightly exasperated by her capriciousness. 'You're not a Talent for nothing. There are more ways of doing things than blasting out left, right and centre. That's not like you anyway. Get in touch with the other like-minded folk. I'll help you there without Mom and Dad knowing. See what you can do to help *change* public opinion. It can be changed, you know. And you'd make a damn fine lobbyer. That way you can *help* the Queen.'

'She'll never be released.' Zara was not about to be consoled. Rojer thought she was enjoying this wallow in sentiment. 'She'll die in that awful place, friendless, childless, alone, with her home all blown up . . . ' Zara put her hands to her face, weeping desperately again.

Despite 'sensing' that she was working herself up, Rojer couldn't stand his pretty sister in tears. He took her into his arms, and she leaned exhaustedly against him, crying more piteously than ever.

I'll take over, Rojer, his mother said as she came down the hall.

No need, Mom. I can handle it. I'll soothe her. You know I always could get her to sleep when she was a baby.

Yes, you could, at that. There's a strong affinity between the pair of you like— Damia broke off and Rojer knew she had been about to name Larak.

There is, Mom, so let me use it now to calm her down.

It took time, and it meant Rojer had to forgo the few free hours he had hoped to spend with the Hive pieces but Zara was more important. He consoled her with lavish affection, support and understanding, until, spent with such an emotional storm, she fell asleep.

When she appeared the next morning, she was calm and her usual self-effacing self though there was a sadness in her eyes that wrenched Rojer's heart.

She's over her menses, now, Damia said very privately to him. *Thank you for calming her down. You're a sweet boy as well as a clever one.*

Sweet? Rojer replied in disgust. *Zara's too tender-hearted for her own good.*

His mother continued, but not to him, to his father and on such a subject that Rojer was surprised to be included.

Then he realized, he *wasn't* included: he was catching a private conversation he ought not to be able to 'hear'. He'd've shielded had his mother not been discussing Zara with his father.

She's a dysfunctional Prime, Afra, Damia was saying with deep regret and distress. *Father can't expect her to do Tower service. She'd wilt under the stress. And with everyone knowing she's a T-1, they'll expect her to go to a Tower.*

Everyone is not your father, nor Gollee Gren who has a lot more to do with placing Talents these days than Jeff. Certainly we must inform Gollee of our anxiety and our assessment. Zara can be trained for other duties, less emotionally laden. She's got good thrust . . .

Erratic as her sympathies . . . His mother's tone was peevish.

Well, I'll admit that I felt a pang of sympathy for the Queen . . .

YOU?

Rojer was equally startled, and relieved.

Yes, I. It's an attitude that won't endear me to many, but to be honest, Damia, and we have always been honest in our private thoughts, there was something pathetic about that Queen! Pathetic, awkward, and . . . valiant, I think one could say.

There was a long pause of silence. *If one isn't swayed by conditioning,* his mother admitted slowly, *and unfortunately, I am biased about Hivers – I can't help it – one could call her brave to leave the pod. Of course, she had to, didn't she? No oxygen, no food.*

Rojer nearly cheered to hear his mother admit this.

I worry more about Zara's 'Dinis, Damia went on. *They do not understand her perversion . . .*

Not perverse surely, Damia. Wayward, or maybe deviant, but not perverse. She's an extremely sensitive girl . . . I'll work on reassuring her 'Dinis.

Oh, I think they'll pull round once they're over the shock of hearing Zara defending the Queen.

I don't think she's defending the Queen so much as

empathizing with her. And she's thrown up a very tight mental shield about her thoughts. We must allow her the privacy we always permit other Talents, Afra said.

She's not adult yet.

But nearly. I seem to remember . . .

Afra!

There was such an intimacy in their minds that Rojer hastily closed off the intriguing conversation.

That mental exchange was not the only one he inadvertently 'overheard' in the next few days for there were 'pathed messages filtering in from all the Primes. Some of the messages Rojer would rather not have heard: others were curious and fascinating. Especially the badinage his mother enjoyed with her father, or her pithy remarks to her brother, Jeran, and her sister, Cera, both of them Towered Primes. Rojer now caught Laria's reports from Clarf. Those he was glad Zara couldn't hear.

There was a faction on Clarf that mirrored the Aurigae City wish for summary execution as public as possible.

He also caught all the reports from Heinlein Base. The Queen had remained stationary for seventy-six hours, ignoring replenishments of the foods she had been seen to eat. Xenobiologists and xenozoologists were doing their best to be sure the offerings covered all nutritional requirements for they were certain she would be laying the eggs that strained her lower body to the point where striations or cracks were visible in the bulb of it.

There had been several more failed attempts in laboratories within the Alliance to vitalize the larvae and their numbers were dwindling rapidly. That was when someone suggested that perhaps the remaining larvae should be sent to Heinlein Base in the hope that the Queen could hatch them. Perhaps she required attendants for the egg-laying and, with these missing, she would be unable to function.

Some of the larvae of each type were therefore 'ported into the base, to see if their appearance would activate the Queen. Men seemed to dominate the push to give the Queen the larvae. Women seemed less inclined to sympathize with her condition. For, apart from eating again, the Queen had done nothing else, though her egg-filled bulb continued to expand.

However, when the decision to give her some of the three types of larvae was implemented, Rojer got Zara off by herself to give her what he felt should be good news.

'The least they can do,' was all Zara said in a disgusted tone, though, for the rest of the day, Rojer thought she was more cheerful. Certainly she was on hand to see a screening of the transfer. The scene was even more dramatic than the Queen's emergence.

The Queen rushed to the larvae, running her upper limbs across each sac, emitting a low hum. She deftly turned each larva so she could inspect all round, then she awkwardly swept a path to the nearest building. This, the experts said, had to be some sort of instinctive behaviour for the paving had been brushed clear of any dust or grit when the base was cleaned for her occupancy. She ran back to collect the day's green offerings and piled them in the big entrance hall. When she'd done that, she patiently rolled each larva to its new site, with many pattings and turnings and hummings. The day's efforts seemed to exhaust her for she resumed the immobile post-prandial position, propped up by her hind limbs.

Biologists and zoologists – including two eminent human orthopterists – argued over what sort of 'bedding' would suit her needs, and chose straw and wood shavings, as well as several types of artificial chips, bits and bobbles. A quantity of fine artificial 'wax' and natural tallow were added to the offerings, in case she was more apiarian than insectoid. When she settled on the shavings, heaping them in mounds over the larvae, more was sent in. Rojer had a private smile for the things Cousin Roddie had to do as the Observation Talent.

Zara brightened at each new concession granted the

216

'prisoner' and kept within viewing distance of the screen, waiting for the next development. Her mother let her because, as Damia privately admitted to Afra, she was more use in the house than in the Tower. Zara was certainly not the only one so involved in what happened at Heinlein Base. Queen-watching had replaced piece-finding as a galactic pastime.

Two mornings later a frantic call from Zara reached them as they left the Tower. Damia nodded once at Afra and Rojer and they all 'ported into the main room.

Oh, look! Just look! She's laying! Zara cried, frantically gesturing at the screen. Morag, Ewain and Kaltia erupted from their rooms and thundered down the steps. For once, Damia didn't reprimand them.

The Queen had propped herself up on all frontal limbs, her bulb half-hidden in the mound of shavings which seemed to heave and enlarge.

'Can't they allow her any privacy!' Zara demanded, her eyes vivid with her angry protest.

'We can't see anything, Zara,' Ewain said, flopping down in the nearest chair with a disgusted expression on his face. 'And we watch the Coonies and the Darbuls when they give birth. What's wrong with watching her?'

'Ewain's right, you know, Zara,' Afra said placidly, 'we see nothing of the process itself: merely the result of eggs.' But he cast a look at his daughter, adding, *Your sensitivity is commendable if unnecessary, Zara. Insectoids do not share human feelings of embarrassment. In her Hive, helpers and attendants would be swarming over her at such a time. Privacy is probably a hardship for her.*

Rojer knew he wasn't supposed to hear that private remark and he shook his head, wondering why he was getting all these unexpected confidences. But Zara plainly had only extrapolated what *she* might feel during the birth process, and not the species' differences. She gradually subsided.

217

'Biology Teach's doing a special on orthopterus, on account of the Queen,' Ewain said casually, eyes glued to the steady rise of the shaving-topped mound. 'It said insects lay enormous quantities of eggs at a time. They'll be bursting out of the bedding any moment now.' They did, shiny white covered pearls, hundreds of them. 'Wonder what variety she's laying now?' Ewain continued conversationally. 'She must've been pregnant – or whatever Hivers get – egg-full? – before her ship was wrecked. There wasn't anything else in the pod with her.'

'Some insects eat the male after mating,' Morag said, casting a quick glance at her sister. 'Maybe that's what caused all the scrabbling we heard in the pod . . . '

'That is quite enough, Morag,' Afra said firmly.

'But, Dad, Biology Teach said we got to observe the Queen for our project,' Morag protested, her voice almost the whine her parents deplored in her.

'Then observe, but keep your comments for your class hour.'

Morag obeyed. After such a putdown from her father, Rojer knew she wouldn't dare provoke Zara any further. Anyway, Zara seemed oblivious to Morag's taunting, for her gaze was glued to the screen, her expressive face tender. Her 'Dinis were seated close beside her but they apparently were not picking up on her emotions. Rojer made a tentative probe at her but she was shielded so tightly he doubted that either of his parents could have 'heard' her thoughts and feelings just then.

It did take the Queen hours to finish her laying. Rojer left when he got bored and spent an hour with Xexo, trying to build on his *Beijing* success.

There were new pieces. The *KLTL* had calculated the point at which the Hive ship was probably hit, and quartered the area. Rojer wondered if that had been Thian's bright idea for it had produced quite a lot of flotsam and jetsam: some of it too twisted or melted to be useful, but each fragment, splinter and scrap was gathered up.

218

There were some big sections of hull, warped and melted but the art of reconstruction might be able to render the original from the remainder.

Neither Xexo nor Rojer was as interested in the bigger pieces as the smaller ones that had remained intact, easier to match and piece together. These newest pieces Xexo and Rojer first sorted into the appropriate subdivisions where the most likely matches were possible.

'If only this one didn't have that little hooky edge,' Rojer said, having vainly tried to mate two very likely looking bits.

'Hooky place?' Xexo flipped the bit he'd been fiddling with to Rojer.

'That's it! That fits a treat!' Rojer said, crowing with delight. Xexo rushed around the table to see and grimaced.

'And I handed it over to you!'

'I give you leave to report it, though!' Rojer was quite willing to defer. Lately his name had come up in his parents' conversations and he'd closed up, rather than hear them discuss him. They had such high standards, standards he might not be meeting. He wished he hadn't become so acute a telepath.

When Xexo returned from making that call, he was grinning from ear to ear. 'Brace yourself for a surprise or two, lad,' he said but refused to explain. 'Oh, it won't hurt you to simmer a bit. This fit's original, by the bye. I'm the first to report it. And I made it a joint discovery. Only fair, Roj. Now, let's see if *my* hunch is right because I think we've got part of a gyroscope here. I know it sounds far fetched because gyroscopic drives are ancient history in engineering usage . . . '

'Gyroscope! Of course it is!' Rojer cried, reaching across the board for half a dozen shards and scraps which, with little fussing, came together into a whole ring. Xexo's eyes bulged at the result.

'They won't believe this: two sets in one day . . . '

'Well, we always thought the first match would be the hardest . . . '

'You report this one on your own, Rojer Lyon!' Xexo said, turning the band. 'Might not be part of a drive. They might have used it as a compass leveller or . . . Go report it.' And Xexo shooed him out of the basement.

Rojer reported it in as unassuming manner as he could, relieved when he got an automated answering service. It asked for details and he gave piece numbers and the sequence in which they fitted together. He was asked his name and the time of the match and he was thanked for prompt reportage. The nice thing about machines, Rojer thought, was that they couldn't be impressed by rank. They took you as you were!

He and Xexo tried to build in their match but then Rojer's time sense alerted him that his leisure time was over. He and Morag had to exercise the ponies and their 'Dinis wanted to come along. Damia asked them to get more greens, if they saw any ready for picking, but they didn't need to hunt. Ewain and Kaltia came along, stuck up on their ponies with their young 'Dinis still able to ride pillion. Zara stayed at home, glancing up at the screen and the Queen half-covered with shavings and eggs.

When Rojer and his group returned to the house, Zara was once again in floods of tears.

'She might be dead. Has anyone looked? They don't report the sensor readings. She's exhausted, delivering all those eggs, Mother. Oh someone has to help her! I'll call Grandmother Isthia myself if you won't.'

'You will not disturb your grandmother. Either one of them. And you will stop this hysterical nonsense immediately.'

Rojer recoiled slightly at the force of his mother's peripheral 'pathing. She was both trying to calm Zara and making certain the girl could not project a call. Even Damia couldn't 'path all the way to Deneb without some assistance. For that matter, Rojer was on hand –

but his sympathies were oddly on Zara's side.

'Ah c'mon, sis,' he began in a drawl, sauntering across the room to them, 'Look there now! They just put food right by her palps. Roddie's getting good at making deliveries.'

'Roddie . . . ' Mention of their cousin surprised Zara and she blinked her tear-filled eyes and looked back at the screen, seeing the neat piles of food in easy reach. 'How d'you know Roddie did that?'

He sensed that it mattered that a member of her family, sidereal or not, was involved in actively succouring the Queen.

'He's the only Talent up there, isn't he, Mother?'

Damia agreed with him vocally and mentally, glad of any diversion for her daughter's over-sensitivity.

'I know he 'ports the fresh food in daily. And, if you'd stop and think a minute, she has been assisted in every way as soon as her needs were seen. Like the shavings. Every xenbio and xenzoo's watching the screen as closely as you. Stop fretting so much. And if you're really worried, I don't think Roddie'd mind if you shot him a query or two. Do you, Mother?'

Damia regarded him a moment longer and Rojer knew he'd surprised her.

'If it would ease your anxieties, Zara, I don't think Roddie would mind. But you're not to bombard him with inane questions,' Damia said, raising a stern finger. 'He has duties to perform and he can't be distracted any more than your father and I, even if he isn't a Tower Talent.'

'Mother, you never liked Roddie,' Zara said, picking up on that aspersion.

Rojer felt his mother relax: her remark had been a deliberate attempt to keep Zara diverted from the Queen. Zara had always perversely stood up for Roddie, simply because her brothers and sisters detested him.

'Look, Zar,' Morag said, 'she's eating!'

Zara was instantly back in her chair, eyes glued to

the Queen's activity. Her movements were slow, but she'd laboured mightily and she would be drained. Rojer watched until he saw her carefully putting seeds and pips to one side and then he went to seek his father. With everyone else involved in something else, he'd have a chance to speak to his father who was taking an evening swim, without being interrupted. He descended to the pool level and shucked out of his clothes.

They swam a companionable few laps and then Afra caught the edge and turned to his son.

'Something's on your mind and, for the first time in your life, I can't get a hint of it,' Afra said.

Rojer grinned, having the opening he needed.

'That's just it, Dad, I can block and I am also hearing a lot of exchanges that I don't believe I should. But I swear, Dad, I'm not *trying* to hear.'

Afra lazily swirled his free hand and both feet to keep balanced in the water and he smiled thoughtfully.

'I'd say that you were coming into your full strength as a Talent. Your mother and I thought you might after the pod transfer. It was about time for you. You confirmed it by 'porting us neatly to Heinlein and then back here.'

'You were in on those . . . Weren't you, Dad?'

Afra chuckled, the sound reverberating in the pool.

'No, actually I wasn't. I let you do the work.'

'I did those 'ports all by myself?'

'I'm surprised you didn't realize it. I assure you that I wasn't involved.'

'But I thought you were the focus . . . '

'Only for lifting the pod.'

'Then . . . '

Afra nodded. 'Your mother would rather that we tell you tonight after the younger ones are in bed.'

But the news, and his father's pride in its purport, was so vivid that Rojer caught it.

'They have? I'm to join the squadron?' he cried jubilantly. Then Rojer gasped. 'I should have listened to Thian!'

222

'You've already conducted yourself quite adequately on the *Beijing*, Rojer. Do you think you can contain yourself until later, when we can discuss this in my study?'

'Sure, Dad, sure!'

But it was hard not to let his joy escape. Zara, being so sensitive, caught the edge of his elation but no specifics. So he deliberately regaled everyone at dinner with the news of the double find, and let her believe that success caused his jubilant mood.

The youngsters went to bed and then Zara, probably with some prompting from her mother for she started yawning much earlier than usual, went off to bed.

Damia winked and led the way into Afra's study which was completely shielded.

'You've been very good this evening, dear, and we appreciate it because the news is not generally known. Father said there's a hold on it. But the B-Squadron which went to track down one of the three Hive ships that did escape the nova has been located.'

Afra took up the narration. 'There're three ships in Squadron B: the 'Dini *KTTS* . . . '

'That's one of the class Aurigae ore built . . . '

'Yes, and so are the two human cruisers, the *Arapahoe* and the *Genesee*. This may be premature but the High Councils want to have a Prime out there, to relay messages. Your brother has done so well in that capacity that, even though you are not quite sixteen, your grandfather, and Gollee, feel that you are able for the duties and responsibilities.'

'Dad, I can't teach like Thian could . . . '

'That wouldn't be one of your duties. The complement of the *KTTS* have enough Basic, and both human captains have sufficient 'Dini for necessary exchanges. It's the heft of your Talent that's required.'

'Oh,' and Rojer grinned. 'Stevedoring' was a long-standing family joke. 'But why, Dad, might it be premature?'

223

'The squadron has discovered that the Hiver ship is decelerating. Their apparent destination is a G-type star system. When the message capsule was sent, the Hiver was closing with the heliopause. It also had not despatched either scouts or probes. It is thought that this system may contain a Hive colony.'

'Wow!'

'Precisely. A reasonable enough assumption since this G-type star is not that far, spatially speaking, from the Hive homeworld. The feeling is that these are refugees, not colonists.'

'Wow! And we're going to attack it?'

'Ah, now that has not been discussed, much less decided. Considerable reconnaissance is required. In the matter of how Hive colony worlds are protected, even the 'Dini High Council has no expertise. That star system is galactically opposite to Clarf, north in a manner of speaking and rimward.'

'And that's why a Prime is needed to 'port the findings of reconnaissance probes and scouts!'

'Exactly! To expedite data delivery and receive necessary orders. You have always been discreet, Rojer.'

Rojer let out a sigh, only then realizing he had been holding his breath. 'I'll be a clam with my shields at maximum.'

'Not quite, dear,' his mother said. 'You'll be on call at all times, but there are no Talents above an eight on either of the human ships. So you can't be read.'

'You'll be going out with supply drones which are badly needed,' his father added.

'I don't mind what I go with so long as I go.'

Afra placed his hand on Rojer's shoulder and gripped it tightly, allowing his pride to flow through. Rojer glanced at his mother. There was a slightly sad look in her eye that made Rojer appreciate his luck was her regret.

'Mom!' He reached out to touch her cheek and she held his hand to her face briefly. He sensed that she had

224

accepted, if reluctantly, the disposition of yet another of her children.

'It's all right with me, too, Rojer. But for you, it does mean deferring your training in engineering. According to Xexo, you've shown considerable aptitude in that area. And you aren't really the staid sort that would thrive on Tower life.'

'I'd do it, Mother, you know that.'

Damia lifted her eyebrows. 'You've had little choice. Nor more had I at your age.'

'But, Mother, it's not a question of choice, is it? Talent has responsibilities . . . ' He stopped.

'You learned thoroughly, didn't you?' she said, smiling.

'Yeah, I guess. You brought us up real good, Mom. And we have choices, you know. You're seeing that we do. Even Zara . . . '

'Oh,' and Damia clicked her tongue. 'She is becoming a problem with this mercurial instability . . . '

'She'll be all right,' Afra remarked soothingly, 'though she'll probably surprise all of us eventually.'

'I think so, too, Dad,' Rojer said stoutly, to reassure his mother. And himself. 'Ah, when will I have to go? And do I take Gil and Kat with me?'

'You certainly do. They're only just out of hibernation so they'll be fine. Not that it did Thian's pair any harm to do theirs on Clarf,' and Afra smiled when that remark got a chuckle out of Damia. 'As to when you leave, we'll inform your grandfather that we've asked you and you've consented. It's not going to be easy, but you have Thian's experiences as a guide. You are a civilian and you are to be protected so don't have a fit if someone summarily throws you into an escape pod and tells you to get yourself home. Primes are *not* expendable.'

Rojer grinned, imagining the ruckus his grandparents would make if anything did happen to a Prime grandson.

'We'll keep in touch, too,' Damia said, combing her fingers through the white lock which Rojer kept short.

'We're only a thought away wherever you are.'

'I know, Mom, Dad, but I don't think you ought to tell Zara where I'm going. I think she'd freak out.'

Damia nodded, pursing her lips. 'I must ask Elizara to come visit her namesake. Maybe this is just a phase she's going through. It's not like my family, and certainly not like your father's.'

'All our children are individuals in their own right, Damia.'

'I know!'

11

Captain Osullivan of the *Genesee* himself welcomed Rojer Lyon on board and politely but firmly took control of the courier pouch that Rojer had been sternly charged to deliver only into the captain's hand. His personal carrier, with drones attached like oblong satellites around it, was 'ported by the efforts of Callisto, Earth, Aurigaean and Denebian Primes. That gave Rojer some indication of how very far from his part of the galaxy the B-Squadron was.

A thought away, indeed, he thought. More like a hoarse whisper.

That's all you know about it, young man, said his grandmother's unmistakable voice, fainter than usual but clear. *I can't abide cocky youngsters.* There was, for Rojer's peace of mind, the ripple of amusement in her tone.

The two drones directly obstructing his hatch were shifted and it was opened. Neither he nor his two 'Dinis suffered any untoward effect from the atmosphere on board: the *Genesee*, being the prototype Constellation-class vessel, had an extremely efficient oxygen regeneration program: *sgit* plants played a large part in air filtration.

Rojer shook right hands with the captain: with his left hand, Rojer released the documents pouch to its stated recipient. Osullivan, a tall man in his fifth decade, fit, slightly balding but urbane gave not the slightest reaction, as others behind him did, that such a young person had been entrusted with the courier pouch and had helped bring the drone supplies. The captain then introduced Rojer to the lieutenant who would be his aide while on board. He also issued an invitation for Rojer with Grl and Ktg – whose names he had no trouble pronouncing – to join him and his officers at dinner at 1930 hours. He then excused himself, courier bag clasped tightly to his side, and, nodding right and left to the dawdling crewmembers to get back to their work, left the bay.

Lieutenant junior grade Lin Xing Tsu, a slight, wiry young man with so close a haircut that his sallow scalp showed through his black hair, immediately picked up Rojer's one duffel and led the way to his quarters.

Lin was obviously proud of the *Genesee*, recently commissioned and on her maiden voyage, and described her amenities in glowing detail as they traversed the passageways. As they passed some of the more important features, or Lin indicated which lift to take to reach the gym, sickbay and commissary, Rojer began to feel more assured. He, Gil and Kat were shown into a stateroom, not quite as large as the one Thian had occupied as described by Damia, but certainly not the cramped cabin that had been his brother's first accommodation on the *Vadim*.

'Can I get a little something to eat . . . to tide me over until dinner?' Rojer asked because he had left Aurigae just after breakfast, arrived before lunch at Callisto where the drones were attached to his capsule and arrived after the noon meal on the *Genesee*.

Smiling, Lin inclined his head. 'Sure thing! Considering you brought us several tonnes or more of food, you're entitled to a decent meal. Betcha all the edibles are already in the galley and storage.'

As they made their way back to the mess-hall, Rojer asked, 'Is there a piece table aboard this ship?'

'A peace table?' Lin slowed to glance back over his shoulder in surprise at Rojer. 'We haven't declared war yet. How can we make peace?'

'Not that kind of peace.' Rojer spelled out the correct one. 'You know, Hive ship pieces . . . Putting them together?' His explanation fell on puzzled ears. 'On the *Beijing*, they had all the pieces, in scale of course, of the Hive ship that was caught by the nova shock wave. The one that the *Vadim* squadron found? People are trying to put it back together . . . '

Lin still didn't understand, so while Rojer continued to explain, he glumly realized that he'd have no more chance of participation. By the time this mission ended, the wreck would probably have been totally reconstructed. He'd so wanted to be part of that effort.

'Maybe Lieutenant Gander would know,' Lin said helpfully, 'he's the morale officer.'

'You have seen a tape of the Queen's emergence, haven't you?'

'Queen? Didn't know there were any left on Earth! Or is it Procyon that has a royal family?'

'I'm referring to the Hiver Queen that was found alive in an escape pod.'

'You don't say? A live Hive Queen? Oooh! Wouldn't want to see that!'

'Actually, she's quite beautifully coloured,' Rojer said, speaking in the most diffident manner. This was a warship, chasing a Hiver vessel, and their attitude towards a Hiver Queen would reflect that. 'They've put her in Heinlein Base on Earth's moon.'

'Thought that installation was decommissioned decades ago.'

'It was, but it's been reopened to accommodate the Queen. She can't get out of there.'

'Who'd want to get in?' Lin wanted to know.

'Your ship's really been out of touch,' Rojer said, shaking his head.

'Oh, we know what we need to know,' Lin assured him affably. 'We're more interested in what's likely to happen than what has! Here we are,' he added unnecessarily, for the smell of roasting meat wafted appetizingly along the corridor.

A meal was cheerfully set before him.

'A single zap and you'd never know it wasn't freshly prepared,' the cook's mate said as he was served a piping hot plate. 'We allus has somethin' for the watch. You really a Talent, kid?'

'So they tell me,' Rojer said, grinning. He didn't mind being called a 'kid' by a seaman so grizzled he was probably older than Grandfather Raven. Then Rojer half-goggled at the multi-coloured pictures on the sailor's massive forearms: tattoos, he thought they were called.

'Where'd you get them?' he asked between attempts to cool his food enough to put it in his mouth. The plate had been well zapped.

'Ah, now these, me laddie buck, are the result of a wager . . . ' Settling into the seat opposite Rojer and Lin the mate proceeded to embellish a tale almost as garish as his forearms.

'Mr Lyon here,' Lin began when the tale was over and duly appreciated, 'says they caught a Hiver Queen. Got her locked up on Heinlein Base.'

'Do they?' and the mate was either sceptical or not easily impressed.

'She's laid eggs,' Rojer said, hoping to generate some interest.

'Well, laddie buck, in a month or two, we may see more eggs'n she'll ever lay,' the mate said, rising to his feet. 'Aye, wouldn't doubt we'd see more. That's a Hiver system we're coming to. Knew we'd find one sometime. Glad I've lived to see the day. I'm Denebian, you see, so vengeance is mine! Enjoy your meal.'

'Th . . . thanks, I am.' Mentally Rojer was glad he'd kept his remarks neutral. He was amused, though, that all the startling events he had witnessed recently were unexceptional on the *Genesee*, and philosophically, resigned himself to the situation.

Mother, Father, Damia said, initiating a call to her parents, still at their breakfast on Callisto.

Yes, Damia? her mother replied. *Something is the matter. Jeff, I told you that yesterday when we exchanged Rojer's capsule. And it's . . . Zara?* There was gratifying surprise in the Rowan's tone. *Whatever could be the matter with Zara? She's the most pliable of your lot.*

Not any more, Mother. And quickly Damia conveyed a summary of her daughter's recent aberrant and capricious behaviour. *I don't know where she gets these notions about the Queen . . .*

Unusual that, the Rowan said. *Especially across such distance, and with only a tape to stimulate the reaction . . .*

D'you mean – others have reacted the way Zara has?

Yes, indeed, Jeff put in. *There's a growing minority who feel the Alliance has been authoritarian, peremptory and high-handed. Which is muddle-headed thinking. After all, the creature was humanely rescued from sure death. There was no planet on which she could have landed before oxygen and food supplies ran out. She may be isolated but that's as much for her own good. There've been two attempts to . . . eradicate her from 'human soil' already.*

We hadn't heard about them . . . Damia was indignant. The Queen *was* in responsible protective custody: by observation alone much could be learned from her about others of her species. She wouldn't be released but, on the moon, she was certainly no threat to anyone.

You haven't heard because it's been kept top secret. Young Rhodri is to be commended once more for prompt and effective action, Jeff said.

Mind you, the Rowan added in a terse caustic tone, *there*

231

were a few snide remarks about the prolificacy of plummy jobs held by one particular Denebian family . . .

Damia heard her father's amused chuckle. *Our critics simply fail to appreciate large families: but we're by no means the only Denebian family with phalanxes of progeny. And certainly not one family at that: there're Ravens, Eagles, Cranes, Gwyns, Lyons and a healthy sprinkling of Terran Reidingers, Owenses, Grens, Maus and Thigbits in the top echelons. That isn't really a monopoly – just clever family planning.*

However, the remarks were just short of libel and slander, and decidedly snide, the Rowan said, irritated.

Irrelevant, all of it, Jeff said. *So far the Queen has been cared for to the best of our small knowledge. High Council 'Dinis are in accord with ours that she be treated with care as any prisoner of war. The old Geneva Conventions – and I don't know how old they actually are – have been scrupulously applied. The difference here is that she has never seen her keepers, curators, whatever. Which may be pure serendipity.*

Why?

We have to assume that, after centuries of space battles and the one landing the Hive managed on the 'Dini Sef colony, her species know what Mrdinis look like. But they can't know what humans look like, never having encountered us in the flesh as it were. There is a school of thought that she could be approached by a human representative, in a friendly manner. That way we may find out . . .

Father, that is totally reprehensible! That's . . . that's taking advantage of a helpless . . .

You too? the Rowan put in.

Me, too, what?

You feel that she's helpless, alone, isolated, friendless, worldless? Her mother's tone was sardonic.

Not particularly, Damia remarked dryly, *but Zara does!*

Zara? Yes, she's always been particularly sensitive, hasn't she? But how would she pick that up from looking at a tape? That's real distancing, the Rowan said thoughtfully. *Still, there's a use for that sort of Talent, too.*

Damia caught an undertone in her mother's mind. *Mother, she's not fourteen yet. And . . .*

And . . . Jeff Raven prompted his daughter when she faltered, although what she was finding hard to say was the reason for her contacting her parents.

Lately she's been almost . . . dysfunctional as a Talent. Cross her off your list of prospective Tower candidates!

Not fourteen yet? the Rowan repeated. *And presently dysfunctional? She's just started menstruation? Well, the dysfunction could right itself when her cycle settles. Is that what you wanted to tell us?*

Damia heaved a sigh. *Yes, I felt you should know.*

The Rowan projected sympathy but again Damia felt that undertone, and a flash of keen interest and some satisfaction.

I will not say that you were not a handful at that age, dear Damia, her father said, a ripple of fond amusement in his tone.

I was never *dysfunctional as a Talent.*

No, that you weren't. There was a shade of irony in the affectionate wave that washed over Damia and she relaxed.

I just wish I knew what to do to help Zara right now, she said wistfully. *We've tried so hard to support and encourage her.*

There isn't a parent in the universe who hasn't felt inadequate and at fault at one time or another, Damia, Jeff said.

Like your father, and the Rowan's mental touch was as full of affection as Jeff's, *I feel that you are being unnecessarily anxious about Zara. Perhaps you aptly chose to name her after Elizara who has such amazing empathy for her patients. There's no disgrace in having a Prime medical Talent.*

I doubt Zara has the stomach for a medical career, and Damia shot a tableau of Zara's reactions to limp animal bodies and the preparation of meat for cooking.

Surgery's only a minor part of medicine. More is done through bio feedback, metamorphics, mental conditioning, and genuine compassionate therapy than intrusive methods, the Rowan said.

233

Consult with Isthia and Elizara. Either would have some insights that will help you.

I felt you two should know first, Damia added lamely. Why had she expected her parents to solve her parenting problems when neither she nor Afra could?

Because you are closest to us, dear heart, said her father, having picked up on that thought. *Don't be hard on your daughter when she is what she is.*

She is what most people aren't right now, sorry for that wretched Queen. The mental tone in which Damia said 'wretched' indicated that she didn't apply the usual meaning.

Leave it, Damia. Just love Zara, the Rowan said. *And consult with Isthia and Elizara.*

Damia withdrew then, but not without a farewell surge of affection and approval from both parents. Wanting to sort this out now she'd admitted her reservations about her daughter, she checked the time differences. And swore under her breath. Isthia would not enjoy being awakened from sleep. When she tried for Elizara, she touched a mind that was intensely occupied in something vital. So Damia desisted, waiting for a more opportune moment to reach the two healers.

Maybe her parents were right: Zara would settle when her cycle did. She'd wait a few months and meantime give Zara the benefit of unconditional support. That was, after all, what Afra had recommended. He'd lived through her mother's vacillations and vagaries . . . and her own. He had always shown how much he understood – and loved – her. And he was very gentle and understanding with Zara. That might be all the child needed.

When Rojer, Gil and Kat appeared at the captain's mess for dinner that night, his presence was welcomed by officers keen to hear more details to flesh out the official communications that Rojer had brought.

'Bare bones of the matter,' Captain Osullivan said. 'I

234

believe your brother went on with the *KLTL* to check on the exact location of the nova and where the Hive homeworld was supposed to be.'

'Did you know about the great Hive wreck, sir?'

'That was the last communiqué we've received,' Osullivan said.

'Then you don't know that three pods escaped . . . ' Rojer asked.

'Three? But they only mention capturing one . . . '

'That's the only one so far *located*, sir . . . '

'Any survivors?' asked one officer.

'Any live survivors?' asked another.

Captain Osullivan held up his hand for silence as his usually orderly mess erupted into minor bedlam of information-starved queries. 'Shall we let our guest explain in his own time? Then, if there are additional questions, they can be dealt with in due course.'

Rojer took a deep breath, sending his recall back to the proper sequence of events and gave as comprehensive a report as possible. The only thing he left out was his own participation, limiting it to mention of nameless Talents. He had 'picked up' that most of them identified him as a 'kid'. He didn't want them to add 'cocky' to that.

'We have tapes, gentlemen,' the captain said when Rojer had wound down, 'but these can wait until after a very good dinner. Provided, I might add, by the arrival of Mr Lyon and eight supply drones. We'll all be the better for a meal.'

However, there were questions put to Rojer that he was not able to answer. Some he knew nothing about and others he replied to not as fully as he could, but as fully as he should. When pressed by the engineer-ing officer, Rojer had the chance to describe how the great Hive ship was being painstakingly reconstructed. This venture, aided and abetted by so many autono-mous groups throughout the Alliance, aroused the interest of many of the officers. They were suddenly obsessed

235

with the notion of initiating their own piece table.

Once again the captain's table erupted into excited babble. When order was restored, Rojer had to disappoint them because he hadn't brought his spec files with him. It hadn't occurred to him that the *Genesee* wouldn't have their own on board. Every other ship, world, city, town, settlement in the Alliance seemed to.

'While it would have been a nice leisure-time activity during the long pursuit,' Captain Osullivan said ruefully, 'I think we will soon be concentrating on more immediate concerns, especially if that is indeed a Hive-colonized system.' Then he leaned on one elbow towards Rojer. 'With your permission, Mr Lyon,' Rojer felt awkward being so formally addressed but he tried to look relaxed, 'I feel you should personally report all these details to the *Arapahoe* and Captain Quacho, and the *KTTS* and Captain Prtglm. I'll signal them to join us at 1230 tomorrow for the midday meal. Is that all right?'

Rojer grinned. 'Anything you say, Captain. Did you want me to 'port them aboard?'

Osullivan cleared his throat and Rojer 'heard' that the captain had overlooked that possibility. 'Ahem, yes, that would save hours of time and a good deal of fuel that we might urgently require in the near future.'

'That's why I'm here, sir.'

Rojer saw amusement on faces about the table and 'felt' a generally benign acceptance of him. The general opinion was that the 'kid' was being very useful.

The next day Rojer was more fluent in his account of all that had happened since the last official bulletin had reached the three ships of B Squadron. Captain Prtglm was as large and charcoal grey a 'Dini' as befitted its name. It was also the most fluent speaker of Basic that Rojer had encountered, even more so than his parents' friends, so, although he used more technical language and empha- sized certain phrases with body movements, he knew the captain of the *KTTS* understood every word he said.

'I doubt not that squadron approaches a Hive-held system,' Prtglm said, nodding its poll eye politely towards Rojer when he had finished. Then Prtglm added a gentle tlock. 'Captains do not agree with whole mind but Prtglm is old captain. Longly pursued Hivers. Have also brought new device for early viewing. Not sensitive to sensors.'

It gestured for one of its aides to bring over and unwrap a warty-looking object which had the sheen of plastic, even about the obvious jet mouths that ringed one end of it.

With eager excitement, Commander Metrios and the *Arapahoe*'s engineering officer leaned across the wide table to examine it and then looked at Prtglm for explanation.

'Hive sensors read metal. No metal in this probe. Undetected is. Good look round gets.' Captain Prtglm emitted the rasping noise of 'Dini laughter and, when the aide who had unwrapped the 'probe' said in a spate of 'Dini too fast for anyone but Rojer to translate, all the 'Dinis had a good rasp over that, too: even Gil and Kat joined in; more in courtesy, Rojer hoped.

He pretended to look puzzled. The substance of the remark was that, ' 'Dinis now had an instrument that would provide even humans with as long a look as was required to be sure of what to do next.'

Thian had mentioned something about the dichotomy of human and 'Dini attitudes as far as aggressive or offensive action was concerned, so Rojer wasn't as upset about such subtle censure as he might have been. Someone who hadn't lived with 'Dinis all his life might take umbrage at the subtle insult of such a remark.

'A totally plastic probe, huh?' Captain Osullivan said. 'Compact, and looking like a meteor or an asteroid. Just the sort of debris that litters space. But have we ascertained whether or not this system has an asteroid belt?'

'All space has floating and flying objects of no definite description,' Prtglm said, stiffening its bottle neck.

'The captain would certainly be correct in that, sir,'

the *Genesee*'s astrogator replied, smiling at Prtglm and signing approval and respect.

'I meant no disrespect, honoured Prtglm,' Osullivan said suavely and inclined his body in apologetic movements.

'I'd worry about ion trails, sir,' Commander Metrios said. 'Those'd be picked up . . . '

'What if it left no ion trail?' Rojer put in. 'I mean, it doesn't have to *go* there, I could send it. No trails then.'

Slowly, with obvious elements of disbelief in its turn, Prtglm swivelled its poll eye down to Rojer, and blinked.

RESPECTFULLY, LARGE HONOURED PRTGLM, RJR IS ONE OF THOSE WHO CAN PUT THINGS AND PEOPLE WHERE THEY ARE NEEDED. SEND MESSAGES TO DISTANT MINDS. Then Rojer made a most obsequious bow. Beside him, Gil made a barely audible click of approval.

Prtglm had ignored Gil and Kat from the moment it stepped into the ready room. So had the rest of its contingent because all the 'Dinis knew that had immediately identified Rojer's friends as younglings with few hibernations.

THIS IS THE HUMAN TALENT RJR LN, Captain Osullivan added quickly. THIS SHIP IS ALREADY INDEBTED TO HIM FOR NEWS AND FOOD SUPPLIES, AND THOSE SUPPLIES FORWARDED TO THE *KTTS*.

Prtglm clicked and clattered, even tlocked once in surprise but it regarded Rojer without blinking. With a very slight movement of its head, it also examined Gil and Kat who respectfully presented uncovered poll eyes to the KTTS captain.

'Rijor,' and Rojer did not worry about misplaced vowel sounds: the fact that Prtglm would use his name at all was sufficient notice. 'You are Tower?'

RJR IS TOWER TYPE SENDER RECEIVER NOW. Which was true. Adding a title of any kind to his name, at his obvious age, would have arrogance beyond excuse in the eyes of such a prestigious 'Dini.

YOU ARE ABLE TO SEND PROBE TO HIVE SHIP, AROUND HIVE SHIP FOR PERFECT SCAN?

'Well, lad, that would certainly help a great deal in deciding what to do next,' Captain Osullivan said suavely. 'We've got to know a lot about that system and which ever worlds the Hivers are using.'

'I can send something that light and little—' and Rojer pointed to the lumpy, metre-long, quarter-of-a-metre-wide probe, '—anywhere you want it to go. And it won't leave ion trails.'

The briefing that followed was as heady an experience for Rojer as finding that first match of Hive ship pieces.

'We'll have to make certain there're no sensor devices or mines outside or just inside the heliopause first,' Captain Osullivan said, 'before we let you go inside.'

'No such devices are used by Hives,' Captain Prtglm said and then flicked its forearms open in a gesture that meant it knew that its reassurance was insufficient for its human colleagues, and they'd complete that search first.

By the time the squadron reached the heliopause, Captain Osullivan admitted there were no early warning buoys. 'But there was no harm, and no delay, in making certain of it.'

Once inside the heliopause, they examined the astrogator's diagram of this solar system. It was so far from Earth and the Nine Star League that it hadn't even a number on human charts: the 'Dini ident was a long series of consonants and 'Dini numerals which were shortened to Xh-33. It had ten planets, having no asteroid belt where a fifth planet would have been in Earth's system.

When the 'Dini engineering contingent produced a round dozen of the plastic probe lumps, Rojer said that he was quite able to handle several in the air at one time.

'A juggler, are you, kid?' Commander Metrios asked, mildly sceptical.

From the beverage counter in the ready room, Rojer 'lifted' four mugs and three glasses, two saucers and a knife, a fork and a spoon and had the cups gyrating like compass points, the glasses were circling the room – well above everyone's heads – while the two saucers made a Möbius strip path around both groups as the knife, fork and spoon dipped into either mug or glass at random. This sort of juggling had been a favourite pastime at home for him and his siblings as good practice for Tower work. He didn't mention that his parents would have scolded him for showing off in such a childish fashion or that the probes would take a lot more concentration – plus generator gestalt – but as soon as he'd figured he'd made his point, he neatly returned everything to its original position.

'A most accomplished juggler you are, kid,' Commander Metrios said.

'How much difference is there from that exhibition to handling the probes, Mr Lyon?' the captain asked.

'To be honest, sir, I'd better stick to no more than three at a time.'

'Even so, we'll cover a lot of ground in a much shorter time than if we had to wait for the probe to get there by . . . ah . . . ordinary transport methods,' Osullivan said. 'When you're ready, Mr Lyon.'

Commander Metrios still radiated a certain amount of scepticism as he led Rojer to the bridge station where a couch had been placed for his use during gestalt. With the ship in flight, the generators were humming nicely. It took Rojer only a moment to lift them to the requisite power to 'port the three probes: a second each to lob them on the parabolic courses about their target planets.

The outer planet, predictably a small cold hunk with a heavy core, then a larger but equally sterile one, and the third was no more interesting, though it had several moons. On his second foray, Rojer sent the first probe around the gas giant. It was not a ringed planet but it had twenty moons and lots of debris, which interchanged when two or more moons were close enough to affect gravitational pulls. Rather a show for the astrogation officer, a very pretty woman named Langio, who was enchanted by

240

the lunar dance. The fifth in was the largest, with awesome surface activity and again possessing a herd of moons: some of which had man–made ruins. Rojer was asked to take that probe in for closer examination. That suggested that the moon had been mined at one time.

The sixth planet displayed more extensive ruins, enough to suggest that it had once been habitable before its atmosphere had drained off and it had lost the necessary warmth from its cooling primary.

Captain Osullivan called a halt to Rojer's day then and told him to get some rest. Rojer was only too happy to comply. He was exceedingly tired and wished he hadn't been such a show-off. Prtglm's doubt had incensed him. He might still *be* considered a youngling by his own kind as well as 'Dinis but he was 'a useful kid' and he wanted to prove he was.

When he reported to the bridge the next day, all three captains were present again and their manner suggested they'd new plans for him.

'Mr Lyon, we'd like you to send one probe to the Hive ship. We've been lucky that the outer planets do not have warning mechanisms on them but, if the seventh planet is Hive settled, Prtglm is confident that it *will* have monitors in space. Today let's scan the Hive ship.'

Rojer was quite willing to limit himself to the one 'seeing' rock.

'Now,' said Lt-Commander Langio in her quiet voice, 'we know the Hiver's present position, just past the eighth planet, but we don't dare risk extending our sensors that far to get you good definition.'

'I don't need it, Commander,' Rojer said easily. 'Hive ships are always the same shape . . . '

'Not always same size,' Captain Prtglm added.

'True, but as there isn't but one out there, that isn't a consideration.' Rojer nodded to Commander Metrios who ceded control of the generators to Rojer so he could achieve

241

the necessary gestalt. He'd seen where Langio had sited the Hive ship on the astrogation chart: he picked up the lumpy probe and 'ported it in a wide parabolic curve towards the Hiver.

The com officer gave a grunt of surprise. 'Getting readings,' Doplas said. 'Can you hold it still a minute?'

Rojer obliged and then followed his directions so that, by the time he retrieved it, the probe had done several circumnavigations around the Hive ship without, apparently, alerting the ship to the probe's presence.

Rojer wasn't nearly as tired as he'd been yesterday but that brief hour's work now occupied every area of the *Genesee* and every specialist on all three ships of Squadron B. He was relegated to the sidelines which he tried to take philosophically. That lasted until dinner time when he was politely, if absently, asked to eat in the main mess-hall. He didn't mind that because Gil and Kat kept him company. The food was nearly as good as he'd gotten at the captain's table and there was not nearly so much formality. And a lot of the crew tried out their 'Dini on his pair . . . with often amusing results. Gil was particularly good with pronunciation problems but the methods by which it taught caused great hilarity and provided an interesting evening's entertainment for everyone. He was proud of his 'Dinis and told them so.

He was roused from a sound sleep by an irritating noise and finally realized that his comunit was squawking for attention.

'Hmmm? Yes, whacha wan'?'

'Captain's compliments, Mr Lyon, and can you come to the ready room immediately?'

Grumpily, Rojer obeyed but he didn't wake Gil and Kat. They were dead to the world. Someone should get a full night's rest. Although he was in officer territory, it was still a hike to the ready room. If he'd been wider awake, he'd've 'ported, but a Talent never did that without full control of his faculties.

'Ah, there you are, Mr Lyon,' the captain said when he arrived but there were scowls, an irritated tlock and snubbing switch of the upper torso by one of the younger 'Dinis on Captain Prtglm's staff, as if he'd deliberately delayed his appearance. That they'd been up all night was obvious by the smell in the room, and the numbers of discarded mugs, half full of cold liquid which orderlies were clearing away as well as serving fresh drinks to both human and 'Dini. 'I'm happy to say that your efforts bore extremely ripe fruit. There you are!'

On the big tactical screen Rojer sleepily noticed a Hive ship. Only something about it wasn't quite right: it had coloured marks all over it: different coloured marks that hadn't been on the original scans.

'I'm not sure what I should be looking for, Captain,' Rojer said, too sleepy still to pretend to understand.

'You're looking at an unarmed Hiver, is what you're looking at, lad,' Commander Metrios said, smiling with tired triumph. 'She's a new ship: not so much as a scratch on her hull. She's not on search or armed to invade. That's a colony world and she doesn't expect us. And it doesn't know we're on its doorstep.'

'Yes, sir,' Rojer willingly agreed, hoping that was all that was required of him.

'This time a Hiver will not escape,' Captain Prtglm said, and his body mirrored satisfaction and triumph.

'If she doesn't have weapons, she can't defend herself,' Rojer said blankly.

His comment caused all conversation in the big room to cease and he became the unhappy focus of every eye, especially big poll eyes.

'Where's the glory in attacking an unarmed ship?' he asked, looking directly at Captain Prtglm. The silence continued, but it had a different quality: a quality that made Rojer terribly uneasy. 'You've a message you need me to send to the Alliance?' he went on, thinking that was why he had been sent for. The silence was almost

243

deafening and he was too muddle-headed with sleep to be able to 'read' the conflicting ones. 'Or do you want another probe sent out?'

'A message and a probe, lad,' Captain Osullivan said and then signalled to one of the orderlies. 'Some coffee for Mr Lyon, please. He'll need his wits about him.'

When Rojer settled in the couch on the bridge to 'path to Earth Prime, he heard and 'felt' not so much animosity as cynicism and dislike: not outright hatred but definitely contempt.

What he did hear, almost spoken aloud the thought was so strong, was: 'How can we be sure the kid'll send what's written?'

The captain handed him the message. 'This must be transmitted verbatim, lad.'

'Sir,' and Rojer raised his voice so that he'd be heard across the wide room, 'a Prime, which I am, has the duty to send what he is given to send and forget what he is not supposed to remember. I've been trained in Tower ethics since I was old enough to use telepathy for distance speaking ten years ago. And that is why I was sent to serve on the *Genesee*, because I can 'path accurately over distance. When you're ready, Mr Metrios, I'll need every erg those engines can give me right now.'

To be sure he had made his point, he read the message in a low voice that would be audible to the captain, Commander Metrios and the com officer so that they'd know he had sent what he was asked to send and without comment. He kept his mental tone even and bland but inadvertently he caught his breath as he felt his grandfather's touch: clear despite the distance involved.

That's some report, Roj. You been stirring things up?

Me, sir? No, sir.

Jeff Raven had not held his important position as Earth Prime and the strongest T-1 in the Nine Star League without sensing what sometimes was not 'pathed.

244

He altered his voice after his official acknowledgement of the communiqué to a less formal tone.

Giving you a bit of a rough time, huh, Roj? He was sympathetic but bracing.

Nothing I can't handle, Granddad. I guess I'm just not used to naval ways.

There'll be a reply to this, I'm sure, Rojer. Let's set an arbitrary time every hour on the hour for reply. That'll make it a tad easier on you. What is your current time?

Rojer looked up at the digital and told his grandfather the ship's time: 0505. Then, out loud, he added, 'The message has been acknowledged at 0933 Earth time, Captain, and has already been forwarded to the High Councils. Earth Prime asks me to be ready to receive a message every hour on the hour: or 0600 Ship's time.' He slipped out of the couch, making himself straighten up. 'If you don't need me now, sir, I'll get back to my 'Dinis. If they wake and find me gone, they won't know where to find me.'

Rather awkwardly, Captain Osullivan gave him a pat on the back. 'Do that, lad. Do just that.'

The fourth time Rojer arrived on the bridge for the appointed hour, to his immense relief he 'heard' his grandfather's alert.

'The generators, please, Commander,' he said, nodding to Metrios. He lay back and let the gestalt extend his range. He also pushed down all the negative feelings he'd been subjected to during the last four hours. Hell, he was only a kid. Why was he getting the stick? It's not as if he could *warn* the Hivers. Or even wanted to. If only he'd been more awake, he would have sensed the vibes in the room and kept his mouth shut. No-one here could tell what he was thinking. Were these some of the reactions his parents and grandparents had had to deal with when they were among the unTalented?

That message put the cat among the pigeons, lad, his grandfather said, chuckling. *Here are their orders. Repeat mentally and vocally after me. There must be no misunder-standing.* Rojer said that much aloud. *To Captain Etienne Osullivan, aboard the AS* Genesee *in response to telepathed message received 0933 this date by Earth Prime. Reply 1300 hours precisely from Earth Prime Raven to Aurigaean Prime Lyon. Message reads: No action is to be taken against unarmed ship. No action must arouse the suspicions of the colony world that it has been penetrated. If squadron can launch additional recon-naissance units of the new type, details of the inhabited planets and moons would be of inestimable value in formulating strategy. Re-peat, further reconnaissance may only be undertaken if there is no risk of disclosing Alliance presence in the system. When the recon-naissance is completed, or risk of discovery imminent, Squadron B is to retreat behind heliopause, maintaining discreet surveillance of system. Do not, repeat, do not engage enemy. This is by order of the High Councils of the Alliance. Gktmglnt and Admiral Tohl Mekturian presiding. End of signal. Earth Prime Raven sending.*

Aurigaean Lyon receiving at Earth time 1300:10.90 and acknowledging.

Well done, lad.

I'll hope they think so, Granddad.

They will. And you are entitled to call yourself Prime, you know, since you're doing the work of one. That was delivered in a firm admonitory tone which made Rojer wriggle a little in pride. Grandfather would not have said something like that if he didn't mean it. Then his voice took on its 'official' tone. *A message capsule has also been despatched. That's what took so long, getting it written down. Naval types! Get ready to catch it. Confirmation of the message, signed, sealed and pick it up for delivery . . . Now!*

'A message capsule's on its way, Commander,' Rojer said, sitting up and gesturing for Metrios to keep the generators up to peak. 'It's coming in now.' And the slim message tube dropped the last inch on to the carpeted floor by the captain's feet. Rojer grimaced, wishing that he had managed an absolutely perfect landing. 'This way, sir, you know no-one's been able to tamper with it.'

246

Someone, somewhere on the bridge, gave a low whistle. The security officer glared around but the culprit was not identified.

Captain Osullivan pressed his thumb to the seal of the tube and it obligingly popped its lid, the rolled sheaf extruding. The captain opened it, scanned it and grunted. 'Good transmission, lad. Every comma and dot in place.' He handed the flimsy to the com officer. 'Send a coded fax to the *Arapahoe* and the *KTTS*, for captains' eyes only.' He was silent a moment, looking at the forward screens and the distant glow of the G-type star. None of the planets that Rojer had sent probes to were visible, just a tight pattern of winking stars of all kinds. 'Mr Lyon, have you had lunch?'

Rojer shook his head, unable to say that he'd gone to the messroom but the moment he'd been seen, the place had gone very quiet. He'd left, his 'Dinis tlocking in distress behind him.

'Then it's high time you did eat. We need your particular talents again and we must be extremely delicate in our investigations. Engineering, security, astrogation, exec, join us in the ready room. And Doplas, inform Captains Quacho and Prtglm that we'd like them to join us if they'd signal the time to be 'ported over after lunch.'

12

Of all her relatives, only her great-grandmother Isthia proved truly understanding of what became known as Zara's Antic. Granny Isthia had raised one beautifully arched eyebrow and said 'You do teach them that where there's a will there's a way! If they implement their teachings, don't fuss.'

Even her father who was the most understanding kind of dad you could want had replied, 'What if she'd been killed?'

'She's half Denebian. We're born survivors!' was Isthia's imperious reply to that.

Zara had actually spent a lot of time and thought on how to achieve her end. The will to the way was also well researched. Eventually her mother gave her credit for that. What really incensed Grandmother Raven had been Zara's shameless and often unethical use of her Talent. The redeeming part of that was that Zara had not abused or misused anyone or more than bent a few laws.

For days after Rojer left – and the nights in which Zara had had horrible nightmares all involving him in lethal situations – Zara had alternated Queen watching with her planning. Ever since hatching, the Queen had been stationary. You couldn't call the use of one palp to draw food to her mouth 'activity' though she did that from time to time. Roddie had deftly replaced foods by the one palp used and put more enticing offerings near the other forward limb. She stayed where she was, her hind end in the mound of mixed shavings and eggs.

A theory was now circulating that this species of orthopterus might require a male fertilization of the eggs after laying, not before. There was endless discussion on the merits of every theory put forth: sometimes rather loud and furious debates in which speakers lost their temper with colleagues in other camps.

These discussions did more to make up Zara's mind than deter her from her wild scheme, for it became painfully obvious that no-one *knew* what to do for the Queen. Something would have to be *done* soon or Zara was afraid she'd be lost. She was sure *she* would know if she could only get close enough to 'sense' the need. Roddie was doing as well as a male could be expected to do. But the Hive Queen was female. It had been females like her great-grandmother Isthia and her great-aunts, Besseva and Rakella, who had 'heard' the Hive response to the arbitrary return of the one scout to survive the Rowan–Raven Repulsion above Deneb. And that act had brought the great ship to Deneb to be vanquished in Deneb's hot sun. That was, of course, before the Mrdini had made contact with humans: in fact it was *why* 'Dinis had made contact with humans. But that didn't exactly exonerate either from current actions in Zara's estimation.

The only female on the Observation Module was the non-empathic Captain Waygella. Why under the suns hadn't either her grandfather or grandmother thought of putting a Talented empath on board that Module?

They hadn't. She *had* to supply the need.

That took timing as well as planning for although there

was a lot of FT&T traffic out of Aurigae, not as much as served her purpose went to either Earth or even Callisto. That's where she had to be unethical – listening in to 'pathed messages to keep informed of what shipments might be made to either Earth or Callisto. She'd secreted in her own room a breathing unit in case she was obliged to go by carrier drone, and a comfortable padded blanket. She'd her travelling clothes ready and a small sac of necessities, including travel food for they used such bars on longer hunting and camping trips. Her 'Dinis, Pol and Diz, were in hibernation which solved that problem. Not that she couldn't keep things from them but it would be unfair of her to seem to desert them for no reason she could explain beforehand.

Time got shorter. The Queen seemed enfeebled and nothing could tempt her to eat more than a few mouthfuls and the intervals between these was increasing.

Zara overheard her parents talking about Rojer on board the *Genesee*. Until he'd managed to get some new sort of probe around the inhabited planet of the Hive colony, he'd had some sort of problem on board. Served him right, she thought disloyally, when he was actively partici- pating in the destruction of a species. And people said the Hivers were predatory, merciless and ruthless. She was even pleased to hear – and certainly did not form part of the majority – that this colony world was swarming with all kinds of Hive life, with well-developed defences, and hundreds of satellites and large ships orbiting. Evidence suggested that the Hivers were even readying for more exploratory voyages. That was, of course, what they did, according to the 'Dini. When a world became too popu- lated, that meant too many Queens, a ship was provisioned with excess Queens and sent forth to find its own world.

Would that procedure alter when the unarmed home- world Hive ship arrived to tell the colony of the nova, and the destruction of their original system? Many thought it would cause chaos in every one of the Hive worlds.

Maybe even, the incurable optimists suggested, curtail their explorations while they established a new home-world. Others were certain that it wouldn't even give the living Hivers a moment's pause.

There was speculation over what would happen if the Hive worlds knew a Queen was held prisoner on Earth? Since it was unlikely that even the B-squadron's quarry would know that the biggest ever Hive ship had been destroyed, why would they care?

Which made this lone Queen's life even more important to Zara.

Miner Representative Mexalgo approached Aurigae Tower for transport to Earth for an important meeting of the Federated Nine Star Miners and Metallurgists Association. That was Zara's chance, for Mexalgo was a large man, nearly two metres tall and close to one hundred and ten kilos. He wouldn't fit in the usual single carrier. A double was allotted him. He also had some alloy samples he wanted to bring with him. Zara nearly yodelled with delight. She was so slight in build that she wouldn't cause an imbalance, especially if she 'lifted' herself. And she was small enough so that she could fit under the second padded couch, with a dark blanket covering her from Mexalgo's notice.

And, when the double carrier was cradled in the yard first thing in the morning, she took breakfast with the family as usual but when she went back to her room, ostensibly to access her morning's Teach, she assumed a crouched position and 'ported right into the carrier. She hadn't quite judged the interior and barked her shins hard against the inner couch and scraped her back along the outer one. She ought to have crouched longways to the carrier, not athwart it. Rubbing her legs fiercely and setting a minor block to reduce the ache, she positioned herself, her sac, and the blanket so that she'd be lost in the shadow when the carrier was open to settle M.R. Mexalgo.

She'd put her Teach on automatic the night before so

251

it would air and turn off at appropriate times, and left a note saying she'd gone to look for greens. No-one would expect to see her before dinnertime.

She had a moment's shock when something very heavy swung into her back as Mexalgo settled himself.

'You'll want to secure those samples to the other couch, Mexalgo,' the stationmaster said, and Zara caught in her breath and shielded tightly against the chance that Keylarian might investigate.

'Why?' grunted the miner rep.

'Tower policy, sir. Wouldn't want you squashed. The pack'll fit nicely on the spare couch and belt down safely.'

That accomplished and the hatch closed. Despite holding her shields down as tight as she could, Zara could 'feel' the initial lift of the capsule.

'Takes longer'n I thought it would,' Mexalgo was muttering. 'When are they going to 'port me? Don't want to be late for that meeting. Awkward having different times on different worlds. Why'nt they synchronize?'

Zara would have laughed at his ignorance and his nervousness. She'd known when they left and when they'd arrived seconds later, and then the hatch opened.

'Miner Representative Mexalgo?' and cool air flooded the carrier. 'I'm T-10 Guanil. Ground transport will take you to the Blundell Building where an air car awaits you. Here, let me undo that for you, sir.'

Neither man had any inkling of her presence and Zara stopped the trembling in her belly. She did exert just a little pressure to keep the hatch from locking. Just that little bit wouldn't be noticed but using the kinetics necessary to unlock it from the outside might be. This was a secured area.

Outside she could hear all kinds of activity but then Earth Prime was an extremely busy facility, especially since the operations against the Hiver species had stepped up. She could pick up a gestalt from any one of the engines she heard moving about outside. But where did she want to go now?

252

She had to decide that no-one would expect to be 'pathed here on the cargo field. And Roddie was bringing shipments in from Earth every day . . . What if she could find one? If not today, then tomorrow.

Carefully she let her senses flow beyond the capsule, just as she'd been taught, to estimate and establish her surroundings. It had used to be a game they'd all played, the reward of the most comprehensive report got one of Dad's origami figures. She didn't have as many as Laria, Thian and Rojer had got, but then she was younger than they were and hadn't done that exercise as often. Morag'd only gotten two.

She was amazed at the size of the cargo yard, as the cradles emptied and filled almost instantaneously. Then she began to worry if hers would be flipped out again and quickly, despite her barked shins and bruised back, 'ported herself underneath the carrier. There was no-one immediately near by so she cautiously looked around the prow of the capsule.

Gradually, as she 'probed carefully, she realized that there were distinct areas: she was in 'live' cradle which was nowhere near as busy as some of the others, where goods were loaded on to and from immense grav-lift platforms that silently went up and down the ranks of drones, large and small. Most of the grav-lift was crated or wrapped. Nothing 'fresh'. Nothing even marked fresh food.

She was suddenly startled to hear voices coming near her.

'OK, use that double, Orry,' a man's voice said. 'We can put the crates in. The Talent's always careful lifting so nothing'll roll out or crash about. Handles his stuff like he would a baby. Don't know why he bothers since she doesn't eat it.'

'Who does eat then? Them in the Module.'

'I doubt it,' said the first voice with a snort. 'It'd be contaminated or something, having been down there by

253

that critter. *I* sure as hell wouldn't touch it. All this choice number-one stuff going to an insect.'

'Big insect . . . OK, strap this down. Harness'll just fit.'

Zara did a scan, as she'd been taught, to assess mass and volume in a capsule. There wasn't much space left. Yes, there was. If she folded into a tight ball, she could just fit on the end of the couch where the fresh fruit had been tied down.

This time she knocked herself on the head and nearly gave her presence away as well by her inadvertent exclamation of pain.

'You hear that, Orry?'

'Hear what?'

'Ah, nothing. Let's get out of the way. Carrier FT-387-B ready for lift. Now like I said . . . '

And she heard the voices dwindle away.

She also felt the lift: a little jerky as the Talent had to expend more gestalt to 'port her weight.

What have they sent along today? And, if she wasn't mistaken, that voice was her cousin Roddie's. She had done her homework, however, and knew exactly where she'd been landed: in bay A, the original facility of the now greatly expanded Module. A second carrier should be in the other cradle. She 'ported herself out of the first one and then hid behind the second. She'd bumps and bruises enough getting in and out of capsules and didn't want to risk any more.

She was no sooner hidden than the door slid open and she 'sensed' her cousin Roddie. His mind was full of his duty and his concern for his charge. He'd ordered some specially succulent tropical fruits – she'd shown a real interest in fruit until just recently: eating and saving pips and seeds. She wasn't even doing that lately. He had to stimulate her appetite, somehow, someway. The xenobs and xenzoos were getting vehement about her lack of interest in the larvae. Those things could die from neglect

254

just like the young of any species. If the Queen didn't make a move to attend them soon, they'd have to be taken from her to join the programme. Two had made successful transitions to the next step in their life cycle . . . Roddie only knew the fact not the reality of the transition.

Zara congratulated herself on being on time. *She* wasn't too late. She'd help the poor Queen. She'd save her. The sounds of scuffling continued.

'Right. The fruit first,' and Zara followed Roddie's mind as he delivered sweet-perfumed melons to the occupant of Heinlein Base. 'Bingo!' he said.

His irreverent attitude towards important things had always raised dislike in his cousins and, despite having heard his mental ruminations, it roused Zara's enmity. She followed his second 'port.

Felt his confusion. 'Hey, now, what's that?'

'What's what, Lieutenant?'

'I don't quite know, Sergeant, but I think I should find out.'

Horrified, Zara took a deep breath and followed the direction of his last 'port and slipped on the congealed juices of many ripe fruits, falling backwards and cracking her head against a larval sac.

For a long moment, Zara was stunned. And then she felt terribly cold: as if every fibre of her body was frozen. Zara paused, knowing perfectly well that the temperature of the base was kept at 32 degrees Celsius. Then she looked down at the motionless body of the Queen. It was a lot larger than Zara realized: taller than she was, though she wasn't tall: short for a Lyon, in fact. Not for a Gwyn. Fleetingly she remembered Rojer telling her how much she resembled her grandmother.

Well, she did, and she was here for a purpose. And she had part of the answer: 32 degrees Celsius was not warm enough for an egg-laying Queen nor the eggs around here. Zara sensed terrible hunger, terrible weakness, fear

255

of leaving a task undone. Solitude! Hunger! Cold! Strange-
ness everywhere. Cold! Hunger!

Zara Raven-Lyon? What are you doing down there? She
stared up at the Observation Module, aware she was drip-
ping rancid fruit juice.

*She's cold! She's bloody freezing to death! She's frozen, that's
why she can't eat. Turn up the temperature. Get more shavings
down here to cover her and her eggs or you're going to lose them
all.*

*How under the seventy suns of the Alliance do you know that,
Zara Lyon?*

*Hive minds are female. The Rowan and everyone else who
heard the Hive Many Mind were female. I'm female! She's cold!
Turn up the heat!*

*I've already turned it. And I'm turning you up here to face
heat of another kind, young lady!*

Zara felt him touch her, to 'port her to the Module. She
resisted, grinning.

*Did you forget, Cousin Rhodri, that I'm T-1? You can't lift
me unless I want to come.*

I suggest, said another voice with great authority and no
humour, *that you lift yourself into the Module immediately,
Zara Gwyn-Lyon!*

*Grandmother Rowan, don't make me until she's warm enough to
eat because she needs help and I'll give it to her if no-one else will!*

Why you cheeky little snip!

A male chuckle spared Zara from matching strengths
with her grandmother. *She's come a long way to do this,
Rowan,* and it was her grandfather. *Since she's brave enough
to be there, and may be correct in her diagnosis, let's give her the
chance to prove it. Otherwise, the experts are fearful we will lose
the Queen.*

Over the next two hours, Zara removed what she could
to reach some comfort for herself in what became midsum-
mer midday tropical heat. But the Queen began to move,
began to eat, and Zara pushed more and more food close
enough for her to grasp it with her palps.

256

When the bales of shavings appeared, Zara piled them around the eggs and the larvae. Her cousin sent her down something to drink to ease her own parched throat, a sweat-band and replaced towels as soon as they became sopping.

Then slowly, the Queen worked herself free of her egg pile, crawling forward on her upper limbs. Zara, keeping a respectful distance from those long arms and powerful-looking palps, remounded the shavings. The Queen continued to eat. When she stopped, Zara moved as far from her as she could, with the larvae in between. The Queen busied herself with adding more shavings, as if criticizing Zara's efforts. Then she went into stationary mode.

Zara could sense nothing.

You've done what you set out to do, Zara, now report to the Module, her grandmother said but she didn't sound angry even if her statement of what Zara was to do *now* was not something Zara would, or could, disobey. *I suggest that you shower before you join us on Callisto.* There was a thread of amusement in that addition.

'I'm in for it though,' Zara thought, 'but I did do what I set out to do. And the Queen will live now!'

To her surprise those on the Module did not attack her, or put a guard over her. The first thing Captain Waygella did was hold her nose and suggest a clean-up for the first priority.

'We've got a good recycling plant in the Module but, child, you'll use up all the deodorants for the month.' So Zara was led, at a jog trot, to the sanitary facility, someone thrust a big towel in her hand and someone else a knee-length tunic and some soft-soled station shoes. Only when she picked up her suit, after a long shower, did Zara realize the pong she'd given off. At arm's length she pinched two fingers on the suit leg and thrust it into the disposal. Then she scrubbed the fingers again.

She was just opening the door, noting a female soldier

257

outside when she was arbitrarily 'ported to the shuttle and beside the carrier she'd hidden behind.

In you get, child, her grandfather said. *We'll spare you what publicity we can.*

Zara 'sensed' that Jeff Raven wasn't exactly angry with her, more surprised than angry, but it was only him she could be sure of on that score.

She was right about that for when she arrived at Callisto, she was met in the yard by Gollee Gren, her grandfather's first assistant, and the man who decided where Talents should be placed when they were old enough to have official assignments.

'You have surprised all of us, young Zara!'

'But, don't you see, Uncle Goll, I had to do what I did. No-one else *knew*.'

'Zara, honey,' and he put an arm about her shoulders, sort of guiding her towards the path that led to her grand-mother's house, 'the only thing that saves you from being sent for ever to a boondock Capellan transfer station is that you did know. And you did save the Queen.'

Zara began to feel a little better and lengthened her step to match his longer stride. His arm was comforting across her shoulders and she 'knew' that she'd need comforting if her mother was in Grandmother's house. She didn't even dare 'sense' if her parents were there.

I'm here, and she felt the cool serenity of her great-grandmother lap over her. *Your mother and father are far too busy pushing big-daddies about the Alliance.*

Then they were on the steps and the door was open. Great-grandmother Isthia and, Zara's eyes widened, the woman she was named after was there as well, Elizara. That sank Zara's spirits. She'd've known where she was with Mother and Dad, even with Grandmother and Grand-father, but Isthia and Elizara . . . ! Uncle Gollee's arm was still strong on her shoulders and she felt the touch of both her great-grandmother and the medic implacably – if kindly – gathering her to them.

Rojer woke when he heard the klaxon of red alert. He scrambled into clothes, wondering for a brief frantic second if he was supposed to go to his escape pod. But this was red alert, not abandon ship. He was supposed to report to the bridge for either yellow or red alert. He pushed his feet through the legs of the fatigue suit, found the ship shoes with his toes at the same time as he poked his arms through the sleeves.

STAY HERE. WILL RETURN FOR YOU, he told his sleepy 'Dinis as he closed the front fastening. Then he 'ported himself to his station on the bridge and just missed colliding with Commander Metrios who was lunging for his station.

Rojer opened his mind and found the captain's. The alert was not for danger to *them* but to the incoming Hiver which seemed to be under attack.

The previous day, Rojer had put several probes into geosynchronous orbits about the inhabited planet, high enough to avoid many Hive units, and about the moons which previous probing had shown to have weapon emplacements of some kind.

These planetary probes were showing unusual activity and the lunar ones indicated that long-range torpedoes were being aimed at the incoming vessel.

'Doesn't have an updated security code, huh?' Metrios remarked to their gunnery officer, a Lieutenant-Commander Yngocelen.

'Either that or they know that vessel's coming in loaded with Queens and they don't need more. Bearing in mind,' Yngocelen added, 'what we know of their colonizing rationale and what seems to be happening on the planet.'

'Yes, but it's their own species, isn't it?' the astrogator said, her voice puzzled.

'Like I said, maybe they don't have today's password. Wouldja look at that barrage! Damned glad we don't have to run it!'

'They're not hitting a thing. Look at the blasts!'

'Maybe a shot across the bows?' suggested the exec.

'Their markmanship's not great, Ynggie,' Metrios said contemptuously. 'And the incoming's not in range, not by spatials! Why'nt they wait?'

'Call for you, Captain,' Doplas said, 'signal from Captain Prtglm.'

'On screen.'

'This is how they fight, Captain Osulvan,' Prtglm said. 'Barrage will continue until ship is either destroyed or retires. Then it will be followed until it is dead.'

'But it's their own ship, Captain.'

'The Queens do not like to share, Osulvan,' Prtglm replied.

'Perhaps the incoming ship has not been able to identify itself as being a Hiver, or that it comes from the destruction of the homeworld.'

'That does not matter, Osulvan. Too many Queens! The extra die!'

'At least we're learning where their surface-to-space missiles are launched,' Yngocelen said, his hands busy over his terminal. 'I'm logging them in.'

'Any chance they'd exhaust their supply so we'd have a clear run in?' Metrios said.

'Not a valid theory, Commander,' Prtglm said.

'Wooops!' Doplas said and one of the probe screens suddenly went blank.

The loss of one probe did not mitigate the volume of destruction that could be followed.

'This is different,' Prtglm said suddenly as the missiles which had begun to land on the surface of the incoming ship altered to miss.

'They can't miss. They're in range,' cried Ynggie. 'How can they possibly miss? They're bouncing missiles off the hull!'

A rasp of 'Dini laughter caused all talk on the *Genesee* bridge to stop. 'They need the ship unharmed. They wish to force the Queens to leave it. This is a new tactic. Very new. Very interesting.'

After a while, it didn't seem so to Rojer who had to rub his eyes every now and then as the battle, millions of miles below, was relayed by the probes to the interested audience. Due to relay time, they didn't realize exactly when it was over . . . except there were less tiny sparks about the third planet.

'Watch, allies,' Prtglm said, intoning in such a deep voice that everyone obeyed. 'Observe that escape pods now leave ship.' One probe was fortunately in the perfect position for such an observation.

'They're bloody well sitting ducks, if those bugs have the range,' Ynggie said.

He groaned as each of the sixteen pods leaving the safety of the Hive ship was blasted to bits, seconds into its escape trajectory.

'Now, how do they take over the ship?' the exec asked. 'No Queen minds to tell the ordinary ranks what to do . . . and they haven't stopped firing, have they?'

'What to happen is not known. Observe. This is not usual pattern.'

What happened took far longer than forcing the Queens to abandon their ship. Rojer had, in fact, fallen asleep on his couch, weary of watching screens. The com officer roused him with a few gentle shakes to his shoulder.

'We need you, lad,' he said kindly, but his face was haggard with fatigue. 'It's over and we've got to report it.'

'Wha . . . happened, finally, sir?' Rojer knuckled his eyes but a cup of steaming coffee was put in front of him and he took it gratefully from the astrogator Langio.

'The incomer ran out of ammunition, by the looks of it,' Metrios said, pausing before he sipped from his own cup. 'Then a big shuttle blew a hole midships – probably a cargo or docking area. Prtglm said that once Queens got on board, they'd take over control of the crew. But that's only supposition because as Prtglm kept saying . . .'

' . . . on and on and on . . . ' Doplas muttered, rolling his eyes.

' . . . The 'Dinis have no precedent for the behaviour we witnessed. Now everybody, except you, Rojer, can stand down from red alert. Nor shall I keep you up much longer, either,' Captain Osullivan said, and surprised Rojer no end by giving him a friendly buffet on the shoulder as he extended the notepad.

Grandfather was sleepy, too, but he was instantly alert when he recognized Rojer's voice and overrode apologies.

Rojer delivered the message, speaking it aloud, which of course made it much longer to transmit.

Well, that is stunning news. Then his grandfather chuckled. *The Squadron would have had a very warm welcome had it ploughed right in there as some would have liked. Don't repeat that, Rojer.*

Of course not, sir, and Rojer even managed to keep his face straight. *We were on red alert. For hours. I'm not sure how long the fighting did last.*

That's irrelevant, Rojer. That it occurred, with such ferocity and duration, with such a result, is! Caution, and more caution, are needed. Even the most bellicose 'Dini will see that now. That battle may have saved many human and 'Dini lives.

But, Grandfather, for Rojer realized that the official part of their contact had been discharged, *there're now four Hive ships that this world can use for colonizing. That's not good.*

Perhaps, Rojer. But they haven't left that system yet. Maybe they won't. I'm nattering with you, lad, because I've sent Captain Osullivan's report and there may be an immediate signal back. Can you stay awake? I can feel you yawning along with me.

Rojer grinned. He saw Captain Osullivan's eyebrows raise in query. 'Earth Prime wants me to stay in touch, sir, in case there's an immediate reply to your report.'

'Oh!' And Captain Osullivan began to pace up and down the narrow walkway along the stations. Many of the other officers had left the bridge and the duty helmsman had

262

been replaced. A lieutenant manned Doplas' seat but the nice astrogator was still at her desk, blinking frequently as she stared at the display in front of her.

Fraid we'll have to leave you where you are, Rojer, his grandfather said, *and that goes for the squadron, too. Repeat aloud 'Message for Captain Osullivan aboard AS* Genesee, *report received. Data being analysed. The squadron is to remain in present positions unless enemy traffic requires resettlement. All activity on subject planet is to be reported on an on-going basis: in twelve-hour intervals unless increased activity suggests imminent departure of enemy ships. Reconnaissance by probe must be continued and the scope increased if at all possible. Additional personnel will be teleported at further notice. High Councillor Gktmglnt and Admiral Tohl Mekturian. End message. Rojer, I think your brother will be joining you. May even be replacing you.*

Aw, Granddad, it's getting exciting now! And they don't think of me as just a 'kid' anymore!

Professionally and personally, I'm delighted to hear that, but I do believe that you may have witnessed the only 'exciting' part that will happen for a while. Be that as it may, you're stuck there a while longer . . .

Hurrah!

Thian is six weeks at least from a point where we can 'port him from the KLTL. You're stuck on board till then.

That's all right with me, sir. Commander Metrios is giving me some naval engineering courses, so I'm not even missing schooling.

Ha! was his grandfather's surprising comment. *You're not the only one of my grandchildren who takes the initiative. Since you couldn't possibly guess what your sister Zara did . . .*

She got to see the Queen?

There was such a pause that Rojer wondered if he'd lost contact and then he heard the low chuckle. *You're not adding precog to your other Talents, are you, Rojer?*

No, sir, I just know she was in bits over the Queen.

On the contrary, she put bits together, Rojer. You may be

proud of your sister. She's staying on Earth, living on Callisto, and studying with Elizara. Meanwhile, there's a female T-4 on the Module, monitoring the Queen. Zara discovered the poor creature was freezing to death. Temperatures in an egg-laying chamber are degrees higher than they would be anywhere else in a Hive.

You mean, Zara did all this from Aurigae? Rojer was overwhelmed by his sister's abilities.

His grandfather gave him a summary of his sister's adventure, which astonished Rojer thoroughly because he hadn't thought she'd ever do something as wild as that.

Sometimes, Rojer, we don't know what we are capable of until we have unexpected goals to achieve! Zara's happily placed with Elizara now, to the relief of all of us, I might add. Now, as I can feel you yawning, you get to bed. We've a waiting game to play, but for now, we can all get some rest.

The End – For the Time Being